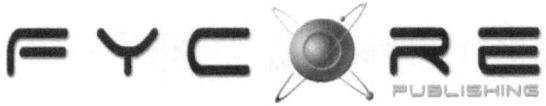

CAMOUFLAGE
Author: Victoria E. Kain
Graphic Illustrations by: |www.gritography.com
Layout Design by: Fycore Publishing
Development Editor: Jane Adams
Publisher: Fycore Publishing
www.fycore.com

International Publisher Author Number: 1403427755160
International Standard Book Number: 9781619100060
International Digital eBook Number: 9781619100275
Library of Congress Control Number: 2014931290

I0587196

Additional Formats May be Available for Pre-Order:

PHYSICAL		DIGITAL	
Trade Cloth	$29.95	CD/MP3 (Audio Book)	$15.95
Hard Back	$27.95	PDF Book	$12.95
Soft Back	$16.95	eBook	$9.99

For Inquiries or Additional Orders:

131 Sunset Ave Ste E#353
Suisun City CA, 94585
Office | (800) 470-FYCORE
Facsimile: | (800) 531-0190
Email: | publisher@fycore.com

Text on left margin (vertical): www.fycore.com   Fycore Publishing

CAMOUFLAGE

6th Book Edition
"I'll be Brief" Series

TM

I'LL **BE** RIEF

"Great minds read between the lines"

Author: Victoria E. Kain

CAMOUFLAGE

The "I'll be Brief" Overview

Victoria Kain values the time of her readers and will always be "Brief." She introduces her new suspense Novel "Camouflage." Gabriella McPherson, is a fourth generation Native American who enters the world of espionage with her Uncle after the death of the father she never knew. They fight to protect the family's fortune by concealing the birth of the child she carries and is completely unaware of who the child's father is after having been artificially inseminated. The unborn child will inherit millions according to her late fathers Last Will and Testament and they must evade murderous business partners who seek to destroy her and the unborn child. In the aftermath of the fight for survival, she falls for the man who she believes she is not permitted to love and is shocked when the actual father of the child is revealed to her after it is born. It is a fight for love, truth, time and ultimately "life!"

Kain's imagination goes wild once again as she delves into the world of the greedy minds of ruthless people, clawing their way to untold riches! All of Kain's books are rated for "A" all audiences! Another key feature of books in the Brief Series is; they can be read in one day. This affords people "time" to relax and read a good book! We hope you will enjoy this book and others from her collection. As promised, I'll Be Brief."

"CAMOUFLAGE"

By Victoria E. Kain

Author: Victoria E. Kain

CAMOUFLAGE

TABLE OF CONTENTS

~ CHAPTER 1 ~

A Charge to Keep

A CHARGE TO KEEP

Clarissa McPherson, was the eighth child born to Wisdom and Anna Mae McPherson in the desolate city of Hatchechubbee, Alabama. There was much history behind this great city, but its original residents had an abrupt exodus and there were many tales told about what happened here but those stories were told only around the camp fires of those that lived here decades earlier. Hatchechubbee was an unincorporated community in Russell County, Alabama and was located at the junction of Alabama State route 26 and County route 65 about 6.5 miles west-southwest of Seale Alabama. It had a post office which opened on August 17, 1855. *(americantowns.com)*.

It would always be difficult for the school aged children living there in Hatchechubbee to learn how to spell their great city's name. They were assured by their minimally educated teachers, that in time, they would surely learn to spell it eventually by breaking it into syllables *(Hatch-e-chub-bee)*, and then they were cautioned to practice spelling it piece by piece until they could put it all together as one proper noun they would never forget. Sadly though, only the gifted children would get it right and the others simply stopped trying if they stayed in school long enough. There were other small cities surrounding Hatchechubbee that were not as hard to spell yet they suffered some of the same injustices as the residents of this old town.

Residents in other areas felt superior in many ways to the people of Hatchechubbee. Hurtsboro, Marvyn, Crawford and Opelika were some of the other surrounding cities to Hatchecheubbee which were once thriving places to call home for many Cherokee, Choctaw and Chickasaw Indians from the east and the west that resided there. Over time, they all were forced to leave their homes where they had lived for many moons. They were ultimately told they had to relocate and leave Georgia, Alabama and the Carolinas because of special treaties made by Government officials and other powerful white men at that time.

Many of the Indians left their homes peacefully after promises were made by the Government to relocate them to another state where they were supposed to be able to make a new reservation as their home and would have their own land once again. Sad to say, this did not happen as it was told to them. In order for them to obtain this land, they would be horrified when told they were required to travel on "foot" to the new location which was hundreds of miles away. The requirement for them to travel this far was cruel, unjust and borderline criminal. Though they tried to comply, many of them died in route of disease and other issues before they reached their new promised land.

Even with the mass exodus, there were others who did not leave Georgia and Alabama. They chose to stay but had the arduous task of finding a safe place to live where they could etch out a new homestead for their families. Some even felt unsafe, and hid their families from the authorities on the same land they had grown to know and love and some even adopted the White man's way of living in order to survive which created much chaos in their culture. They became slaves to the land and the men that now owned "it" and them. Some of the McPherson clan were one of those families that were able to evade the mass exodus from Hatchechubbee but would find much difficulty in living a life without their family "tribesmen" to help support their families. It would mean making many changes in their culture and their lives in order to survive.

The location where the McPherson's resided in Alabama was widely known by all who lived in the area. The land was filled with many wild turkeys and excellent deer hunting. Food was plentiful and the soil was rich black dirt that was superior for growing vegetables of all kinds unlike the red clay dirt common to many Georgian residents. It was thought that this was one of the reasons the land was sought after by the government and the greedy men in those regions. After the exodus, the reservation was deserted and only a few Native American descendants still lived in those parts of the old home land.

Since the land no longer belonged to Native Americans, the ones who remained would have to accept the difficult new rules for hunting and fishing. They no longer had the freedom to feed their families as they needed to, but would have to abide by seasonal rules and if caught hunting outside of those timelines, they could be fined large amounts of money or other punishments that would be imposed upon them. They would now have to travel to get food or sneak to hunt on the land out of season, no longer being permitted to roam free and openly provide for their own. With these new rules the now illegal residents on the old reservation would sometimes travel up to thirty-six miles to the next largest city, which was Opelika, and about twenty-three miles to Marvyn which was another small town nearby for food.

These cities were sparsely populated as well and only a few folk who owned the town by way of land and money had inherited everything many of their forefather's had handed down to them. The towns were rural with no street or traffic lights for many decades. The city of Marvyn had a small country store that provided everything from kerosene lamps to fat back. That was pork meat from the hog used for breakfast or cooking vegetables in the South. The store doubled as a mail drop off point if the residents ordered from any mail order catalog. It also carried a variety of candy and other treats for children, such as broken crackers and the Johnny cake cookies that were popular back then. Kids didn't get much of that, but when they did, it was truly a special occasion.

These were the pick of the day for a child's taste buds when they were able to get them along with a grape pop, which had not graduated to the label of "soda" as of yet. Anything that you couldn't get at the store in Marvyn you travelled to Opelika. There, you had a few other dry goods and specialty stores to choose from, but money was always in need and work was scarce.

Roads were not paved in Hatchechubbee. It was the custom to walk everywhere and over time, there were paths grooved out from people walking on the roadways for centuries going to and from their destinations. The roads were usually clean and gave a clear vision from one end to the other for its traveler to keep them from getting lost in the dark, or getting off track. Most Native Americans were good trackers and used Gods sun, moon and stars as their natural compass.

Deep, dense foliage lined the roadways and presented a cooling effect on summer days. On the flip side, the forest was mysterious and dangerous if you walked those same roads at night. Travelers found themselves walking alone on many occasions. They would sing songs their forefathers sang to them as children and occupied their time and minds, keeping them focused on their destination and their footsteps precise. This was their insurance that they would avoid encountering a snake or anything else that might be travelling the road with them.

They'd sing so as not to become afraid because of the multitude of superstitious teachings that ran high among Native Americans. Foxes and wild boars and other animals were prevalent in these parts and any human noise might scatter them, as well as keep the traveler's journey unmolested by any other unknown predator. If you were fortunate enough to know someone with a horse and buggy, you rode instead of walking which was always a rare treat. Most folk walked to be unnoticed in the event it was necessary to hide. It was also a natural thing to do and served the purpose of keeping people healthy and strong. It was widely known that Native Americans lived very long lives unless there was a war. The senior McPherson's were well known in these parts.

Wisdom's father and mother had resided here until they passed away before the new treaties were made. They had escaped the trauma of the mad exodus the tribes would face. They had died old and satisfied on the reservation with no regrets except wanting peace with all men that never came during their lifetime. They had prayed for rain along with praying for their children to survive the oppression they knew would soon be encountered. They had nothing to leave Wisdom and his brothers except strong family values that would soon be eroded away and a history that ran deeper than the roots of the red wood trees.

Wisdom was only seventeen and barely a man by the world's standards yet old enough to procreate when he met and married Anna Mae. She was only fourteen years old just having her menstrual cycle for the second time. They were very young like all others who lived in these parts and had nothing to begin their lives with except each other and the few things left behind by the tribe that belonged to their deceased parents. They stayed in the old home shack for a while and upon leaving, took what they could to make their own dwelling elsewhere. When their families still lived in the area, Wisdom had been taught to speak English by the older tribe officials.

He was very intelligent and would occasionally be used by the elders to interpret to English speaking visitors when he was young. He had a great future but it was cut short by the exodus of the tribe. Even though Wisdom and Anna Mae had not had time to fully mature and really get to know each other before they married, they immediately began bearing children at a very young age which was normal. Bringing new babies into the world was what Wisdom and Anna Mae would begin doing every year after their marriage. Initially, procreation was considered a joy and a blessing to them. They felt it was a spiritual requirement, a beautiful way of life. They enjoyed their intimate time together and treasured the quiet moments they had with one another.

Over time and more children, life would began to beat them into submission and eventually take its toll on them. Stealing both their enjoyment of their sexual intimacy and robbing them of any opportunities to share happy moments with each other again. Life would become hard and marital pleasures would soon be short lived after each baby was born. The thing they so loved about each other at first and the time spent together at night would become a thing of the past as each toddler cried demanding the attention of one or sometimes both their parents. Leaving them exhausted and deprived of everything else they needed for themselves.

Years would quietly slip away like the dew on the ground that they saw each morning as they walked the beaten path down to the pasture to milk the cows. It was their daily ritual to churn milk to make butter that they would sell for that day to care for the growing needs of their family. Soon their sexual desires faded altogether like a thief in the night and became more of a nemesis than a mutual arrangement for them to bond. It became a duty to perform the marital dues and soon even that time would be shunned because of the fear of becoming impregnated once again. On many occasions, Ana Mae would try to avoid having relations with her husband at all cost. Often she would fail miserably when he resorted to forcing his affections on her when he felt the burning urge to relieve himself of the day's exhaustion. As a dutiful wife, Anna Mae conceded to the sexual encounter to satisfy her husband and soon the inevitable would happen… another baby would be on the way.

Sex became a duty to produce another human to help work the fields that were now getting out of hand and Ana Mae stopped refusing her husband. She reasoned that once she was pregnant, she would have several months of free sex without the fear of becoming pregnant, because she already was with child. It was a pitiful way to reason, but it was the only way she could cope with her new plight in life. After all, they followed in the footsteps of their parents and grandparents. The old house they now occupied was comfortable for them and too small for their growing family. They had dreams like all other young couples.

When their babies slept, they pondered what it would be like living in the big city with all the bright lights and fancy things that city folk had. Their dreams would soon deteriorate away with each new baby that was born as they realized they would never be able to afford living in the city raising their kids. It was becoming more challenging each day to get what they needed on the farm they were working. Over time, they knew they'd never leave the area and stopped dreaming at all. They knew it would never materialize and just focused on raising their children like they raised corn, tall and strong. Things seemed to be going well for many years for them but with the hard winters, getting things they needed was becoming more difficult to provide for so many in their family. Now they had seven children knew they didn't want any more.

The babies seem to keep coming and child birthing was hindering Anna Mae from being able to help Wisdom and the other children with much of the harvesting of the crops they planted. They still managed, but barely. A year went by and Anna Mae was now pregnant again with her eighth child. Clarissa was born at a time when Wisdom and Anna Mae's marriage had begun exhibiting some of the same serious problems most marriages experience when there are multiple births and little means to care for the family. Anna Mae named Clarissa after her mother-in-law in hopes that it would soothe her weary husband's heart as he toiled late into the night to keep them fed and clothed. There was no outside work for the minorities in the area, especially not for the descendants of Native Americans. It was beginning to take increasingly more to provide for their families.

Anna Mae took in washing from some of the land owners but it still was not enough. It was beginning to take a toll on Wisdom because he only had one son and the rest were daughters. Naturally, all of them had menstrual cycles at the same time which prevented them from being able to help out in the fields with the mounting work on the farm. Wisdom and his son took care of the majority of the work each year, which was back breaking to say the least. At this point, having so many children didn't feel like such a blessing, since they had started at such a young age with no support from family. This was snow balling into a very stressful responsibility and adding a dangerous strain on Wisdom and Anna Mae's relationship.

Author: Victoria E. Kain

Daily, the stresses escalated to the point that the couple forgot how to have fun with one another. They only knew hard work and the children always needed something which stole the few private moments they could have had. Soon all that was left were minor intimacies when the children were in school or when Wisdom would take a lunch break from plowing the field to be intimate with his wife.

It seemed that after Clarissa was born, Wisdom and Anna Mae began blaming each another for what they didn't have. They referenced that maybe they should have left when all the other tribe members left the area pointing the finger at each other, indicating which one of them was responsible for that decision. Sadly, they didn't realize they both were ultimately responsible for the children they had. Their lives were now taking an ugly turn on them because of what they had chosen to do, even though they loved their family and each other. It was difficult to look at themselves in the proper light with the massive responsibility staring them in the face. No "village" of people to help raise the children as their parents and grandparents once had. No grandparents to rock the babies at night so they had time for each other. Or, the old mothers of the tribes who used to cook for the families which gave the young mother's time to bond with their new born. Back then, it looked much easier when their parents were caring for them. Now, the stark reality was that the children had no one else to go to besides them.

They would feel the pain of having no support at all and would began to feel hatred for the white officials who they felt had caused their suffering. Following in the footsteps of their parents was becoming more difficult to accomplish each day as they slowly forgot the old customs and adopted new ones to fit their drastically altered lives. With the turmoil of raising a family, Wisdom talked with older men that were scattered about at the feed stores and ultimately began to sell moonshine. It was a growing trend in that area and the men explained how much money he could make, even though it was illegal for everyone except Whites.

Since the other men were doing it, he decided to give it a try as well. Living way back in the woods would be a great cover. He could hide his stills and sell the moonshine when he had to. Like everything else, Wisdom knew that with the money from the moonshine, he could buy more things they needed and spend less time in the fields. His baby girl Clarissa was almost a year old now and the alcohol sales were increasing, but with those sales came other distractions. Women… and lots of them. Wisdom would soon be tangled in a web that would destroy him. Selling moonshine would become secondary to his interest in being in the company of other women. He felt a comfort with them that he no longer felt with his own loving wife Anna Mae. The freeness and a lack of responsibility he experienced when the women lay with him, made him feel powerful. They asked for nothing in return and he became like an addict waiting for his next fix.

This behavior was not anything he had been taught by his elders and he would soon forget all the good values and morals he once had. Wisdom was unfaithful to his wife Anna Mae on many occasions. At times he felt remorse, but as soon as the weekend rolled around, remorse left him for his carnal pleasures. All the years Anna Mae had faithfully served her husband and their dreams were now crashing down on them like a tree falling from the aftermath of a terrible storm. Their relationship would tumble many times and come to rest in a quiet place in their hearts, knowing that the rubble from the storm that had swept their marriage away could never be cleaned up again. Shortly after the infidelity with one woman in the town, talk had it that a baby was born to this woman down the road from where Wisdom and Anna Mae lived.

The woman's name was Tooninee, *(Too-nine-e) and she* was only 19 years old and unmarried. She was said to be a prostitute in the town and was one of many that Wisdom had begun keeping company with. It was thought that women who lay down with men and had children by them outside of the sanctity of marriage were considered loose or tainted… but the question was, what made them more "loose" than the men that lay down with them? Was it because the man didn't get up from the bed pregnant? Or was it that there was no evidence that he had ever been there at all? Did anyone ever consider that the woman in these situations may have been made to believe that they would be cared for by their lying suitors and they simply trusted the wrong men.

People knew that true prostitutes didn't allow themselves to get pregnant for their Johns because it would hinder them making money. In the case of Tooninee it may have been just as was mentioned…she trusted all the wrong men. Unlike the other women who did their do and went on their way from the men they visited, Tooninee had tried to hold on to the men she was with, but it always failed for her for some reason. Some said that she had fallen in love with Wisdom, but already had three other children by different men. She was very attractive from a distance, but close up, you could see that life was already taking a hard hold on her from her past years of promiscuity. The child born to her by Wisdom would not be much older than Clarissa who was his youngest child with Anna Mae.

There would only about one years' difference in age between the two girls but they would never grow up together. As the hushed gossip continued in the town, it was confirmed that Wisdom truly was the father of Tooninee's last child. Doing the math showed that the infidelity was taking place at the same time Anna Mae was pregnant with Clarissa. It was sad, but this was the way it was then and unfortunately, not much would change over the centuries as Clarissa would find out on her own later in life. She would ponder why her parents did what they did, and learn a hard truth about life, love and loyalty. It would become an unspoken truth about infidelity in marriages.

If an unmarried woman had a baby by a man that was married, she would say nothing about who the child's biological father was and keep that baby's father secret from the people who lived in her town as well as the child itself. Never divulging the identity of the father under any circumstances would be her duty until death. On the other hand, if a married woman who was separated from her husband became pregnant by another married man and her husband made up with her and came back home to her before it could be known that she was pregnant, the woman would then let her husband *think* the baby she was carrying was *his* child unless there was some other way that this horrid secret would be let out of the bag before or after the baby was born. If the baby could blend in with the other children they already had and no one could tell whether the child belonged to the couple or not, they fed "him or her" with the rest of the children and fought silently at night on the weekends until the relationship either ended or one of them fell asleep in death.

The child would eventually grow up and find out the truth on their own because no one would ever admit their wrong doing. The couples took the information of the deceitful conception to their graves. The turmoil of infidelity caused the relationship with Wisdom and Anna Mae to deteriorate over time because Wisdom never stopped being unfaithful. Clarissa being the youngest felt the worse of her parents failing marriage. Her mother was never the same after her father was unfaithful to her and she began drinking to hide her pain and shame.

She knew where his stills were and when she needed something to soothe her nerves and loneliness, she helped herself to his stock while hurting the rest of the family. The children were affected in many ways by the conduct of their parents. They would not notice it initially, but time would tell in their own lives, years later how their parent's examples had destroyed the comfort of their home and how it affected the way they would ultimately live as adults. Their lives were changing significantly. Their parents were very unsteady as they saw less of their father on the weekends. Years went swiftly by and Clarissa was almost fifteen now and her parents had pretended all these years that all was well, saving face in the small community where they lived. It was amazing how parents hide things they did to seemingly shield the children but ended up exposing them to much worse than they ever imagined. Wisdom continued to farm by day and sell whiskey at night, buying the pleasure of all sorts of harlots, though no affection was lost for his beloved Anna Mae.

Anna Mae still put up the front to others like nothing had happened, even though everyone as far as Society Hill knew about the infidelity. When Anna Mae would see Tooninee at the Rolling store, they would face each other like two gun fighters waiting to draw on each other. Clarissa remembered her mother speaking to Tooninee one day as they stood at the back of the Rolling store truck getting their goods. She wondered if the money Tooninee was using came from money Wisdom had made at his whiskey stills.

Anger welled up inside Anna Mae's heart but she kept quiet like she always did. The woman, Tooninee, seemed bold with her antics, probably because many men she would lay with bragged to her about their families which made her sad. Now she would taunt Anna Mae with her adultery and spoke to her in a curt manner, trying to show that she had something over Anna Mae.

"How y'all doing these days," she said to Anna Mae, boldly looking her in the face as if she dared her not to respond in kind. It seemed as if Tooninee wanted to pick a fight with Anna Mae so she could tell her what she had done with Wisdom. Being the lady Anna Mae was, she put on a good front and responded politely...

"My family is doing tolerably well, thank you." Anna Mae took the conversation a step further not wanting Tooninee to have the last word. "Ms.," she called her, giving her the respect of a dignified woman knowing everyone else in town simply called her a whore.

"The weather sure is hot today, aint it?" she replied," pulling her thick hair up off her shoulders. Flaunting the fact that it was clean and beautiful. Tooninee's hair was cropped short and wrapped in a dirty head rag that was common for women like her. She looked a bit foolish because she hadn't expected any conversation from Anna Mae.

She didn't say much else to her either, except exchanged glances and there was an understanding that took place that day between them.

They both went back to their prospective corners never coming out to the rolling store again at the same time after that meeting. Tooninee learned that day that if you weren't born "with" something, you could learn to live without it. Eventually she left off seeing Wisdom anymore. Someone else would have to fill his time up at night. It must have been something about Anna Mae that made Tooninee realized that even though Anna Mae's husband had cheated on her, he still took care of her better than he did the women he laid down with. She must have remembered the clean fragrance of Anna Mae's freshly washed clothing and the neatness of her appearance. It was a life that Tooninee had always wanted but had been denied by every man she had known. They never spoke again after that day.

Things would change in Anna Mae's life as well. Being the dutiful wife, she was always in the kitchen or on the front porch when her husband was plowing the corn fields. It was customary to keep an eye on individuals plowing because sometimes the horse might be spooked by something and injure the person and no one would even know it. Anna Mae always stood in the kitchen window, preparing dinner during the coolest part of the morning after breakfast. She would watch her husband go up and down those rows all day until late evening. Clarissa was a big girl now and this day she had been visiting one of the neighbor kids that went to school with her.

Parched from walking in the hot sun, she quietly waltzed in the house nonchalantly dropping her hat on the table. It had been a long walk and she desperately wanted a glass of water to quench her thirst. This day, Clarissa walked into the kitchen for a glass of water but was horrified as she stood in the doorway frozen, unable to move. Here her mother was, standing, leaning over the sink at the same window where she prepared their meals each day, but to her surprise, she was not standing there alone.

There was a man in the kitchen with her mother at the window towering over her. They both were intimately involved and no one was watching Clarissa's father dig deep in the dirt of the field outside as he tried to keep the rows and the mule straight. All of this was taking place while her mother committed the un-for-getable act at the kitchen window that day. When her mother finally opened her eyes and saw Clarissa standing in the doorway, shock caused her to let out a death scream at the top of her lungs. Her secret was out and her voice would echo through the woods filling up the dense trees and foliage with the sound of sheer panic! Her scream was so intense, it could be heard by her husband as he stopped plowing to identify the sound of his wife's voice, amplifying through the trees like a siren. He stood erect behind the plow never looking back. He knew the worst thing he could have ever imagined had happened. He was still frozen as he listened to his wife's next words that told him that she had finally gotten revenge for what he had done to her for years.

"GET OUT OF HERE CLARISSA!!! GET OUT! She screamed, almost choking on the words that came from her lips. The man gathered himself and exited through the side window like a thief. Clarissa was mortified at what she saw and stumbled clumsily out of the room, not knowing what to say or what to do. She finally ran like a blind man, running into things as she made her way to the front door and to the porch and down the dirt road she went crying uncontrollably. It would be the worse day of her life. Clarissa was now part of an ugly secret that she would take with her to her grave as many adults had done. She wanted to keep running and never come back to her home, but had nowhere to go but deep into the woods. She stayed away as long as she could that day realizing it was beginning to get dark and she was becoming afraid.

Eventually, common sense motivated her to go home. Not knowing what she would find once she arrived, she approached her home with much caution for the first time. She sat on the familiar porch that seemed like a stranger to her. For a while, she waited for the other children to acknowledge her presence and inform their parents that she was back. Surprisingly, her mother had prepared a magnificent dinner and acted like nothing had happened. That entire evening, her mother gave her the strangest look and Clarissa avoided making eye contact with her. Her father sat quietly with his head down in his plate as if he had lost something in it that he knew he would never find again. For the first time, Clarissa felt sorry for her parents.

She knew that her father knew what had taken place even though he did not personally witness it. From that day forward Clarissa was confused and daydreamed about moving away. She no longer knew what to think about her new relationship with her parents, but understood that it would never be the same now that the family loyalties were completely shattered. There was nothing more to look forward to at home. Her positive thoughts about her parents were dead forever. Finding forgiveness for them for doing what they had done to the family, would be difficult. But, as life would have it, Clarissa would have her own situations in her family years later. Weeks went by very quietly and then the bomb was dropped on the family. Anna Mae was pregnant again and acted like it belonged to her husband, although she knew it wasn't his. It was if she had finally gotten even with Wisdom.

Wisdom even pretended to be happy for a moment. It was the most pathetic thing Clarissa had ever experienced. She could now tell there was a strain in her parent's marriage the size of the state of Alabama. They knew it would never get better or go away. The peace they use to have would never exist again because all the innocence and trust was gone in the relationship. On the weekends, Clarissa's father went down the road to camp meetings which were like gatherings or parties held in secluded areas in the woods. People brought food to sell and there was music and dancing and Wisdom provided the moonshine for all who came out.

It was the place where men met women to have a good time and for many, it was a meeting place for infidelity for the married folk and a brothel for others who needed to release pent up frustrations from working in the fields all week. It was their way to forget the oppression they still felt internally. With every passing week, Clarissa's parent's marriage became increasingly strained. Eventually, her father began staying away from home the entire weekend all together. Talk in the little town had it that Wisdom had found out the baby his wife was carrying was not his. Needing someone to talk to, Anna Mae must have divulged her secret to one of the women she thought she could trust. Like all others, when people are in bed at night, somehow, secrets get told in the dark.

Anna Mae still stayed home with her children as usual and although they were not babies anymore, when Wisdom did come home from his weekend fiasco, they argued and fought all night long, until the children wished their father would stay out on the road so they could have some peace. One by one as the children became of age, they left home. They couldn't take their parents broken relationship and fighting anymore. The four older girls married the first man they knew and left home. Soon, the next daughter did the same. Now it left only Keye, another sister and Clarissa. Keye, never married. He loved his mother and seemed to feel sad for her plight with his father and wanted to be there to help her cope with the new baby coming and all.

CAMOUFLAGE

He vowed never to leave home, but a bad thing happen and changed everything in their lives. Keye met a woman in the city and began his own secret romance. Being naïve, he fell for the lies from this older woman's lips and didn't know she was also married during the affair. His time would come swiftly and tragedy would strike the family a fatal blow they all would feel forever in their little community. The news came late one night while Anna Mae slept alone and Wisdom was out on the road as usual. The sheriff came to the house that night and Anna Mae groggily stumbled out of bed and got up and went to the front door. She thought it was her husband and began complaining about how late it was before she even opened the door. There was a relief just thinking he had come home. Like a teenage girl waiting for her boyfriend to finally come to see her, she soon realized that it was not her husband at the door that night. The sheriff then gave her the sad news that her son Keye had been found murdered. Anna Mae dropped to the floor howling like a wounded animal that had just been shot.

She moaned so hard and loud, that it woke up the children that night, and later some of the neighbors said they had even heard her moaning as well. Upon seeing their mother laying in a heap on the floor, the children all ran to her, trying to console her. Thinking their father was dead, they began to cry as well. Then they would be told that it was their brother Keye whose life had been taken. He was gone forever. Now they all began to weep together that lonely night. None of them would rest as they mourned their loss.

It was the saddest day ever for them. It was even sadder that Anna Mae had whispered to her daughter that she wished it had been her husband Wisdom that was killed rather than her son, for she knew that her son loved her and she loved him dearly. It was a common case in situations of infidelity when a woman's husband was cheating on her. If she had a son, he unknowingly became the male protector for his scorned mother. They looked to their sons to support them by protecting the home from intruders when the unfaithful mates would leave them alone.

The sons protected the household when the father was out gallivanting. Keye did so out of love for his mother and family. He felt it was his duty to take over as the man of the house in the absence of his father. Now, it was a bitter time...it was. Back then, when people were killed, the authorities didn't look for the killers like they do today. Unless someone told what they saw or the killers emerged, then they were never caught. They went Scott free. Later, the details of the killing was revealed. It was said that Keye was killed by a group of men that found out he was seeing a White women on the other side of the tracks. His mother never knew about this. The other part of the secret that Anna Mae kept was that she had been sending her son out on the weekends to follow his father to see where his father was going. Not realizing that each time her son went out, he became exposed to the women of the night.

He was unprotected and vulnerable but she did not realize that he made many other stops in his quest each week to find his father. He too was beginning to find pleasure in the company of these same women his father had been intoxicated by. The long silky hair, the smooth sweet smelling skin, the piercing eyes and fragrance of their perfume was irresistible. Anna Mae had plotted to catch her husband in the act and was going to leave him for good. Instead, she sent her only son to his death by exposing him to the streets, innocent and unarmed. Not knowing that people told lies to get what they wanted, Keye fell into the trap of a married woman which took his innocent young life. Clarissa's brother knew nothing about their parent's infidelity. She had kept the secret, but now regretted not telling Keye what she knew.

She would always blame herself for his death, thinking the truth may have saved his life. Keye, on the other hand innocently thought his mother was being wronged by his father for staying out each weekend and leaving them alone. It would end in a sad way. They never found out who killed Keye but heard it was a group of men. Someone said it was the husband of the woman he had gone to see that night. The authorities didn't seem to care at all that Keye had died at the hands of a jealous husband and his friends. It was a horrible time to remember. Days later, the funeral would prove to be even more horrible. The embalming during that time was not the best when a person was beaten to death. Technology was limited and they couldn't hide the scars when someone died the way Keye did.

When they got up to look at him for the last time, you could see the scars and blunt force indentation on Keye's head and cheeks where he had been bludgeoned like an animal. The scars were deep and still red from not being healed. The mortician could not cover the deep indentations of the object used to kill Keye which made the viewing unbearable for the family and friends. Clarissa's mother fainted and her father was visible distraught. The minister had to close the casket because of the distress that was being caused to the people who came to say goodbye. The image would be a haunting one, etched in everyone's memory. All the neighbors and even Tooninee were there…We figured Keye may have had a run in with her as well on one of his nights out. Keye was buried and it was quiet at home.

It was as if his death had spooked them all. The world seemed much darker on the old road. Clarissa's parents were devastated, but knew they were responsible for their son's death. After Keyes death, Clarissa's parents gravitated towards religion. They seemed to think it would right the wrongs they had committed and that God somehow would look the other way on their infidelity in their marriage if they went to church. It was as if it were an afterthought to try and forget what they had done to each other and to their family. Sunday service became the connecting point in their hypocritical lives. The children that were still at home were now subjected to a strict household. Everyone went to Sunday school and never missed choir practice whether they could sing or not.

They pretended to like their new lifestyle but couldn't escape the past. They never forgot Keyes death and Clarissa's mother never seemed to trust her after she walked in on her and her lover that day in the kitchen. She feared her daughter would tell who the man was that she saw her with that dreadful day, but Clarissa never did. It soon became obvious that Clarissa's mother had been unfaithful to her husband long before he began cheating. Now it may have explained why Keye looked nothing like the rest of them. Little did Clarissa know that her life was about to change drastically when she turned seventeen years old and met a boy named Danny? Life was a strange thing. One minute everything would be okay and the next minute, all hell would break loose. That would be the best way to describe Clarissa's life after meeting Danny.

He was already nineteen and said to come from a decent family. That was always a plus in those days. He met Clarissa at school and began courting her secretly. As all boys did, he said all the things Clarissa had never heard before coming from a man, but realized she enjoyed listening to these things very much. It seemed that it would finally be her turn for a way out of the old Reservation town for good if only Danny would eventually ask her to marry him. Each day, this thought was in her head continually. Soon, they became somewhat of a secret couple, sneaking to the woods each day after school and on the weekends to see each other when her father was gone away and her mother was drinking herself to sleep each night.

It was the first time she was almost glad her parents were distracted by their own sordid lives because it left her free to escape and be unnoticed to do what she wanted. There were many places to hide back then and Danny found a cozy little spot in the woods just for the two of them to meet each day for hours at a time. He exposed her to many of the wrong things at that age and convinced her that the sun and the moon set between her beautiful lips and she wanted to believe every word he uttered. Not knowing how dangerous it was to be where she was, everything sounded so real and perfect to her. She just knew the question she waited to hear would soon come. Over time, naivety would cause her to fall hard. She would give in to his relentless begging and pleading and lying. Finally, he said those three fatal words, "I love you."

They were followed by the fatal question. "Will you marry me?" Her excitement was more than she could handle. Hearing those words coming from him, she readily agreed to marry Danny believing this was her ticket out and all she had to do now was to say "yes" to everything. After all, he had said the magical words that she thought were the key that opened all doors to happiness. Marriage would be next and they would be happy. It was all in line with what she knew. What she didn't know was that, those words meant nothing, if there was no true love or respect behind them for the person they were being spoken to. Soon came the heavy petting and all the other things that should have been reserved for the wedding night.

It seemed that everything was moving too fast and out of control to the extent that she could no longer hold back and was overpowered by Danny over and over again. Sadly, the words "I love you," had caused her to let down her guard and lose her virginity in those woods. As she lay on the ground collecting herself from the dirt, she now felt that their hideaway had become darker than she had ever seen it before. It was as if her eyes were opened and she realized what had happened. She was expecting a different reaction from Danny but did not get the one she sought. Their little love nest had now become a very uncomfortable and dirty place to be and Danny seemed distant.

There was something that had instantly changed about him. She was cautioned by Danny not tell anyone of their secret or they might not be able to see each other again. Clarissa agreed believing that the love of her life had promised to come back and officially ask her parents for her hand in marriage and had even briefly spoke of a wedding.

What could be wrong with giving in to these beautiful words, "I love you," she thought to herself. As she kissed him goodbye and walked home not knowing that would be the last time she'd see him in that way. She vowed to patiently wait his arrival at her parent's home for him to take her away. After that day and night, weeks went by and Danny had not come up the road to the house to speak to her parents. Her mother would see her looking out the window and ask, "Who are you looking for Clarissa?" she'd say.

"Nobody Mama," Clarissa would respond, still hoping and looking out of the door with every sound she heard. She didn't see Danny again, even after school. Finally after many more weeks, Clarissa came home from school feeling ill. Upon her mother's examination of her, she quickly discovered that her daughter was going to have a baby! Anna Mae seemed reluctantly elated, almost in a sadistic way. Knowing that her daughter would soon experience the pain she herself had suffered as a young girl giving birth to all of them.

She now knew that her daughter would understand what she had gone through in the kitchen at the window that day, thinking that her lover somehow wanted her enough to take her away from it all but soon would find that he only left her with another mouth to feed and empty promises. It was all lies! Clarissa's father was immediately told about Clarissa's pregnancy when he came home. His first inclination was anger and wanting to give her a beating, but her mother cautioned him because of her condition. Later in the evening, after digesting the situation, he realized there was a simple solution. He realized his circumstances and remembered his own frailties. Calmly he stated, "I will have this boy marry you," he said.

"After all, it is the right thing to do." They all seemed satisfied that Clarissa would marry Danny and the problem would be resolved. She felt better too believing they would soon be married.

The boy and his parents would take the responsibility for what had happened to their daughter and he would marry Clarissa and take her to his family's home, which was the custom. The next day came quickly and Wisdom, Anna Mae and Clarissa were on their way to Danny's home to speak with his parents. They walked briskly and had lively conversation with hopes of settling the matter of their daughters' pregnancy quietly. Though imperfect, Wisdom and Anna Mae were still dutiful parents even with their own flawed relationship with each other. They realized they had set bad examples for their children and prayed to somehow right the wrongs they had committed even though the last child Anna Mae bore would be the thorn in Wisdom's side forever and the family shame they all would wear.

Arriving at Danny's parent's home, they approached the modest house very boldly. Accepting the normal invitation, they entered the home and were seated. Danny's parents were not aware of what had happened with their son but as they all sat in the front room of the tiny home for this untimely meeting, they called Danny in to join them from the bedroom. As he promptly entered the room, oddly enough, there, trailing behind him was a young girl holding his shirttail like a toddler holding onto their parent's apron. Clarissa's eyes were fixed on Danny and his eyes were fixed on his parents. They didn't know if this could be his younger sister that had followed him out of the room, but soon they were mortified to deduce that the girl was clearly pregnant and almost ready to burst with a child.

Danny was frozen from the time he caught sight of Clarissa and her parents. He stood like a statue on a mountain as if he were mute and unable to speak. Clarissa, still waiting for Danny to ask her father for her hand in marriage, had completely blocked out the swollen belly of the young girl that stood next to him. Finally, Danny's mother spoke to break the awkward silence of everyone. "This is Danny's wife," she said, nervously. Everyone's jaw dropped. Wisdom then spoke about Clarissa's condition and Danny denied having anything to do with Clarissa at all and called her a liar. His wife though visibly young, spoke harshly as well, boldly calling Clarissa a whore and home wrecker vouching for her husband. She even went as far as stating that Danny would never do anything like that because he loved only her. Clarissa began wailing knowing she had been tricked by Danny to give up her virginity with the empty promises he had made to her.

Everything was a "LIE!" Her parents were shocked and knew there was nothing more to be done about the marriage and collected their distraught daughter and began taking their leave. During the visit with Danny's parents, Anna Mae had examined Danny's young wife. She would never forget the features of the town whore Tooninee and the resemblance of this girl to her. It was later found that this young girl that was married to Danny turned out to be Wisdom's illegitimate daughter by Tooninee the town whore who had caused him to become unfaithful to Anna Mae.

What a disaster this was! If all of this were true, it would make Clarissa related to Danny's wife and the babies they both were carrying would be related as well. It was a biological nightmare which was now repeating itself. Clarissa was glad the meeting with Danny's family was finally over and as they all walked home, this time, it was with their heads hung low. Clarissa walked behind her parents and watched them unsteadily climbing the hills they had to travel to get back to their home. She realized the mess that had been made and was swiftly realizing how easy it was to be fooled into believing something when you wanted something else so badly. They arrived home but didn't say much to each other. That night, they didn't hear their parents arguing, it was deathly quiet in the house.

Under the circumstance, Clarissa's parents had no choice but to help take care of her first baby. They soon picked out a name for her, which was "Terra" and she would soon be on the way. They did as they had always done and pretend that everything was good. It seemed that one blow after another soon beat the family down very low. Over time, things changed in the McPherson household drastically. Clarissa soon realized what it must have been like for her mother to want to be a child again but couldn't because she was having a baby of her own. Running through the woods frolicking freely was a thing of the past like a lost dream turned nightmare. She would never see those days again.

She reasoned that, at least her mother had a husband to help with her children. Clarissa didn't know it then, but she would never see a wedding day. She would go through life searching in all the wrong places for the love she desperately wanted and needed. Only finding it once, she would foolishly let it slip away from her, never to see it again. Now realizing that once she became sexually active, things would change in her body and mind. She no longer wanted to be under her parent's rules or their roof and soon began seeking ways to leave the dark road where she lived in Hatchechubbee. After having her baby, she quickly began learning things about men. Most of them did the same thing…they all would lie to get what they wanted from women. She also learned that they would do small things for a woman but always squelched on the big things the woman really needed.

Basically the men only gave the women what "they" wanted them to have and not exactly what they asked for. She watched men in their antics for a while and finally, she met a man named Vincent at a Camp Meeting places like what her father had. It was the same kind of place that caused her father to fall prey to Tooninee, and the same woods where she and Danny had conceived the child she now would raise without him. Sadly, it was also the same place that took her brother Keye's life so soon. What was it about these trees that beaconed their visitors to come and recline under their smooth limbs? The cool breezes that blew ever so gently over their skin making it come alive, soothing their worst day's anxiety.

There was something strange about this meeting place where everyone that was lonely flocked to. Soon she began having frequent conversations with the man Vincent. They met often at this meeting place in the woods. They seemed to get along very well and it was quite different being with a man instead of a boy, but she would soon learn the difference between the two. Vincent didn't mind that she had a child and was ever so attentive to her. He would give her and the baby gifts and the family seemed to like him too. Secretly, Anna Mae had hoped that Clarissa would marry him. Time passed and Clarissa mustered up the courage to ask Vincent to help her get a place of her own so they could have more private time together. She felt that if she told him some of the same lies men had told her, maybe she could come out on top and get what she wanted from them first.

After all, she knew what Vincent wanted from the beginning. That was clear when they first met. At least this way, she would get something out of the deal before she would give in to his wants. She had learned that a man would say or do anything to have his way with a woman. She would play the game but learn that there was a new twist that would arise from this new man in her life. Vincent, like Danny, promised her everything and even found a small house for her and Terra to live in. She was excited about being able to receive what she asked for from this man and soon would move from her parents' home and away from the small town once and for all!

She moved to Opelika the first weekend after Vincent had gotten the house for them. He cheerfully gave her the keys and bought furniture and set the house up very nicely. It appeared that he had money coming from somewhere, but it wasn't her business. She just enjoyed what he gave her. Clarissa was feeling very hopeful that he was a keeper and waited to be intimate with him. She was trying to be cautious and learn how not to be too anxious for a man. That seemed to be the trouble with new relationships. When everything was set up nice and cozy with a small room for her daughter and a room she and Vincent would share as an unwed couple, she hesitated still, but reasoned that the man had done so much to move her away from her parents' home, that she fell prey and began to feel obligated to him. She would soon learn that the obligation was the new trick. She didn't realize if she had waited, it may have turned out differently for her.

The first night they stayed in the house, she gave in to his desires for her. Once again, she heard the same words that Danny had spoken that day in the woods. He lied about her being the sun, moon and stars. Now, here she was with another man who was saying the same sorts of things to her. This time, her ears were not as tickled by these words the man was giving her. She knew that he only said these things when he received something he wanted and needed first. She did not believe him on the first encounter, but after several times of him saying these sweet things to her, she was beginning to have a measure of trust in him, but still much too soon.

Out of sheer gratitude, she still felt a sense of obligation to him and began cooking and cleaning the small house like she had watched her mother do while growing up at home. For weeks, they were a non-stop couple. All was going well until the fatal day came when she had to go to her parents to take care of her mother who had become ill. Vincent took Clarissa and Terra to her mother's home and dropped them off. They stayed for only two days to help her mother out. Vincent seemed comfortable with her being gone. Besides, he had never had any issues before. When her mother was feeling better, Clarissa packed her and Terra's bag to go back to her own home and caught a ride with one of the ladies that lived in town. She arrived back in Opelika and noticed that the front door was ajar. As she walked through the door, she notice the house appeared almost empty. She went to turn on the light switch and the power was off. She ran to the sink realizing something was wrong and there was no water. After searching the house, the only furniture left was the bed in her Terra's bedroom. Everything was gone to include Vincent! All the pretty furniture and even the food and dishes! Tears welled up in her eyes, but she forced them back. That night, she would have to sleep in her daughter's bed or sleep on the floor.

Clarissa was devastated! There was no note from Vincent, no clue as to where he had gone or why...he just up and disappeared! She did not tell her parents initially. Later she found that she was pregnant with a second child and to make matters worse, he had given her a sexually transmitted disease.

It was the beginning of a vicious nightmare for her love life. Crying was not an option with this news…, she was MAD!!! Now, two men had come into her life and taken advantage of her and left her to fin for herself. This was an insult! What had she not learned about men that she needed to know? She had no role models and all the family values were down the tube. She would have to learn on her own, but "like this?" She thought. She went looking for Vincent in all the places they had gone. She wanted to let him know she was pregnant, but couldn't find him anywhere. It was as if he had vanished. His friend Jack Balor, ran the Camp Meetings they frequented. He told Clarissa that Vincent was a drifter and had not been in the area long when she met him.

He said that Vincent worked on the railroad and when work was good, he made good money and then lived it up with the woman of the day until it ran out, and then he would run out. Then Clarissa sat down and cried! She thought she wouldn't, but she did. The tears just came on their own hearing this information. It was time to cry and she didn't hold back. She had no place to turn and could not go home or pay the rent on the house Vincent had gotten for them. Jack was a nice man, but he was married with nine children and his wife was only 24. His quiver was truly full. At least he seemed to love his wife and made sure they had what they needed. His business was prosperous and he offered to help Clarissa get the money to leave the area.

She thought he would want to lie down with her for helping her but thankfully, he was not that kind of man. She was happy to see a decent man even though the fact that she had a disease probably was the reason he didn't want to lie with her. She thought back to the woman Tooninee and began to sympathize with her plight in life. She understood that this was what men did. Women were looking for love and men were looking for one thing. Jack gave Clarissa a job working at the camp sites where people came to eat and drink…he cautioned her not to get close to any of the male customers or women because they were only there for one thing. This was something that Clarissa felt her father should have taught her, but never took the time to do so which had caused her two huge mistakes in her life.

Here at Jack's place, she was to watch the liquor and ensure that everyone paid when they drank. Whatever else she saw, she was to forget it and not talk about it. If she saw anyone in the camp that looked suspicious, she was to take the cash box and run and hide. Jack would collect it from her later. Clarissa worked for Jack until she was ready to deliver her baby. She had made enough money to see a doctor each month to be treated for the STD and prayed it had not adversely affected her child. Part of the money she saved would get her and the children to Chicago to stay with a hometown friend of Jack's who promised her work and a room she could rent until she got settled into the new city.

The baby was born right on time and was named "Brenda." Fortunately the disease did not affect the baby at all. Clarissa would plan to move to Chicago when the baby was six weeks old so she would be okay to travel. Soon, she would say her goodbyes to Jack and thank him for his kindness. He had been the kind of friend a man can be to a woman if he is faithful to his wife. He wished her well as they left the area. Their long ride on the train would deliver them to this intimidatingly large city. Being her first time in a big city, Clarissa was fearful. There were so many streets and lights and people. It was crowded and many of the streets were dirty and the people seemed unfriendly. Jacks friend Cody and his wife Lilly were good people. They met her at the train station and took her and the kids to their home. They allowed Clarissa to live with them rent free for another four weeks at their home since she had just had the baby. They understood the situation because they had kids of their own and sincerely wanted to help her which made her feel more comfortable. She would have a lot to learn in this new city.

She settled down in Chicago and began working for Cody in his store. She worked there until she saved enough money to get a place of her own. It was on Cottage Grove and was over the landlord's grocery story on the first floor. It had two bedrooms, a kitchen, living room and a bathroom. The first night, she cried herself to sleep. She realized she had been through a lot at home being pregnant out of wedlock and couldn't believe how her young life was turning out now with two mouths to feed.

Cody and Lilly had truly become Clarissa's first friends in Chicago and she would always be grateful for their help. She would be there to support them whenever they needed help in the business when times were hard and they couldn't afford to pay anyone. She soon found another job that paid more and took it so that she could afford the rent in her new place. Living with Terra and Brenda, and no man to help out, the next two years were difficult. Being alone was the worst part of it all for her, especially when she saw other couples walking and holding hands in the malls or in restaurants. She would see them as she rode the bus home passing by the shops and diners. The city was cold and uncaring. There were many who had migrated from the South and other locations to Chicago. They wanted the same thing…to get out of the woods and live in the "big" city where they thought everything was supposed to be beautiful, but it really wasn't.

Time went on and Clarissa's basic needs were being met. As soon as she thought she had escaped the fate of another bad relationship over the long months of being alone, she realized she felt okay being by herself. After all, it was just the three of them now. Her confidence level was increasing and she was gaining back the self-esteem she thought she had lost forever. Though unfriendly, her new home in the big city was not the best but she was adjusting to being alone and spending time with her girls. Daily she reflected on her life as a child and shuddered at the thought of being in a relationship like her parents.

It was a fearful thought she quickly dismissed, knowing she wanted the real kind of love that would weather any storm that came up in the relationship. She tried to focus on teaching herself to seek out that type of companionship. All was going well on her job until one day at the plant where she worked, a group of managers came through with the big boss from New York. Being a good worker, the bosses brought the group of people to Clarissa's station and observed her skills in handling their products. That morning she was very chipper and smiled and worked effortlessly as they all complimented her on her skills. As they were retreating, they all shook her hand for a great job she was doing. Each hand shake was good until she noticed one of the men in the group shook her hand and held it a little longer than the others did.

Clarissa had a surge go through her like a lightning bolt. She knew that was not just a regular handshake and reciprocated by looking directly at the man as opposed to looking away as she had previously done. They had connected! It was like electricity going through an outlet. Sparks were already flying within her body. She watched the group go into the next section of the plant but they were still in view. She found herself glancing over at the man that had gingerly held her hand and noticed that he too was glancing her way. With a rapid heartbeat, she knew it had been a while since she had even touched a man or anything else for that matter, but swiftly rationalized that she was not dead!

CAMOUFLAGE

The next day came and only the man that had held her hand came back to the plant for inspections. The others had gone on to another location. This man came into Clarissa's section again but this time he was alone. He formally introduced himself that morning. All the women were fluffing their hair under their hair nets. "Good morning ladies," he politely stated. "I am Eli Chambers, District Manager for the Brand Ox Corporation. I will be with your location for the next few weeks reviewing stats and look forward to working with each of you." His voice was melodious and all the women were swooning after his introduction but he seemed to take a fancy to Clarissa and ignored all the other women. He gave her special assignments ensuring they personally worked together each day. Each morning he'd come to her station and she began feeling special when he was around because he doted on her and paid her so many compliments.

She was taken in instantly because she had never had that much attention from a professional man like Eli before. By the end of the first week, he even bought her lunch in the cafeteria. He bought one other employee's lunch but Clarissa knew that was for cover up so as not to show favoritism in his boss's eyes. It would conceal his underlying motives. The days went on and Eli became more and more comfortable with Clarissa. They talked about their family and life and seemed to like each other. He soon began harassing her for a phone number and when she kept refusing him, he playfully threatened to follow her home one day if she didn't give it to him.

Finally she reluctantly gave in to him. She realized that this was risky with Eli being her boss and all, but her mind told her that she was human and needed a man to take an interest in her. Besides, she didn't have much adult conversation or company for that matter and welcomed his calls. She was still a young woman and had missed the attention she was accustomed to getting from the locals when she was back home. Men whistled and made cat calls when she walked by. It wasn't often, but it did happen. Little did she know that the relationship would be brief. Eli began calling Clarissa each day after work. They talked until late in the night and even though he was aware that she had children, he never asked to come over. Instead, he began asking her to have dinner with him at the company apartment where he was staying.

Several times she refused him and by the third week the women at the job were cackling like runaway hens about how good-looking Eli was and how they wished he would show them as much attention as he was showering on Clarissa. Clarissa played it off at work, but after work, was fueled by the desperate women's coaxing statements and feeling privileged for the first time having a gorgeous professional man chasing after her. She wasn't accustomed to this much attention and having been alone for some time now she soon gave in and accepted Eli's dinner invitation. One thing led to another and they made a connection.

Clarissa and Eli, began spending all their evenings together for the next weeks. Times had changed and Clarissa was being careful to ensure that she was protected when she was intimate with Eli. However, she noticed that after they had been intimate a few times, Eli seemed to spend less time with her each day at work but would call her after work. He became more and more distant the closer his time came to leaving the plant to the extent that he began sitting with other women in the cafeteria during lunch and ignoring Clarissa altogether. Clarissa was through with men at that point and couldn't figure out why this continually happened to her. He would make up with her for his aloofness at work and would want to be intimate with her at inopportune times and a few of those times she did not have time to protect herself. A few more weeks passed and she became sick one day. She knew she was again carrying a child.

This time, she was grief stricken like she had lost someone in death! She began to wonder if he did it on purpose because it was a way to control her. She would not dare consider an abortion but couldn't take it anymore by being ignored at work and hounded at night when he left work. She would gain the strength not to let a man get away with not taking care of his responsibility any more. She went in to work that next morning and boldly approached Eli during break and told him that she was pregnant with his baby…His reaction was something that made her want to puke …there were some women in the background when she told him, but she didn't care anymore.

This was about her! Eli was going to pay. Not for the other children she had, but for his… She boldly approached him…

"I am pregnant Eli," she said, a bit nervous, but stern and waiting for his response. Eli never looked up from the clip board he was writing on…

"Well, you may want to take that up with Human Resources for maternity leave or FMLA," he said smugly, never even acknowledging her presence. Everyone was looking on. He thought she would go away, but Clarissa had become strong and determined not to be taken advantage of again. The other two fathers had gotten away, but not this one she thought. "I will take it up with H.R. and let them know that their District Manager has impregnated one of their workers after hours and now threaten the reputation of this "Family" oriented company that they promote so boldly," she shouted. Eli quickly put his clipboard down and ushered Clarissa into his office.

Once the door was closed, he tried to console her by pretending to be putting on a show for anyone in the plant that may have heard them. "Why didn't you call me aside and give me the good news about our baby," he said, smiling a cheesy smile and holding her hand under the desk so that no one could see them through the glass window in his office. Clarissa was stunned at his flip side reaction. "You just acted like I was an invisible monster out on the plant floor a minute ago and I'm supposed to believe what you are saying now? She asked angrily." "Yes," Eli stated, smiling and continuing to console her.

"I am elated that you are having our baby! I just couldn't let those biddies out there know what we have together." After all, I need a job to support my baby and you, don't I?" he cleverly responded, now closing the blinds momentarily and hugging Clarissa and giving her a kiss, groping her all in one motion. Clarissa was frustrated and confused. She didn't know how to handle this Jekyll and Hyde approach from Eli and didn't know which one was real but accepted what he told her...at this point, she had no choice. Eli assured her that he would be there for her and the baby and gave her the rest of the day off stating he did not want the mother of his child on her feet at all. What pregnant woman would not want to hear those sentiments from her baby's father? But she had been lied to before she had no choice but to believe what the snake had said. She took the day off with pay and left.

Eli began caring for her and the girls but it was to be kept a secret so that he could keep his job. Clarissa played along with this, believing that he would be there for them. At this point, she would do just about anything to keep him there with her to go through the pregnancy with her. She wanted to have one baby's father there by her side to have that feeling all other women had with their babies. Besides, she couldn't let this happen a third time. Their relationship seemed fairly sound for a while and the pregnancy went well. Eli's contract was extended but it was heard in the plant that he was angry because they asked him to stay longer. He had hoped he had a reason to leave. After the extension date, Eli had to move out of the company apartment.

They gave him a stipend and he moved Clarissa and the girls into another house where he wanted to live. It was a much nicer home in a better neighborhood and Clarissa felt good about what was happening, but they could not use the same address at work. No one could know they lived together now. She used her same old address until she ended up having to get a P.O. Box for her payroll check to be mailed to her. Things looked well on the outside until the company began cutting back on the work at the plant and Eli had more work to do than he did initially. He began drinking when he would come home and became very aggressive. The baby was almost due now and their relationship was beginning to shift from good, bad to ugly. One day right before the baby was born, Clarissa's father passed away.

Her mother was all alone now and wanted Clarissa to move back home with her, but Clarissa refused. She realized she had followed in her parents footsteps in taking care of her children and now understood what she needed to do this time where men were concerned. She vowed never to return to Hatchechubbee. She was back home only to attend her father's funeral but would not stay long. It was the very reason she didn't bring the children with her so she could travel light. She didn't want to leave Eli with them either with his sporadic behavior, even though he offered to help. She decided to leave them with Cody and Lilly. They had girls the same age as Terra and Brenda to play with.

Once she arrived back home in Hatchechubbee, it was amazing how things looked to her after having been gone for just a short while. Now it was understood why her mother and father did the desperate things they did. Realizing there was nothing back there in those woods and anybody that came around and showed you the least bit of attention were considered special and exciting. For the moment, your emotions were out of control, sweeping you up like a dirty floor making you feel alive in the calamity of a lovers' enchantment. How soon though, the ugly mornings would come and go from the memory of that night of passion and the feeling of being somebody, dwindled to a crashing down of your very soul. The only thing you inherited was finding yourself with the ever so familiar morning sickness weeks later.

That wonderful memory would soon be choked out of you and become only an afterthought, a gleam in your eye after the child from that encounter came into the cruel world. They would forever be the reminder of your night of pure lust, but you would never have to find a reason to love your child. You just did! Clarissa's father's funeral was over very quickly and she left immediately afterward, heading back to Chicago. She had to work the next day and knew that her friends she left the children with had to work as well and could not keep them any longer than a day or two. Eli didn't seem to mind her being gone but she was beginning to have her suspicions about him on that note as well. On the bus ride back to Chicago, she slept uncomfortably and daydreamed about what her life could have been, if only...

Thinking about how she wanted to find a good man for herself because she knew that Eli was strange and never spoke of marriage. She didn't know what a good man really was? No one seemed to have one among the women she knew. They all were flawed, but some were just better than others. She felt she had apparently looked in all the wrong places and couldn't figure out what was so wrong with her that she seemed to repel men from wanting to marry her. What was it that she did or didn't do that stopped her from landing the right guy? It seemed that she was only giving birth to daughters and she feared constantly that this trend would rub off on them. She prayed that this baby was at least a male. This baby with Eli would tell a bitter story. After she returned home from burying her father, she eventually gave birth to her third daughter and named her "Micah." She took off only four weeks and went back to work. It was a happy but sad time for her and the girls. Eli began abusing Clarissa when she refused to give him money she earned after their secret of having a relationship got out at work and Eli lost his job with the company.

He blamed everything on Clarissa and used her as the scape goat for all his troubles. It also was found that he had other children in another state as well that he did not pay child support for. The company allowed Clarissa to keep her job knowing that before Eli arrived, she had been one of their best employees.

Author: *Victoria E. Kain*

When Eli would drank and become intoxicated, he would attack Clarissa and she never fought back. She'd go to work with bruises over her body and the same old Biddies that swooned over Eli initially, would now sneer and shake their heads whispering as she passed by,

"I'm glad, I didn't get involved with that thing" The whispers were audible and Clarissa dropped her head in shame as she worked all day standing on her feet beside them. She didn't know how much of this she could take. Soon the day came when Eli was very drunk. He began to attack the children, this time Clarissa fought back hard and literally ran him out of his own home altogether. She found another place for her and her three girls and moved out of his home for good.

She was determined never to go back even though the baby was still young and Eli begged her to come back to him. Because her salary was much lower than Eli's, the places she lived after that were all sub-standard but she managed. Her children were seemingly happy and they grew up right along with her. She was finally realizing that she had nothing in the way of a true companionship and the examples that had been set for her did not give her the best beginning. She continued living her life according to what she understood about relationships always trying to be fair but never again being afraid to defend herself if needed.

Eli's daughter would soon be three years old when she met one final man that she would have any relationship with. This man, was everything she ever wanted. Clarissa was now in her late thirties and wiser settling into life. Carlos was loving, kind, handsome and an intelligent man. He seemed to be in love with Clarissa, along with being an extremely wealthy man, which she had never considered seeking for herself but felt it was a bonus. The only drawback to this was that he too was married. She was devastated about this fact and was determined not to allow her feelings to be crushed again by her emotions for a man she knew she was in love with but could not have completely.

Fear stricken, she thought she understood how to play the game with men and play it safe. She tried not to feel what she was feeling but didn't realize that when you were in "love" everything you did mattered. Knowing Carlos could have any woman he wanted, she thought she would hedge her bet, by reopening communications with Eli, who was now a reformed alcoholic. She soon realized she was in love with Carlos and wanted no other. He was able to care for all of her needs and did so. She knew she had found true love and it felt like nothing she had felt before…A year had gone by and Carlos had expressed is love for her over and over again. He truly seemed to want to be with her. A year and six months had gone by and they were inseparable, knowing it could go no further, Clarissa once again wanted to let herself down easy knowing she could not have Carlos. She secretly went to see Eli.

She felt that if she lay with him, she could protect her feelings of possibly being let down if Carlos's wife found out about them and he had to leave her. After the encounter with Eli, she realized she had done a wrong thing and did not want to see him again. When she was with Carlos, everything in her world was complete. Their love was real and like clockwork the weeks came and she was pregnant with yet another child. This would be her fourth child out of wedlock, but she knew that Carlos loved her and would take care of them the right way. Carlos was elated that she was having a baby. Clarissa was only aware that he had two step sons from his wife's previous marriage.

For the first trimester, he showered Clarissa with anything she wanted until one night as they sat pondering over their faded future. Carlos spoke of getting a divorce from his wife who was very mean and contentious. Clarissa would soon hear the words she longed to hear again…"Will you marry me," he asked. Carlos was willing to divorce is wife. Clarissa was the happiest woman on earth…she agreed in a heartfelt way to marry Carlos and would feel as if everything would be alright for them after all.

That night, she went to sleep and dreamed that Eli came for the baby she was carrying. She woke up in a cold sweat, perspiring as if she had been running a marathon. The dreaded thought came to her that she had been intimate with Eli during the same time that she thought she may have conceived the baby with Carlos. This made her very fearful that their beautiful relationship would be lost if she were carrying Eli's child.

To have everything in a relationship that she wanted and to have made such a foolish mistake of seeing two men at the same time, shattered her dreams of happiness. She was clearly in love with Carlos, but now would have to wait until the child was born to know who the father was. The one thing that had been missing in all her other relationships, she now had, but had developed the wrong thought process and brought an outsider into the relationship that could destroy the union she had with the man she truly loved.

She did not know who the father was but desperately wished the child belonged to Carlos. She hated that she had been unfaithful to him and now she sadly remembered walking in on her mother's indiscretion. Clarissa cried in private and soothed her own wounds simultaneously praying for her situation, realizing that just when you think you have it all figured out, you have to start back at square one.

She had been taught by her parents example that if a woman was pregnant and wasn't sure who the father was, she just kept her mouth shut and assumed the baby belonged to the man she was with. You would find out later after the baby was born, but what a horrible process. It would later be found that it was the biggest mistake of her life. Clarissa's relationship with Carlos ended abruptly before her child was born.

She didn't know why he left her, but he did. Before he left, he put her in a better neighborhood than where she was initially and paid her rent for three years in advance. Now she would live in this uncaring city once again, with no one to help her survive. Love never stayed with Clarissa long, but it did visit her once in her life time. She would always cherish that feeling knowing she had been loved by someone that truly wanted her.

Several months went by before the baby would be born in the dead of winter unlike her other children who were born on bright sunny days. They say that hind sight is twenty, twenty. But what Clarissa had just witnessed in her young life as a child, she felt she would rather have been born blind from birth than see some of the ugly things she had seen. She had no idea how life would soon change for her, but still hoped for the best against all odds. It would be years later in her life that she would find out the truth of why Carlos vanished from her life. She never married and never saw another man after Carlos. She wanted to end the intimate relationship with love, holding onto the memory of someone holding her close and whispering in her ear the words she longed to hear..."I love you."

❖   ❖   ❖

~ CHAPTER 2 ~

Finding Our Voice

Author: Victoria E. Kain

FINDING OUR VOICE

Chicago was extremely cold that winter for obvious reasons. Everyone was accustomed to snow and ice, but what happened here was downright unheard of. Everybody knows the Windy City, and its nickname, "the Hawk" because the cold just sneaks up on you and catches you off guard. This year, it did just that. It caught us all off guard. It was the worst year of Clarissa's life. In all the years of living in this God forsaken place, it had never been this cold. It was said that even Lake Michigan froze for a few days, but only the rich would know that because they could probably see the lake from their living room windows. However, we, the poor, lived so far from the water that it was simply hearsay to us.

What we did hear was that some comedians in warmer areas were heard on the radio making jokes about how cold it was, stating that it was so cold in Chicago that the ducks "quack" froze in midair. There were more accidents on the Dan Ryan this year than ever before. It was thought that it was mainly due to people who were not accustomed to driving in such catastrophic weather conditions. The death toll rose almost ten percent that year because of the elderly and indigent people who could not afford to pay their heating bills and were said to have purchased low quality space heaters to provide heat and their homes caught fire.

The fires consumed them because they were not able to escape their homes in time and no one could get to them because of the icy snow filled roads all over the city. It was almost like the mentality of the casualties seen from the Vietnam era. They clearly expected to lose so many soldiers and they became part of the calculated statistics. Many of the people in the North had come from the south for a better life that year. We never could understand why people left the south to come to places like Chicago, but guessed that when you are living in poverty in one place, living in another place in the same type of poverty is considered better.

Most people here lived in conditions worse than what they did in the south. Who knew what made people do the things they did. Nevertheless, there were scores of them living in high rises which replaced the old southern lean to homes and shacks in the South. The only difference was that the houses in the North were made of bricks and the ones in the South were made of sticks. It was six in one hand, half a dozen in the other, but most people felt they had the half dozen when they left the south. We always hated the winters in Chicago because we didn't have transportation which meant taking public transportation or the elevator train which was always crowded. In special situations we'd take a cab. You never got to where you needed to be on time because of traffic and the cab was always filthy. It reeked of foul breath, armpits and unwashed rear ends. Understandably so, since a million people climbed in the seats each day.

Many people took cabs when they had received their welfare checks or disability checks. In the south, they called it a "crazy check." Again, six in one hand, half dozen in another. If it was the 15th or the 30th when people received money, being robbed was almost a sure thing in cabs or on busses. You either asked someone that you trusted to drive you where you had to go or you took your chances and "If," you were robbed, the robber didn't worry about the police being called, because they never came to the poor side of town. The winters brought many of its own troubles in Chicago, but soon it was over and the spring would appear, erasing all the pain and hurt that had been heaped upon its inhabitants.

After the thaw, people were happy to see the snow melting and the city trucks that threw salt on the streets in the morning became fewer and fewer as the temperatures warmed up and became closer to spring. It was a happy time in most cases. You found reasons to rejoice over what little you may have had just knowing you had survived. But for Clarissa, it was a time of mixed emotions of joy and sadness. Joy of knowing she had loved Carlos and sadness knowing that she was pregnant again with her fourth child and no father to claim it. She could barely care for the ones she already had along with their children.

The two oldest were now old enough to have babies and did, but the unfortunate part was that they followed in their mother's footsteps having children out of wedlock and no fathers in sight. Unbeknownst to Clarissa, she had set a poor example for her daughters who were blinded by the love they had for their mother. They would struggle throughout life, the same as she had done. Clarissa vowed this day, to set a better example for her children and help them get back on track with their lives. She would stop at nothing but would begin from this point forward making the effort. Today would literally be the first day of her new baby's life, if the delivery went well.

Though unborn, baby girl McPherson was only hours away from entering a cruel world which would give her no more respect or special concessions for being the fourth child to her unwed mother than it did the previous three. This child would fall in line as the rest, having no knowledge of who her father was and would never meet them. It's easy to judge Clarissa and many did, but they shouldn't have. We may know of someone just like her. She is a loving mother who gave in to the love of a man…but did not give up on the children she bore. She always took good care and protected them.

Here again, Clarissa lay on what they called a bed but in all actuality was nothing more than a glorified cot. It was specifically designated for the non-paying patients at the small hospital.

She could almost feel the springs in the small of her back, but dared not complain for fear of being noticed by the nurses and doctors that passed by as they deliberately avoiding making eye contact with her. They clearly recognized the bed she was lying on and knew she would bring nothing to their bottom line profits, only requiring free services to deliver a baby she clearly could not afford. One of the nurses scurried down the hallway past Clarissa whispering to another nurse who was working with the patient next to her. She spoke as if Clarissa didn't speak English at all.

"Why do these people get themselves into situations such as this?" They should ban them from having sex if they can't afford to take care of the babies!" the woman said. Clarissa's heart was racing with frustration and pain from the contractions she was having, praying that she could just get up off the bed and go home. Exhausted, she frantically rakes her tired hands through her unwashed hair, hoping no one noticed the stain on the front of her dingy blouse that was too small for her chest due to her current condition. It was crystal clear of her inability to provide appropriate clothing for herself during this pregnancy. She wore in between sizes where she had gained a few pounds in the past. This was the extent of her maternity wardrobe. Here she lay once again, on a small bed in this understaffed hospital room on the West side of Chicago, praying that her child would live through the delivery. She waited anxiously to be told if she would be seen by a physician because, like many others, she had no insurance to pay for her child being born.

In order to envision how significant this experience was for Clarissa, one would have to be there themselves or have lived in such conditions in order to feel the pain she endured. The atrocities that befall many underprivileged people on this earth are nothing short of horrific. Medical facilities in this area were understaffed, overcrowded or lacked sufficient doctors and nurses. Personnel was poorly trained and most of them took the jobs to live slightly above the poverty line themselves. Many employees were void of compassion for those who looked just like them on paper..."poor." You felt the shame and fear of being quietly turned away or left sitting in a lonely hallway waiting to be seen after all of the "paying customers" had been cared for before you.

In this instance, it almost didn't matter what your ailment was because you had to wait until the on duty physician collected enough money from those who could pay to pay his bills for the day and then and only then, would you be seen. More than likely, he would give you sample pills, maybe a shot or something simple to send you on your merry way hoping you would not require any further medical attention to keep him there any longer. In cities like this, you have to remember that there are over two and half million people that live here.

Most live in poverty, in places like Cabrini Green public housing and other such projects where people are simply not able to do any better. Sadly though, many would refuse to go back to where they came from in order to say that they lived "up north." Clarissa felt the same about the North, although it had not brought her a better life, but like many, she fell prey to the grandiose stories about city living and lies and promises told to her by men who only saw what they wanted and when they got that, they wanted nothing more but to be left alone. Her life flashed before her eyes like a Fourth of July celebration as she tried to figure out why things had turned out so badly for her. She finally accepted the fact that she had chosen all the wrong things in her life in order to include the men she chose to love.

They all left her with a special package such as the one she was anxiously waiting to deliver. Although she does not complain about her three beautiful daughters, she realized they were the only thing that comforted her in her time of loneliness and her need for love. Like many women who have been thwarted in their lives by the so-called love of their lives, she cried silent tears inside. If you've ever lived in the Midwest, it is no place for people who are physically weak of heart. It also does not help if you are poor. Once in the North, many realized they had jumped out of the frying pan into the fire only for the sake of feeling as if they now had bragging rights to claim that they were "from" the north, instead of being from down south.

Clarissa continued pondering her life and the decisions she had made over the years while she lay confined on the stretcher. She wondered why she had chosen to leave the south in the first place to come to this horrid location. What was so bad about the south that would cause people to want leave the place? There, you had fresh air, fresh foods, and peaceful nights with no city noise. Oppression seemed to be everywhere. Clarissa tried to console herself by blocking out the mild contractions she was having, dismissing all thoughts of being in this wretched city that had brought her no good fortune at all. She finally soothed her conscience by concluding that having indoor plumbing was worth being in the North, forgetting that even that had changed in the south.

That small psychotic thought process would get her through the night. Even now, she felt as if she had to go, knowing that she could not get off the bed alone and go to the bathroom. She flashed back once again and remembered the feeling she had as a child, having to go in the middle of the night. Never wanting to take that trip alone. She'd wake up one of her siblings to walk with her. Once you arrived at your destination, you ignored the bold stench that permeated the airway when you opened the door.

Although the seat was clean, you carefully perched over the ominous opening daring not to peek into the black pit for fear of being sucked in by the thousands of little critters working nonstop. Your sibling faithfully talked to you through the door to soothe your fears as any true companion would. They knew the time would soon come for them to request the same favor walking down that same lonely path. This was just one of the drawbacks of the south then. It was thought that if you lived in the city, you were deemed to be "something." No one could ever identify what that something was, but you wanted to strive to be that whether it was real or not.

She struggled hard to move up to another level as quickly as she could by thinking that if she met the right man she could somehow change her miserable plight in life. Only to be knocked back down each time but she always got back up! Clarissa had learned to fight for what she wanted and needed. The hospital where she was today was on an old military base that had been closed for decades. Although it was the only hospital for the residents in her area, it was better than delivering her baby by herself or with only a midwife. If you had good doctors that came in to help out at the hospital, they were good folks but didn't stay long. It seemed that they were all just "practicing" medicine on the trusting people who had no other options but to come into the facility with their ailments.

They hoped to hear a kind word or be given true medical attention and not just a pill and be sent home. You never knew what would happen to you once you entered the hospital for anything. You just prayed to survive, and this is what Clarissa was doing today between reminiscing about her past and having mild contractions before it was time to deliver her baby. As time moved forward, she grimaced in agony on the delivery room bed for twelve long hours awaiting the birth of her child. Praying harder than ever before to be able to see her baby's face alive, she reflected on the problems with the delivery and the fact that she had just realized that she was as further along than she originally thought she was.

With no medical insurance, it was difficult going to the doctor for check-ups, and she simply had no indication of the timelines, even though she had delivered other children and was clear that she was pregnant. This pregnancy was very different and she knew she was already in her last trimester. She had all the symptoms, but the doctors kept telling her that she was not pregnant when she would go to them with cramps and other symptoms. At one point, she resolved to believe them and move forward, knowing that something didn't feel right inside her. She knew that she was pregnant or something else was seriously wrong with her.

Either way, the condition was not going to go away on its own. She needed serious medical attention. Clarissa had gone to the doctor numerous times to the extent that the doctors had labeled her as having mental problems and only ushered her out of the waiting room when they would see her come in.

At one point in the pregnancy, they gave her pills to start her cycle. She accepted the pills but did not take them, knowing that they would hurt her unborn child. She prayed and waited for someone to come along to listen to her. Just as she thought, the nurse finally came over to Clarissa and ask her questions.

"What are you in for today Miss?" the nurse asked.

"I am pregnant and have been having contractions." Clarissa stated.

"Have you been seen here before?" the nurse asked again.

"Yes, but they couldn't see the baby on the monitor so they sent me home," she reluctantly answered. The nurse looked at Clarissa as if she had two heads and then called a physician over who examined Clarissa. She was having contractions and knew it was time. The doctor quickly completed his examination and stated that Clarissa was having false contractions and that she should go home and wait until they were closer together. He stated to the nurse that his shift was ending and if Clarissa wanted she could wait for the next physician to come on duty. Clarissa decided to wait. She knew it was time and feared she would not make it back, if she left the hospital.

They insisted that she get dressed and give up her bed and she politely waited in the patient center for another two hours with all the other patients. A new physician happened to come on duty that day and Clarissa was sent in to see him. The new doctor immediately took Clarissa into the examining room and did an ultrasound. She thanked God in her heart for hearing her prayers. The doctor initially heard a very strong heartbeat and Clarissa was elated. Her initial fears were squelched that something was wrong with her baby. She always knew she was pregnant but the doctors could not determine if she was accurate about being as far along as she was from their examinations.

The new physician began looking at the ultrasound and realized he could not see any images of the baby associated with the heartbeat he heard. He scratched his head in dismay and was disturbed by what was simply not there. He tried not to frighten Clarissa and asked her a barrage of questions, which prompted him to admit her to the hospital. Clarissa felt safe now and once again began to thank God for the miracle of having this new doctor there this day. The doctor explained that it was the safest thing to do until he could determine her condition and get answers to his questions about the heartbeat he heard which did not coincide with the blank monitor.

Clarissa was being cared for in the maternity ward. Late that evening, the previous doctors that had originally turned Clarissa away from the hospital came in on the night shift. They were outraged that she had been admitted to the hospital. They were visibly angered with the visiting physician and his decision to admit Clarissa and told him he was insane for taking up a bed that could be given to a paying patient. The new doctor stood his ground and rebuked the other physicians for treating a patient as they had treated Clarissa. It felt good to feel that a man was standing up for her welfare, even though he wasn't her man. The new doctor demanded that they keep a close watch on Clarissa that evening and threatened the other physicians that if anything should happen to her, or her baby, he would personally see that they would be sanctioned for gross negligence of a patient and sued.

The doctors all seemed to cower down and left the room sulking and talking under their breath. The new physician knew that something was different about this delivery. He kept Clarissa on watch that evening. She was treated as an indigent by the workers who had all been coached by the regular physicians. Clarissa had worked in this small town since she came to Chicago and paid her taxes like everyone else, yet she was still treated as if she were from another country, being given the bare minimum service and no respect.

That evening, the nurses on duty were all in their prim and crisp uniforms as they strategically danced around Clarissa's doorway like she was some science experiment, whispering about her.

"Her chart shows she is dirt poor," one nurse said.

"They say she doesn't know who the father is either." another nurse commented, as she adjusted her uniform as one of the young doctors walked by. Clarissa was given no respect that evening but dropped her head in shame because of the way she was being treated. She wondered if she would ever rise above the poverty line to command more respect than what she was receiving this day. She was having some contractions now and decided to rest and not listen to the next group of nurses that gossiped outside her door knowing the shift was about to change.

They seemed to make sure they checked on her…probably because they didn't want to lose their jobs either. They had heard through the hospital grapevine the threat the new physician had put out on all of them. The night seemed to drag on, and sleep for Clarissa was difficult. The only comfort she had was hearing her baby's heart beat all night long. She knew that the child was alive whether she could see it or not. Finally, she slept for a short while and in the early hours of the morning began having heavy contractions. The nurses ignored her multiple requests for assistance until she could no longer stand the pain she was experiencing. Calling the switchboard, she summoned her physician.

When she spoke directly to the doctor who was in the hospital resident's quarters, she explained that she was his patient and was being refused help. He was furious. The doctor immediately came down to assist and brought the entire nursing staff to Clarissa's room and cared for her needs while querying them.

"Nurses!" the new doctor said, "This patient was in need of assistance and no one assisted?"

"Which one of you received the call?" he demanded, but no answer was received. All the gossiping they had done, they were all miraculously mute. With the utmost authority in his voice, he repeated the question and no one came forward. All of the nurses were dismissed to go back to work and another nurse came in to assist the doctor with his examination of Clarissa.

In his examination, he could feel that the baby was crowning. He knew that it would be time to deliver the baby soon. He called in another doctor from a neighboring hospital to assist him with the resistance he was receiving from the local physicians at the hospital. They put Clarissa on the monitor again and still could not see the baby but could hear the heartbeat loud and clear. They did notice that the baby's heartbeat was becoming more rapid which indicated possible fetal distress. The new doctor went into action.

"Nurse, I need this woman prepped for delivery, "STAT!!!" the doctor yelled. The nurses all began to scramble like eggs in a blender and prepared Clarissa for delivery.

The doctor then called in two other specialists to see what they could make of the situation of her pregnancy but not being able to see the baby in her womb with any of their medical equipment. He knew that something was wrong with what was taking place and deduced that someone else needed to know what was happening at the hospital with the patient. The labor and delivery room was abuzz with whispering and low discussions about Clarissa's condition and her invisible baby. Some said she was giving birth to an alien. That was hushed immediately. It was said that one nurse was sent home for the evening when she made a racist remark about a patient and the doctor relieved her of her duties. All the other nurses began to become afraid for their jobs and quieted down and did not show the same reluctance as they had shown before.

There was tension that could be cut with a knife from the doctors and nurses that night. In the wee hours of the morning when the new shift of nurses came on Clarissa, was now exhausted and afraid. She accepted that there was no one there to help her through this ordeal. She braced herself for her fourth and final child and the possibility of losing it as well. Fighting the inclination to believe that she could lose her child, she prayed for their lives that day and promised God she would have no more children this way. Clarissa wondered what it would have felt like to have the baby's father present to share in this stressful time.

She had never known that feeling, and wouldn't have wished what was happening to her on any mother. The physicians from the other hospitals arrived and scurried into the delivery room very confident and assured Clarissa that she would be alright. Their words were comforting for the moment, but she wouldn't relax until she could hear the baby's cry. They then quietly introduced themselves to Clarissa and showed her the utmost respect along with a series of questions.

"I am Dr. Frederickson and this is Dr. Paulina," the doctor stated. "We are here to examine you because you have a unique situation," he said, in a very calm voice that put Clarissa at ease.

"Your baby appears to be healthy by the heartbeat, but we cannot guarantee the physical condition of the child yet. We cannot see the baby which is presenting a problem in delivering it." Dr. Frederickson face now had a serious disturbed look on it.

"We have no idea about the sex of the baby either, but that is the least of our problems," he stated confidently cracking a nervous smile.

Clarissa spoke without hesitation through her pain, "It's a girl," she said, breathing deeply.

"I'm having a girl," she repeated as if they didn't hear her through her shallow breathing the first time.

The doctors looked at each other wondering how she knew the sex of the baby when they couldn't see the baby to confirm it. At that very moment, Clarissa let out a scream and sat straight up in the bed positioning herself to deliver her child.

"My water just broke and I am having this baby now!" she screamed. Getting everyone's attention, all of the physicians looked at each other and Clarissa and immediately called for the nurses. They prepared themselves to deliver the baby. Everything was in place for the delivery and all of the doctors assisted her. They explained that for the sake of the baby she would have to do a natural delivery because they could not see the baby on the monitor to deliver it by caesarean without jeopardizing its life.

They scrambled to find any medical instrument that would allow them to try one more time to see what they should have been able to see on their monitors but nothing worked. As minutes ebbed away and the urgent need for the baby to be delivered drew near, they could hear the baby's heartbeat loud and clear, but nothing more. They knew that time was of the essence and had to save the mother and or the baby if it came down to that decision. Clarissa had no other choice but to agree to a natural delivery, which would preclude the baby being injured by a possible caesarean breach which could have been detected if they had the ability to see the baby in the womb.

Although technology had come a long way, there were still things done in the name of medicine that dated back to the old days. The doctors didn't want to make any mistakes with this delivery because of the delicate nature of the phenomenal circumstances they encountered. They didn't know how the baby was positioned and would do everything in their power to safely deliver this child. Clarissa knew her delivery would mean more immediate pain. But, from past experiences of the joy she felt when her children were born, when she held them, it was worth any risk she might have taken to be able to hold a beautiful life in her arms. She knew this would be her last baby and would cooperate fully with any requests from the men who were assisting her. She would take no chances in harming her baby.

This strange phenomenon had never been seen before in these doctor's medical history, either due to their recent years of finishing medical school or whether the phenomenon had been experienced but dismissed centuries ago from the medical practice, as something that would never happen again. Once physician looked up the phenomenon and rushed in to share it with the other doctors quoting the condition as the child being "Camouflaged." This is where the unborn child was completely "concealed" inside the mother's womb. It was as if the child was being protected from some element outside of its habitat and hidden in its surroundings during ancient times.

This was a strange element to the pregnancy and if the mother and baby survived, it would make this a miracle according to the medical history and the news media. For Clarissa and her child, it was a life or death situation. The delivery finally began, and the doctor prepared the mother to push for her baby's delivery. They had prepared themselves for the worse, but what they thought would take hours took only minutes. With only two pushes, the ordeal was over, and a beautiful baby girl emerged from her mother's womb. All of the nurses and attendants were in shock and looked perplexed. They whispered amongst themselves and nodded in disbelief at the smooth delivery. The baby now lay safely in the doctor's hands as they cut the umbilical cord. As soon as they did so, the baby began to cry.

They were all still in shock to see that the baby was perfectly healthy. The mother also looked radiant, as if she were ready to leave the hospital. It was truly a phenomenon… a miracle! Both attending physicians spoke to Clarissa. "You have a beautiful baby girl, Ms. McPherson!" the doctor said, smiling very nervously. The other physicians were on the phone making calls about the phenomenon. As always, they all wanted it known that they were here to witness this miracle and wanted their names on the blotters of the newspapers and magazines as being one of the attending physicians to bring this baby into the world. Who would ever know that this same phenomenon would happen once again centuries later?

Dr. Frederickson, the visiting physician, immediately made his notes on the recorder about what he had just witnessed. "There was full term delivery, minimal pain for the mother when the process began, and the baby was delivered in perfect health within minutes. Prior to the delivery, there was no visible sign on any hospital equipment that the mother was carrying a child," he continued. "While the record showed that the baby appears that she was on time, the hospital records confirm that she is actually one month premature, but is fully developed and functioning." Dr. Paulina then further stated on the phone to another facility. "The mother's prediction that the baby was a girl was affirmative. We have no idea how the mother could determine this at all, seeing the circumstances of the pregnancy. Both mother and child are healthy and safe."

All of the doctors finished recording their findings. They scurried into private rooms making other assessments out of the ear reach of the other hospital staff. Nurses, clerks, janitors and all were ear hustling that nighty making phone calls to relatives and friends about being at the hospital when this delivery, now being called a "miracle birth" had just happened. With permission from Clarissa, the hospital wanted to run a number of tests on her and the baby to examine the reason this phenomenon may have occurred.

Later they took pictures with them holding this special baby. One photo showed Clarissa, baby girl McPherson and the doctor, with his arm around her. When Clarissa saw the photo, there was a lonely feeling in the pit of her stomach. How she wished that her child's father could have been there to have that photo taken and not a stranger. Either way, it felt good for someone to embrace her on this momentous occasion. Many of the same nurses that had been rude to Clarissa earlier, heard about what had happened at the hospital after their shift had ended and wanted to get in on the action of being associated with the phenomenal birth. However, Clarissa quickly remembered their rude and uncaring attitudes and refused to take pictures with them. She now felt like all the other mothers who had delivered their babies, "with insurance."

Clarissa was given the opportunity to choose the nurses that would take pictures with her family. She now had the opportunity to turn these unprofessional women away as they had initially turned her away. It was the first time she felt worthy of anything and relished in that thought. She felt as if she was now receiving the respect that everyone should receive. It was sad that a human being can receive no recognition unless something big like this happens, and only then do you receive such attention.

She knew it would end at some point as well, but was very happy now because the entire hospital was kind to her. She and her new baby were given a private room and the cost for the delivery was absorbed by the physicians that attended her that day. They donated their services for the treatment she received during her hospital stay. The previous doctors who had shunned her, had no alternative but to concede to the request of the attending physicians. They had to donate their trumped up service charges to her as well, otherwise they would have been exposed regarding their poor treatment of patients who could not afford medical attention.

Prior to the delivery, Clarissa had worried about how she would pay her medical bills for this baby. She no longer had that fear. This child's birth was truly a blessing! She really felt that her baby was special. It was the first time anything this good had happened to her. Before she could leave the hospital, the news of the miracle baby had made the local headlines. It was the first time in the hospital's history that the medical equipment could not pick up a baby's image. In order to ensure that the machines were not faulty, they tested the equipment for accuracy over and over again and then sent the equipment out to other maintenance companies to verify.

They soon confirmed that the machinery was in perfect working order and that they had no other recourse but to believe what they had experienced was a phenomenon. Clarissa was not as much concerned about the phenomenon. She was more concerned about holding her little girl for the first time. The soft little bundle of joy lay next to her mother in their comfortable room which was a stark contrast from the first room she was in at the beginning of her labor. The bed she was in now was twice the size of the previous tiny bed and this floor was clean. The new room had flowers that had been delivered to her from wealthy well-wishers and hospital officials.

She pondered for a moment what she would name her baby, and finally decided that since her little girl's face had been hidden from the world like an umbrella shields our faces from the rainstorms, she named her "Gabriella," and would call her "Brella" for short, like the umbrella. Gabriella would someday understand what that experience was like for her mother. Because of Gabriella's special delivery, her mother received somewhat of a notoriety status in the small town. People no longer shunned her, but when she walked down the streets, strangers would speak to her and stare as if she were a celebrity. She received many special gifts from department stores and rich people from all over.

Businesses sent money, clothing, and other free services to the family. She was excited about all the attention she was receiving and felt that there was something special about her baby that drew people to her. Clarissa gave Gabriella more than she had given the other children and made concessions for her to bolster her potential. It was as if the world was watching Gabriella grow up to see if she was going to do something significant with her life for her family. Time, as always, would soon tell the story of how this one child would grow up to make a difference in the lives of many people. The years swiftly moved by and Gabriella blossomed into a beautiful young lady, doing all the natural things young people do.

Her special birth had no apparent effect on her and she was thriving in every way. Like her other siblings, she never knew who her father was either, except through the same pictures that her mother brought out on special occasions and showed all of them. It was an odd life for Gabriella to only see her father on film. Soon she became accustomed to the senseless and evasive ritual performed by her mother and determined never to question her mother further. She felt that she must not have needed a father if it was this important to keep them all in the dark about their identity. She reasoned further that since her father had made it possible for her to be conceived, she would take the reins of her own life and make the best of it.

Even with this hopeless view of their missing parent, they all learned to look forward to those special occasions where the picture box was taken down from the broken shelf that hung neatly on the wall in the tiny living room. It served as a display to visitors a shallow means of showing that there had been a man in her mother's life at some point other than to produce her children. The stories were told to the children as a way to lull them into thinking that they were just as normal as the next child down the street. Gabriella accepted that her mother provided a good but meager lifestyle for the five of them and she appreciated her efforts. They did what their mother did, which was being thankful and living a simple life on the bad side of a town which gave them no mercy at all, yet they still called it home.

Throughout Gabriella's life, she watched her older sisters follow in the footsteps of their mother. They created a life of misery for themselves by having babies out of wedlock that they could not feed or care for on their own, only because of closely observing the only role model they had. Out of love for their mother, they never seemed to be able to possess the desire or courage to move past where their mother had gone and did not do much beyond going to school and dropping out by the 10th or 11th grade. It was as if it were some unspoken rule that none of them could do better than their mother, showing a weak validation that their mother had set some kind of positive example for them.

All they knew was that they loved their mother dearly and never wanted to hurt her, even if it meant hurting themselves, which was clearly what was taking place. The girls knew their mother had been hurt enough in her life and simply gave up trying to do anything more for themselves. Gabriella on the other hand, wanted to do just the opposite of her sisters. She too loved her mother, but her mind was sharp and she knew exactly where she wanted to go. Her dreams and goals were clear as a bell and each day she visualized accomplishing them one by one. Finishing school and going to college and eventually getting married and having children was in order. It would have to be in "that" order for Gabriella. She had seen enough children born in her household and grew up watching the children when her sisters wanted a short break and had nowhere else to turn but to bribing her with hush money to watch their kids while they would sneak out at night, when their mother was sleeping.

Gabriella was to quiet their children if they awakened in the night and began crying when they realized their mother was gone. Sure enough, those nights at the clubs would only beget another baby to care for and Clarissa would sigh as she saw her daughters growing yet again, with no father to care for the unborn child they now carried. She was too ashamed to chastise them because of the horrible example she had set for them. Remembering the look on her own mothers face when she herself became pregnant at an early age.

Gabriella reasoned that she would not give herself to any man unless it was true love and accompanied by all of the successful trimmings of courtship and marriage. She did not want to follow in the footsteps of any of her role models who she felt had failed miserably in their own lives. Her sisters would laugh at what they considered to be Gabriella's high minded plans for her own life, seeing how they were wasting theirs away with empty promises from men they knew. They chided her every chance they got and this day, as they sat around rocking one baby and scolding another just old enough to play alone, they secretly envied the chance they knew Gabriella had that they once possessed but had thrown away.

They continued chiding Gabriella as they sat looking out the window sitting on a worn down old sofa stained with milk and crumbs from their children who had not been taught to eat at the kitchen table.

"So Gabriella, you think you are going to go to college, huh?" Brenda asked, wiping her baby's mouth while she sat on the floor feeding him his lunch meal. This was her ritual every day. She would feed one and put the other down for a nap and finally get a minute to stay on the phone with one of their fathers until dinnertime.

"That's right! I am going to be the first to go to college," Gabriella said proudly.

"Who does Ms. Thing think she is?" Terra asked, combing her daughter's hair, leaving her curls tangled and bushy. She would soon sneak out of the house and no one would see her for the rest of the evening. They knew her routine and just watched the kids anyway. This was her ritual as well. The two sisters kept the chiding going. They laughed but Gabriella didn't care because she was determined to stick to her goals even if it appeared strange to all of them. She had to break the cycle. Even though they lived just above the poverty line, they were all happy and loved each other as a family. They stuck together through thick and thin and never seemed to waiver.

Over time, with much distress, Gabriella managed to finish high school with honors and was the first of her family to graduate from anything on time. They were all proud of her, but you could almost see a look of disappointment in their eyes. It was as if they did not want to believe that their younger sister had done something they chose not to do. Either way, they did not let on their feelings of shame for their own failures thus far, but made the occasion as happy as they could for Gabriella. It was as if they had missed an opportunity to do something they really wanted to do but tried to rejoice in Gabriella's accomplishments. For the first time, Brenda made a comment that turned all of their heads. "I have decided that I am going back to school to get my G.E.D.!" she said. They were all in shock to hear the confessions of her heart.

Their mother had a faraway look in her eyes as if someone had whisked her away on a private vacation for a moment. She stared at Gabriella, remembering what she had thought about her when she was born. Her feeling that this child would somehow change things for the better in their lives was coming to fruition. She was breaking the negative streak and now her sisters were beginning to see a new role model in their younger sister. Their mother would have to get used to this feeling and embrace it or it could be devastating for them all.

Graduating high school had been accomplished now and she had proved them wrong on this first account of what they doubted she could do. She realized that if the family were to make it, she would have to focus and further her education. She knew she could not afford college but pondered how she would make it happen and these thoughts would plague her during most of her waking hours. She developed a new strategy to succeed. She knew her mother couldn't afford college for her so she never asked her to. There was something pushing her inside and she could not stop the force that was behind her, and worked along with it. Taking a short break after graduation, she decided to enroll in a community college not far from their home.

She knew she'd have to work to pay for books and found a job at a local diner making mere pennies but was able to bring all sorts of food home when they had leftovers in the restaurant. This helped tremendously when her mother was laid off for several months. She helped her mother with bills and rent from her small earnings. She worked hard and stayed home and studied late at night to get her school work in. The years went by very fast. By the time Gabriella was nineteen, she was going into her second year of college, but she had become distressed. She watched all the girls at school having a regular life with boyfriends and nice clothes and cars, but she never seemed to fit into any of the groups at the University.

At one point, she was becoming disheartened. She had hoped to be able to continue school, but it all looked very bleak at this point. By the end of the school semester, the students would always talk about the next classes they would take and what they were doing for the summer. Gabriella had to fain having some grandiose summer plans and pretend that she was taking classes she knew she could never get into. She realized with each passing year that her tuition would be getting higher and her money was getting lower with her expenses and helping out at home. Chicago was a horrible place to live if you were poor and it was the only life she had known since birth. Many times she thought there had to be a better way to live than just existing like this.

She was tired of watching people on television and on the train ride home some days that appeared to have all of what they needed. She would see people in their fancy cars and wondered how some of them may have become successful, or at the very least, comfortable. Most people would not even put their old dilapidated vehicles on the Dan Ryan if they did not work perfectly. It was dangerous to do so. Wishing for things was never her forte, but she knew there had to be a better way for her to be able to make it through school.

She could not ask her mother to do any more than she was doing. Money was always the object of discussion and keeping a roof over their heads was the order of the day. Gabriella's job worked her all night and she slept during the day between classes. She was determined not to stop. The years were tough times, but they seemed to go by swiftly. A faded memory of the good times, just like the pictures of a father she had never known but had only heard about since she was a child were a thing of the past.

Gabriella was nearing her twentieth birthday now and while she had made some progress on her job, she still made very little money to pay for her schooling. She had become a very beautiful young woman with many suitors, but none that she would accept... She had exceptionally high standards and refused to lower them for any man. She took very good care of herself and was naturally pretty.

She had soft blue eyes like her mother and her hair was auburn. She often wondered if she had any features like her father that she could not detect in the haunting photos. She figured she must have had something like him if it was his DNA, but would never know. Gabriella was a very intelligent and a sweet young lady. She was not the sort of girl that would do anything wrong; at least not on the surface. She kept herself chaste for that special person in her life when the time was right. Everyone in the family felt that Gabriella would be the one most likely to succeed in life. Even though life had not given her many solid chances thus far either. The better jobs were always given to the more affluent girls at the college which caused her not to be able to get into the better universities.

She was told that she could further her education in a different way in an effort to help support her struggling family and she desperately wanted to do this. But many of these suggestions came from old men with large bank accounts and lots of baggage. They had other underhanded requests for her to earn the extra money to care for herself. She bravely chose to stand her ground and refused any illegitimate offers for advancement. She kept her good reputation in the community and it ultimately paid off in a big way. Everyone respected her which gave their family a better name other than, "those women who had all those babies." Gabriella's beauty captured the attention of many men, but she was turned off by any superficial attention she received from those who only looked at her outer beauty.

She felt that most men seemed to think this was all women wanted from them: to be told they were beautiful, but never to be looked at for what was within them. Gabriella wanted her life to mean something to someone special and she did not want to be bombarded with empty sexual experiences. She definitely did not want to bring a child into the world the way her mother brought her in. She wanted to have the father of her children right beside her when they were born, if that was to be. While thankful for her mother, an unplanned or unwanted pregnancy was not the way she wanted to begin her life. All had gone well for Gabriella thus far. The further she went in school the more difficult it became to pay for the classes she desperately needed. That same year, just when she thought there might be no way to earn extra money, her sister Brenda had decided to help Gabriella out. She had begun working for one of the baby's father's and was beginning to make a better salary.

"Gabriella, I really think I can help you pay for some of the classes this year, if my job continues as it is." Brenda said, smiling. She was happy that her baby's father was trying to help her even thought she was working with him as a way for him not to have to pay child support. It was sad how self-esteem can be eroded when you have been denied so much as a woman.

Gabriella eagerly accepted her sisters offer to pay for one or two classes. "I would really appreciate that Brenda," Gabriella said, looking at Brenda as if to say, "are you sure you want to do this?"

"Then it's settled! With my next pay check, I will give you the money for this semester." Gabriella knew this was a lot for Brenda, but accepted her offer, knowing it would kill her if she refused it. They already felt that she had gone so far above them that they felt obligated to view her as special.

Brenda continued to work for her baby's father and was doing well. She had begun night school to get her G.E.D. They all were proud of her and she was beginning to feel good about herself. Just when all seemed to be going well and they had made plans to help her with her studying, Brenda came home early from work one day.

She had not been feeling well and was lying down which was odd for this time of day. Gabriella walked into the musty little room and tossed a pillow towards her somewhat reclining sister.

"Stop playing so much," Brella, Brenda yelled.

"What is wrong with you Brenda?" Gabriella snapped, wondering why such a foul mood existed.

"I'm pregnant again!" she growled, with tears in her eyes. "That's not all...they fired me because I was having morning sickness and missed my shift twice." She broke down sobbing uncontrollably.

"I am so sorry Brenda," Gabriella said. "It will be alright!"

"What am I going to do with another baby???"

"Have you told the father?" Gabriella asked, fidgeting, hoping it was not her other baby's father. Sure enough…it was.

"He just looked at me when I told him I was pregnant and then he cut my hours. I thought things were getting better. Now I can't go to work because I am sick all day and exhausted at night!"

"Well, don't give up yet," Gabriella said, "It will be alright!"

"No it won't," Brenda replied.

Gabriella didn't know what else to say to this bad news. Now she would not receive the help she desperately needed and would have to find another way to get some help. She knew it was too good to be true in the first place. It almost looked like they might get out of the hole financially.

They had kept the secret of Brenda giving her the money for school from their mother. They knew she would not like that Brenda was helping Gabriella because she would have insisted they needed more things at the house. After that time, Gabriella was not able to get more work and finally was not going to be able to continue school for the next semester. She didn't talk much about it because she did not want to throw that burden on her family. She was very perplexed about her financial circumstance where her education was concerned.

Exhausted from working all day and going to school in the evenings, she barely made ends meet to take care of her responsibilities. She was tired of fighting off old men with empty offers of the pie in the sky if you lie down with me pleadings. Beer bellies, beards, and fancy cars. She knew where all of that would lead because of watching her own sister's struggle with caring for the children they had with the absentee fathers, and now with Brenda having another one on the way.

Gabriella was more devastated with the thought of having to quit college. She could not imagine having to decide if she should keep a baby or get an abortion. She knew the latter would never work for her moral integrity. Angry and upset, she came home one day from work, exhausted and hungry, and decided to forgo the thought from childhood of never asking her mother about her father. She felt that it was time for some straight forward answers. She knew that Brenda had not told their mother about the pregnancy yet and had been avoiding her. Gabriella figured she would get her question in first, before the news came out about the baby which would set the house on fire. She went into her mother's room and asked her a simple question about her father, naturally wanting to know who he was. She could no longer accept the childhood stories of how fine and famous he was, and yet they had nothing to show for him being in their mother's life.

She felt like her sister's children would feel about their father's when they were old enough to understand their situation. She wanted answers and now she needed money from him to finish school. That was the least he could do for her since she didn't even know him. As far as she knew, he had done nothing for her. She was nervous, as if she was stealing something and knew it was not permitted, but wanted to know if her father was someone she could ask for the monetary help she needed.

Unlike her sisters, Gabriella was not afraid to ask. Everything was becoming more expensive each year and she had come too far to give up now. She felt that she would do just about anything to make it through these next few years of school. She approached her mother gingerly so as not to agitate her.

"Mama, would you tell me who my father is and if he is still alive?" she asked. "Every application I fill out for school asks that question and I don't know if I should put 'deceased', 'divorced' or what?"

She continued: "Having the answer might help me qualify for more money for school. Can you tell me, please?" She spoke very respectfully even though her mother was very touchy about answering and hesitated profusely. Finally, she mustered up the courage to give her daughter an answer that should have been given years earlier, but the pain of her own lost love was too much to bear at that time.

Now she had no excuse to lie to her daughter anymore but even when she really wanted to tell her the truth, it just didn't seem to come out right.

"Gabriella, now you know I told you about your father!" You have pictures of him, and your sisters have pictures of their fathers as well. I told you all the truth about your dads, even down to the fact that you have different fathers and I am not proud of that," she said, looking down at the floor, while ringing her hands as if they were an old wet rag.

"What more do you want from me girl?" her mother asked.

Now, nervous about having been boldly asked about the man Carlos, who she had loved more than life itself. They both sat quiet for a moment as Clarissa reminisced, for she had never told her daughters that she loved this man with all her heart and shortly after he asked her to marry him, he quietly walked out of her life without an explanation or even saying goodbye. It was a tragic ending to Clarissa's love life.

Now, knowing she was pregnant and not knowing if it was his baby or not. She would have kept that secret from him and destroyed the relationship if Gabriella was not his. Since he left before she was born, she never had to face that tragedy. So in a sense, she had cheated fate and always assumed that Gabriella belonged to Carlos. It made her feel that the relationship was real.

She vowed never to tell her daughters this because she didn't want to hurt them with any more negative information than what she had already heaped upon their tiny souls as children. Bringing them into a cruel world with no one to help her give them the life they truly deserved. Clarissa knew they would never have the opportunity to see their fathers or grow up with them. She sat quietly in the room with Gabriella and hoped her daughter would just stop asking and move on with her life as she had. At this stage of the conversation, Gabriella knew she had her mother on the ropes, and she was not going down without a fight for the truth. She did not let up.

"Well, with all due respect mama, I need a little more than this now. I am old enough to understand many things and need to put this to rest," Gabriella responded, now a bit agitated with the short answers her mother had given her. She knew that it would be more difficult to put herself through school for these last years and desperately needed to exhaust all options. It was clear that college had matured her in many ways, and asking questions was the way to learn. She did not let up with her mother. She needed to know more.

"Mama, I need to know more about my father, if I actually had one," she said, flinching, thinking her mother would retaliate and backhand her. She knew that her mother had a strong southern streak in her and backhanding you was one of them. She had anticipated that and had strategically positioned herself across the room from to avoid any hostile actions.

Still agitated, her mother began to use parental authority over her. "Don't get sassy with me girl! Asking me all these questions! I've taken pretty good care of all of you on my own don't you think? And I didn't need a man to do it. So don't ask questions like I was some floozy!" Gabriella could tell that her mother was becoming defensive. She felt that she was reflecting perhaps on how she was made to feel having babies for men who may not have had the same interest in her as she had in them. Gabriella could see her embarrassment and pain. The family already thought Gabriella had exceeded everyone's expectation, so she did not want to put her mother through any more pain. She would soon concede and walk away.

"The fact is, you had a daddy!!!" her mother blurted out, as if she was closing a door to an empty room. "I can't help that he didn't stay around Gabriella! I wanted him to", she said quietly, as if remembering the relationship and pain. Gabriella could tell she had struck a nerve and would give up and bind her wounds later from being sick of the lies being told to her about having a father if he really didn't exist. She was not permitted to know anything about him other than what he looked like. Her mother just didn't want to talk about it anymore. Finally, Gabriella decided to leave. She was sick of the subject of having a father and had decided to let it go…forever.

She reasoned that the next time she had to fill out applications that required information about her parents, she decided to state that her father was simply DEAD! She reasoned that if all she saw were his pictures, he must have been dead. That is what you do with dead people. You show their pictures and talk about them because you know you will never see them again. Gabriella left her mother's house that day with a heavy heart. She decided to go for a walk to cool off and think, but knew she could only go so far in that neighborhood or it could spell trouble for her.

Many women had been assaulted by gang members if they went into the wrong neighborhoods. She only walked as far as to the end of the block where everyone knew each other. She vowed that day that she apparently didn't need a father and would never bring it up again. She also determined she would not play charades with the daddy pictures anymore and if her mother tried, she would excuse herself. Funny thing though, without a word, her mother never brought those pictures out ever again, and the box that held them mysteriously disappeared after that day. Her sisters all wondered frantically where that box was. It was almost like the "Who Moved My Cheese" book Gabriella had to read for a class. No one wanted to change what they had grown accustomed to...except Gabriella, and change she did.

CAMOUFLAGE

Gabriella skated into her third year of college with no money at all, schmoozing with all the folks in the Administrative office, trying to get extra work to pay for classes. She was able to scrape out a little more work from two small jobs. Cleaning houses during the day and some days working in the restaurant as the night Manager. She was always exhausted, but was never able to get much rest at home. Her nieces and nephews were all over the place. It had been a difficult year with work and school. Studying was impossible at the house and she was losing her ability to concentrate at all.

As much as she loved her family, she was tired of the turmoil. She had one more year to finish up her bachelor's and another two for graduate school. Figuring out how to get the additional money for school was becoming a thorn in her side. She had a huge dilemma on her hands. Either she would find a suitable way to pay for the next three years or she was out of school for good! It was as simple as that.

She had no idea what to do. That year, she had met a young man at college and they had become good friends. He attended some of her classes and they often studied together and made it a practice to work with each other since they had similar majors. Over time, things began to get very tough at home. Her sister Terra was pregnant again right after Brenda had her baby, and there was simply no more room in the tiny rundown house.

She could never study in a quiet place and between her sister's kids running and jumping and tearing things up. If she waited until they were in bed, the neighbors played their music on blast late at night or played midnight scrimmage football and the ball was constantly being missed by their wide receiver and hitting the side of the house where her bedroom window was. Gabriella had just about given up on her dreams at this point. She had reflected on how hard she had to struggle to get almost nowhere and it seemed that no one could help her reach the goals she was trying to achieve, while knowing she would have helped them with anything she had. She had entertained leaving home before, but now it was clear that she was tired of all the negative traffic in her life.

Living on the West side of Chicago was horrible enough. Not having enough money to live on and watching your role models bury themselves in children even though you loved them unconditionally. Something had to give. There was never anything to look forward to but street lights that were busted out because the drug lords wanted the corners dark in order to sell their drugs in peace. You would hear gunshots all through the night, only to read in the paper the next day about some 17 year-old being shot and killed by a rival gang member at the end of your block.

You walked to the bus stop and you'd see the chalk outline of the previous night crime scenes and traces of blood on the ground where they didn't remove it all because they wanted to hurry and get out of the neighborhood. Gabriella knew they had it bad, but people who lived on Cabrini Green Projects had it even worse. When an apartment caught on fire one summer, some people were burned alive on the twelfth floor because the fire department refused to go up to save them. The people who lived between the drug dealers and prostitutes doing their business on the hallway steps controlled the building.

She reflected on another news release once about a fire that broke out in Cabrini Green and in order for a mother to save her two children she had to think fast. The apartment was ablaze and she couldn't get to the front door to get out. They could see the fire trucks down below as they stood helpless at the window screaming for help that would never come. Finally, the mother tied sheets together and the neighbors down below on the next floor eagerly agreed to hold the sheets as, one by one, the children climbed down to the apartment below to safety. Then, the mother anchored the same sheets that sent her children to safety and began climbing down the sheets to the neighbor's apartment. They were all full of hope, even the people on the ground that were looking up in horror cheered praying she would make it.

Right before she reached the apartment window to be snatched in to safety, the sheet caught fire in the apartment and was not able to hold her weight, because she was pregnant. Sadly, her children and the neighbors all watched her fall to her death. It was the most tragic story that year. Gabriella decided she was exhausted with living the life she lived and decided to take on additional work at the restaurant to save enough money to move away.

One day on her break, while reading the paper, she happened to see a small apartment for rent. She daydreamed for a moment about leaving her mother's home and quickly dismissed the idea. Reasoning that her mother needed her there to keep a balance on things in the house. She always felt that if she left, her mother would literally lose it.

She tried not to keep reading the ad, but couldn't help herself. The more she read it, the better she felt. She kept flipping the pages back and forth to the ad and saw that the apartment was not far from the school she attended. Then she read it out loud. "One bedroom with a large window overlooking the lake." She thought about it for a moment and reasoned, "This is unheard of for the price they were asking." She began pondering how she could make this happen for herself.

"How could I afford something like this?" she thought. I barely make enough money to do what I need to do living at home! My God, what would I give to have a little peace and quiet?" Gabriella kept reading. "A small island kitchen with an eat-in area, a living room with a bay window. This would be just perfect for me," she thought. She liked the fact that it was on the third floor of the building so that it would be difficult for anyone trying to break in unless they were on that floor. It was quaint, quiet, and clean, all the things she felt she needed but did not have. She had coveted the thought of moving into her own place and was convinced that it was the right thing to do.

She knew her mother would not want her to leave home but rationalized that if she didn't move, she would never accomplish her goals. It was hard enough seeing her mother's feet blistered from standing on them all day working in the chicken plant with nothing to show for her sacrifice, but cuts and bruises and the smell of poultry under her finger nails. It was as if she was giving up on herself since there was no man in her life. Gabriella knew this move was necessary for her progression or she would surely crumble under the pressure of seeing her family's demise. She called the number on the ad and made arrangements to see the apartment. She was able to secure the place by getting the proper references and took her small paycheck and put a deposit down on it.

That took courage because she had never lived alone before or even spent the night somewhere else, for that matter. Once that was secured, she discussed it with her mother. Her mother was not happy and felt sad about her daughter wanting to leave her. None of the other children had ever left her which, in a sense, had validated her in some sad way. She fussed about Gabriella's decision a little at first, and then conceded, looking dejected, as if it was a personal affront to her that her daughter wanted to leave. In reality, her daughter was not leaving her, she was moving forward. To stay would mean stagnating in her current surroundings. Her mother again, had to contend with her daughter's decision.

Gabriella knew her mother had low self-esteem and would think that she did not feel she had provided well enough for them. In time, she reasoned that she had failed her last child, but that wasn't it. With only the desire to move out in order to stay focused on her present goals and not end up the same as Terra, Brenda and Micah, Gabriella knew she had to go. She always wanted more than just the bare minimum. She loved her family and knew that if she did not concentrate on her school work, she would fail. Her goal was to ultimately buy a house big enough for all of them and they could fill it up with as many babies as they chose to.

She just didn't want to start her life that way. Too often Gabriella didn't agree with her mom and sisters' lifestyle which conflicted with hers. She accepted that she was different and this new place would be a little piece of heaven for her. It was quiet and had exactly what she felt she needed. She had everything in it that belonged there, which was just 'herself.' She couldn't wait to get settled. Several months went by and Gabriella was enjoying her new apartment. School was coming along good and her grades were ever better. Gabriella and her friend Pallie, were becoming closer as time went on. She had to keep herself in check with him because she didn't want any babies until she met her goals. The last thing she wanted was to fall prey to a man telling her how beautiful she was and then giving in to him.

One Friday after class, she decided that she would drop by to see her mother and the kids before she went home. She had begun to miss them already. Now having a little get about car she bought from a student who was graduating and moving to Texas. They gave it to her for only a thousand dollars and let her make payments. She could drive instead of taking the dirty old bus. It was a good deal and most of the students drove those types of vehicles to class. They didn't want any fancy or high-maintenance cars being dinged up in the parking lot during the day.

She seemed to be able to do more for herself after she moved out. She felt a sense of freedom and a mound of pressure was removed from her head. This day, as she drove into the neighborhood, it seemed to have deteriorated from the last time she was there. It could have been because she had moved away and the neighborhood she lived in was in a better area and the scenery was more appealing. As she walked up on the front porch that was stained with cool aide from the kids spilling their drinks, she knocked on the door, realizing, even though it was home and family, she was still respectful that it was no longer her home.

When no one answered, she turned the knob like she did when she lived there and walked on in. The door was unlocked as she figured it would be. It was as if nothing on the inside mattered to the people who lived there. It was a horrid reminder of what she had moved from and there was a feeling of gloom still in the air. The only consolation was that she was able to go home to a quiet place when she left. She entered the front room and saw her mother sitting on the couch with several of her grandchildren running around getting into everything possible. She quickly assessed the house and it was still in shambles, or worse. One of the kids was screaming and Mama didn't seem to even hear them.

CAMOUFLAGE

At that moment, Gabriella felt sorry for her mother. She didn't want to see herself in the same shape, at that age. Her mother appeared deeply depressed and she could understand why. It was a minute before she realized that Gabriella had even walked into the house. Gabriella thought that anyone could have walked into that house that day and her mama would never have known it until it was too late. Someone could have kidnapped the kids and she would have no clue to give to the police. But on that side of town, who really would care? She knew that there had to be a better way.

"Mama, how are you?" Gabriella asked. Moving papers and stuff off of the dirty couch to find a clean spot to sit. Her mother looked over at Gabriella with her eyes void of expression. She always thought Gabriella felt she was nasty when she cleaned off a spot to sit. But if she could see something, she didn't want to sit on it like a chicken sitting on an egg, trying to hatch it. Mama wasn't dirty like that. She just didn't clean up behind the kids as often as she should have, along with their mothers.

"I'm okay," Mama said, looking down at a letter she had in her hand. "Well, it finally happened,"

"What happened Mama?" Gabriella asked, now curious about the letter.

"You asked me months ago about your father and I never wanted to talk about him.

CAMOUFLAGE

I feel like this happened to me because I never wanted anyone to know that the man I loved just dumped me. Your father is dead!" Mama finally said it, with tears in her eyes that didn't want to fall to her cheeks. Her eyes just glazed over. This was no shock to Gabriella since she had already listed him as being dead on all of her paperwork for school, when she couldn't get any answers from her Mama. Gabriella realized that since she had never met the man, she would show respect for the pain his death had evidently caused her mother.

Whoever he was to her, he must have meant something to her since I am here, I guess,' Gabriella thought. She consoled her mother, but didn't quite understand her explanation of the relationship she had with the deceased man and didn't ask her about it. Gabriella felt that since she had already buried him in her mind from their last conversation, she thought that maybe her Mama would talk more about it. Now was her chance to ask her about him officially.

"Mama, do you know what happened to him?" Gabriella asked gingerly, hoping not to anger her.

"No, no one will tell me anything, her mother said. "They say since I am not his wife they can't give me any information." Gabriella thought to herself as her mother was speaking,"

Author: Victoria E. Kain

So that's what it was? The man, (my father), was a married man that Mama was seeing and that's how I got here, she reasoned.

"Well, when and where will he be buried Mama?" Gabriella asked, trying not to bombard her, but also realizing it was her chance to get a few more answers. If all else failed, there might be a Will somewhere. Paying for school was seriously on her mind these days.

"That's the thing. They want to bury him here in Chicago," her mother said, drying her tears. Gabriella was disturbed now, wondering why they would bury him in their town if this was not his home.

To clarify that thought before she went full tilt, she asked yet another question.

"Was this his home Mama?" Gabriella asked for clarity, needing to make sense of this senseless conversation about the burial place for a man who didn't live there.

"No," her mother responded.

"The weird thing was that Carlos never liked Chicago and always said he wouldn't be caught "dead" here in the city if it wasn't for me. But his Will stated specifically that he wanted to be buried here where his only family was."

"You see, Gabriella, your father never saw you. He never came to the hospital when you were born, although I tried to contact him and wanted him to see your beautiful face at least once, but he never did," she said.

Gabriella listened carefully, not realizing that this information would serve her well in the months to come as things became clearer about this man they were burying.

"The services are set for this Saturday and I am supposed to arrange it all." Clarissa said. Mama kept talking as if to release her frustration.

"I am burning mad, because he was a wealthy man, Gabriella! Why didn't his wife do this for him? He didn't leave me anything for you!!! He said he loved me!!!" Her mother began to cry again. Gabriella thought that this time her mother was thinking about her father's wealth and realizing it would never happen now. She gleaned from the rest of the conversation that this dead man's wife must have been a tyrant. She tried to console her mother, but it didn't help so she determined that she would assist her with the arrangements to get her through this uncomfortable ordeal and bury the whole thing.

Brenda, Terra and Micah would be as useless as tits on a bull. Gabriella felt, it was the least she could do to help her mother since the other sisters didn't seem to care at all. They knew that this was not their father so it was just another funeral to them. I guess it was my place to play the grieving daughter since he was supposed to technically be my father. "Good Grief! She thought. Gabriella took the letter and read it. She noted that they were very generous with the money they gave her mother to make the arrangements. The signature on the bottom was from someone named Braxton.

This letter could not have been from his wife. She wondered who had sent the message to her mother. This was a question that plagued her deeply. Finally she totally ignored the signer and took the money from the envelope and prepared to make the calls needed for the services. Gabriella felt strange making funeral arrangements for someone that should have been special to her, yet she had never seen them before in her life. Seeing him for the first time like this left her feeling some kind of horrible way. There was a sick empty feeling in the pit of her stomach that made her nauseous. She was clear that she would have this ugly memory as the first and last thing she would ever know about this man. How would she get through this ordeal? She didn't feel much for him other than from a human standpoint of not wanting to see the loss of any human life.

Gabriella focused on why she originally had come to her mother's house that day in the first place. The thing she wanted to tell her mother about, which was coming back home, she couldn't ask her now. She realized that her education was over if she did not get the money for her tuition for the next two years very soon. She also would have to let the apartment go, which frustrated her immensely. With all these new developments with her absentee father's demise, she kept silent and waited until another time. Disappointment was now turning into depression for Gabriella. She would need to see a change in her life soon or she didn't know what she would be forced to do next.

Everything in her life now was horrible, just horrible! For a moment, Gabriella thought about what this man may have been able to do for her if her mother had only had the guts to contact him while he was still alive.

"He may have even given me the funds I needed," she thought. Gabriella was disgusted with the turn of events in her life. She felt like a mere servant waiting for her next chore to come in from her master to be completed for no compensation. She kept herself busy, trying not to think about how pathetic the situation was for her mother and there was nothing at all she could do to console her.

Fear and sadness engulfed her entire being and she began hating herself and could not understand the lack of strength her mother exhibited by refusing to demand support for her all these years. What is it with women who allow the fathers of their children to walk away Scott free from their responsibilities? Making a vow that day, she prayed that she would never be afraid to speak up on behalf of her children if she ever had any. She was determined to keep that vow at all cost, not knowing how soon this vow would manifest itself in her own life.

~ CHAPTER 3 ~

A Time to Choose

A TIME TO CHOOSE

The day of the funeral services for Gabriella's absentee father had finally arrived and not a day too soon. She was sick of the whole ordeal of her mother crying for a man that had literally given her a baby and abandoned her! They both had a horrible time putting all of the things in place that the instructions required them to do. It was as if this man's family wanted to insult Clarissa one last time reminding her that she was the dead man's "whore" and she would receive nothing except the pleasure of seeing him one last time and would be made to bury the man she cheated with as some fatal punishment.

Gabriella felt that if it were her, she would have cremated him and sent the urn back to his wife and kept the twenty five thousand dollars they sent. She was desperately tempted to take from the funds and pay for classes, but the mere thought of finding out that she did that would have killed her mother on the spot.

Gabriella was still stunned from finally see the face of the man that she had only seen in pictures. It was an odd but surreal moment for her to examine herself to see if she looked anything like his corpse considering she didn't even look like the pictures her mother had paraded around for years. She wondered if her mother had not made up all the stories about him being her father. At this point it wouldn't surprise her.

Even in his present condition, he must have been an extremely handsome man even for the age he was. Deep down, she knew he was not her father, but would never let on to her mother about her convictions. She loved her mother enough to follow suit pretending like her other sisters had done all their lives just to please her. Gabriella vowed for the second time that day that she would ensure that if she had children, she would know who the father was. "I will not let this happen to me!" she chanted, as if to hammer the thought into her heart.

Life would soon show her that having control is not always at our disposal. After the viewing, the services finally began and there were no tears from anyone that attended. There was talk that the deceased's spouse did not attend because another private ceremony was to be held for other immediate family members elsewhere. The bottom line was that she didn't want to mingle with low class people. I guess, that was the face of true love of the rich and famous. The services finally ended that day and everyone came back to Aunt Lilly's home for the repast. She was one of the rare relatives who had a house large enough to accommodate the family members of this man and others for a modest meal. Her house was clean and well-furnished and organized and everyone commented on how nicely things were arranged. It was customary that whoever had the best house in the family would open it up for events such as this.

The handful of aristocratic family members of Carlos stayed only minutes after the services and exited the scene swiftly giving the usual, "thank you." They were probably spies of the wife anyway, Gabriella thought as she observed one relative linger afterwards and introduce himself. He was careful not to give too much information about his wealth in case someone accosted him for money seeing that the majority of the people that were left at the house were poor. They only stayed for the free food and drinks until everything all was gone.

Gabriella could not shake the clear vision she had in her mind as to how she could have used some of this man's money but knew her conscience would never allow her to ask for anything. It was an unspoken rule that if you were poor, you never asked for what you needed, you just suffered in silence. It was the stupidest rule she had ever heard but she sucked in her pride and got comfortable in the old wing back chair in her Aunts' house and quietly read the Obituary to herself. She honed in on the name on the obituary and scribbled next to it, a.k.a. 'daddy,' all the while looking around the room to make sure no one saw her defacing her fathers' obit. Seeing how she was to be the grieving daughter and all. Her mother seemed content to play the part of the grieving widow and walked about in a daze.

Gabriella did not feel that she could pretend much longer because she had no feelings for the man. When people came to give her their condolences, she graciously accepted them and swiftly moved on to another area of the room so as not to show a lack of remorse for the situation and the emotional state she was expected to be in. Besides, this was a man she had only seen pictures of since she was two years old. She had never heard his voice or seen him smile. Never a hug or a pat on the back for something she had done well growing up. "Why did they have to bring him back here to my home town to be buried for all the world to see what a mess our lives was in?" she thought. People weren't stupid, they knew this man was nothing to Clarissa's mother because as wealthy as he was, they knew it should have reflected in how they lived.

Well, if for no other reason, the funeral in the town confirmed that she indeed had a father whether it was biological or not. It certainly didn't fit with the lies she made up all her life about not having one. It only seemed to benefit her mother who was being consoled by others who knew Carlos and some actually thought she was the widow. She seemed to like that notion.

Gabriella stopped pondering the day's activities for a while and busied herself with who was at the repass. Her sister Terra was there with her kids and one of their fathers. Why she brought him, no one knew. Probably for the free food and drinks. Gabriella couldn't figure out why her sister kept having babies when she didn't want the fathers at all. Gabriella even tried to see if any of her sisters looked like the dead man they had just buried.

She reasoned that as long as they had the same mother, they were whole sisters and that had to be good enough for her. All of them knew that their fathers never paid a dime for them and never came to see them while growing up. Then, there was Micah, she right before Gabriella. She had chosen an alternate lifestyle. No one knew what she was doing. Children, no man, no job and she continually cut her hair so short that no one could tell whether she was a male or female. We had to look at the birthmark on her face to make sure it was her.

Brenda was there with her children as well. That's all Gabriella could say about her and the kids. They were all bad seeds. There were so many women at this service it was crazy. Very few males were present, which was odd. Who were all of these people and were they all really related to this man who had been buried? It must have been that he fathered a lot of children by the array of woman of all ages that were present and emotionally effected by the loss.

You really couldn't tell who could have been the mothers or the children for some. Everyone probably came thinking there would be money in a Will for them or something. Only two children that were present seemed to even come close to resembling the deceased man. Gabriella thought she saw at least one that remotely looked like him. It was a shot in the dark but it was obvious those children who resembled him were cared for by their aristocratic relatives. It was almost pitiful that Gabriella had to be among these people who she really did not care to know. Her supposed father was a rich and good looking man. Even dead. She could only imagine him in his youth. Besides, it seemed that he only had daughters. Gabriella sighed momentarily and looked away as she thought about the vision of the minister talking with the older ladies in the room.

Even "he" abruptly excused himself from the event shortly after someone handed him a check. It was evident to Gabriella that most of the people there were there only for what they thought they would gain from being at a rich man's funeral. She didn't care because he had done nothing for her and she felt strange about that. She asked herself why a man of such means could know that he had a child in need, yet did nothing at all for them.

She could have no respect for such a man. "Why would her mother even cry for this man?" She thought. It was odd to consider for her, but the realization was that Gabriella had not yet known love and could not understand the strong emotional ties that bind two people together at the most inopportune times of their lives. Love would soon open its window of beauty to her innocent mind and she too would be engulfed in it. As Gabriella walked to the corner of the dining room next to the living room window, she glanced out and caught sight of a strange man exiting a shiny black Town car. The driver had carefully parked in front of the house right at the walkway to give its passenger, a clear departure up to the front door where the family had met. It was odd to see this man coming in when most people of any caliber had already left or were leaving.

He was in a black expensive suit with a crisp white shirt and gold cuff links and no tie. Oddly enough, he was looking towards the window where Gabriella stood. When he caught sight of her, his stare became more intense as he made his way up the walkway. It began to make her feel uncomfortable the way he never took his eyes off her as he approached the house.

Gabriella knew this man was different and had to quickly break the visual contact with him by turning and looking away. She hoped that when she looked again, he would either be gone or at least looking in another direction. Unfortunately, her plan did not work. As she slowly turned around to check his position, she found that he had quickened his pace in approaching the front door from the long driveway. Still with a fixed glare on her, he opened the front door without knocking as if he owned the house he was entering and came into the room with the other guests.

Even then, everyone in the room almost stopped breathing as the man searched the room looking for the face he had seen in the window. He looked across the room as if searching for something lost and when his eyes caught sight of the vision he beheld, he continued coming a little closer to Gabriella as if to get a better look at her. His demeanor was as if he had seen a ghost. The face of someone that he thought he knew well. Gabriella diverted her eyes once as she had repositioned herself in the crowd to shield herself again from the man as he approached the room she was in. For a moment, her thoughts waned and she pretended not to see him at all, slightly turning her back towards the crowd in order to face the window so that it could become her full canvas to see everyone in the room through the reflections in the window pane. She felt like a genius thinking of such a plot to ensure her ability to see what was going on behind her so as not to look desperate or too inquisitive.

As she stood at the window, she couldn't help looking upwards toward the sky seeing that the clouds were fast becoming dark and ominous making the day gloomier than it already had been when the sun was out. The black clouds were forming fast and just for that moment, she stopped thinking about who was in the room behind her. It was clear that it was about to storm and everyone was scurrying out of the door to leave before the rain began. They knew that these down pours could get very ugly during this time of year and they didn't want to be in it.

She realized she had homework for school and wished she were already there nestled in her bed with books and chocolate moon pies that she loved so much around her pillow. She figured since she had to be there with her mother, she would nestle in for the long haul and wait out the storm like those who had decided to stay. Besides, there was a great spread in the kitchen and there was still plenty on the dining room table as well. It was odd that most of these older women were from the south because no one from the north cooked this much food and with such precision. Everything tasted fresh and delicious! Gabriella really wanted to take some home but knew her Mother would have a fit if she did. She didn't want people seeing her children taking food from others as if they were not cared for.

But soon Gabriella remembered she didn't live at home anymore and decided to take a trip to the kitchen and get the best of the spoils so she wouldn't have to cook for the next few days with school and all. She would hide the plate in her vehicle which was parked in the covered parking at the back door. "How convenient," she thought." A clean getaway!

Gabriella was glad people were beginning to leave. It was still making her uncomfortable for this strange man to stare at her the way he did and not say anything. She began wondering what his relationship was to the deceased man. "Why had he come so late?" she thought. "Who is he? Is he a cousin, half-brother, or what?" she continued to ponder. What concerned her most was why she was wasting so much time trying to figure out who this man was that was towering in height above all others in the room.

Before he arrived, she had not cared who was in the house, let alone the room, but now she seemed intrigued. Gabriella wanted to break the ice and ask his name, but realized it might appear too presumptuous or even desperate as if she were trying to hit on him or something. She saw how the other women had swooned him when he arrived and she didn't want to appear that she was trying to get her dibs in on him first. Besides, he might be a business acquaintance or worse, as she previously thought, a "relative."

That would be a bummer, because Gabriella thought this man was very attractive. She decided if there was a move to be made, if he were not a relative, he would have to make it, so she waited. Taking precautions not to let him see her mouth the words she was mumbling under her breath, she decided to go back into the kitchen where her mother and most of the women were.

She figured, being in there, he couldn't see her, and she would be out of sight of everyone, and that included the condolences wishers. Gabriella was still rather shy when it came to approaching men. She thought it was un-lady like to be too aggressive towards a man first in any situation, whether they were related or not. She didn't want it to appear that she was coming on to him. She felt safe in in the kitchen surrounded by the older women.

Being in the kitchen also made Gabriella uncomfortable. She was forced to listen to the old women chatter about how fine the dead man was and how they remembered when they were young. They talked about what they would have done if he had ever been interested in them. Some of the discussion was disgusting. They cackled like old hens in a barnyard. Mama must have been saying something about him. Gabriella hoped she wasn't telling them that she had been with him and that she was his child.

Knowing Mama, that was exactly what she did to make herself feel like she could tell the story of how he really was as a lover. Yeah, that's why the old women were so revved up in the kitchen. Meanwhile, the women in the living room had already swarmed the other man that had come in like bees trying to get the last bit of pollen on their legs before flying off into the sunset. Gabriella reasoned that she understood why they would swarm…he was a looker! She also knew he wouldn't get out of their clutches unscathed. There are usually a lot of hungry women at funerals, especially if a woman dies leaving a widowed man.

They wouldn't care if he had children or not. She resolved to stop thinking about what was happening in the other room. Gabriella's mother was standing in the kitchen doorway and right away noticed the look on Gabriella's face when she walked into the pantry area where she was. "Are you ok?" her mother asked. Gabriella gave a natural response showing respect for her mother's delicate condition.

"Yes, ma'am, I am alright," she said to her. Gabriella and her mom continued to have idle chitchat while cleaning off the counter that was now cluttered with pots and pans of baked-on macaroni and cheese and fried chicken which was the fowl of every event. There were half-empty wine glasses and soda cans to be deposited into the recycle bins.

Her Aunt was very meticulous about cleaning the earth from pollution. Perhaps that was why her house was so clean. Mama's house was just the opposite, but you had to love her anyway for the big heart she had for her children. Gabriella began to fidget thinking that everyone there should be able to eat, drink, and be merry for the moment. Accepting that eventually they all would end up like the man they had just laid to rest. It was a solemn occasion and even though she didn't feel she knew the man at all, she mourned for the loss of life. She hated for anything to die.

Gabriella continued to busy herself with the mundane things of the event for that day hoping it would soon be over and she could get back to her troubled life. She relished in the thought that she had some place quiet to go to when this was all over to reflect and discard the day's activities but remembered the order of the day was for her to figure out how to get her tuition paid for the next few years and pay her rent. This thought had never left her mind. She felt extremely anxious about this matter, but was trying to stay focused about it. With the only man that may have been able to help her financial situation being buried, her options had gone from slim to none at best. Graduation from college was certainly out. She could have kicked herself in the butt for not trying to find him after the futile conversation she had with her mother when he was apparently still alive then.

Out of love and respect for her, she had decided against it. That was the stupidest thing she had ever done. From that day forward, she vowed to ask questions if she needed answers, regardless of what the questions had to be and where the answers had to come from. Sometimes that is the only thing that holds us back in life. Never stepping up and taking control of our own destiny, or making the right decisions for what we need at the time. Reluctantly clearing her mind of her own daydreaming about her needs, she decided to ask her mother the question she had pondered while standing in the kitchen. The thought was taking first place in her brain, even over money issues, and she needed answers. She was determined to ask the question, regardless of what her mother might say. She took a deep breath and dived into the shark infested waters. "Here goes," she mumbled.

"Mama, who is that man across the room out there that just came in? He kept staring at me from the window as he walked up the walkway and he just keeps staring at me now," she said, watching her mother's face trying to see if she could read her reaction. Today, her mother seemed calmer than before. It was something about her seeing this man again even though he was dead. It was like she was putting closure to the relationship or something, but her response was acceptable.

Like a dutiful mother wanting to answer the concerns of her child, Clarissa slowly peeked through the swinging doors to scan the room to locate this man that was visually accosting her daughter. Since there were very few men there, it wasn't hard to find him in the lineup. After all, it was one of the topics of conversation in the kitchen by the older, widowed women.

They too had noticed the shortage of men there. Soon Clarissa's eyes locked-in on the one man that stood out in the crowd. Not only did he tower over all the other guests, he was by far the handsomest man in the room, as well. There was a shocked but excited look that came over her face. Gabriella was confused at the look on her mother's face. It was as if she had seen an old lover. Then, there was a sick feeling that came to Gabriella's mind.

"God, I hope he isn't one of Mama's old beaus?" she thought. Her heart was racing out of control. Then came a side smirk from her mother as if she was happy to see the man.

Finally she spoke and mumbled under her breath.

"Well, I'll be doggone!" she whispered, as if to keep what she was saying a secret. "That is your father's brother, Braxton! Never in a million years did I expect that rascal to actually show up here of all places."

Gabriella's mother went on elaborating on her find...

"No one has seen Braxton since he was in his twenties. He has to be about 32 years old now or so and my, my, my, how handsome he has become."

Gabriella was seeing a side of her mother she had never seen before, but now knew that it was this side that had gotten her the four children she had. She wasn't sure how to take her new knowledge about her mother's personality.

"He looks just like his brother Carlos, your father. They both were fine men," she said, looking down at the floor for a moment as if she dropped something. Even though she showed proper respect for the deceased, she still kept the smirk on her face as long as she could see Braxton. Gabriella realized that her mother must have been honest about her feelings for this man Carlos.

She did seem to know his brother as well. Gabriella quietly swallowed her pride and realized that this man was her Uncle. Her faith was beginning to be strengthened in what her mother had said all those years. She really did know the dead man and maybe...just maybe, he was her father.

At some point you want to believe everything your mother tells you. The fact that maybe this could have been her father was starting to look very real, even though the truth seemed to appear too many years too late. While she wanted to believe, Gabriella was still concerned because there was no resemblance at all. Not even to his brother who was able to be clearly seen right now. "So she really did know this man and his family," she thought. She felt bad about the thoughts she once had about her mother, thinking she had made it all up.

Clarissa never took her eyes off Braxton, and Gabriella wondered what the attitude was that her mother had for her supposed Uncle.

"Well, technically Mama and Braxton are not related. Maybe that is the connection," she thought. Clarissa continued to explain things to Gabriella as they tidied the kitchen area and people began coming back and forth with more dishes to wash as they prepared to leave. She went on to explain to Gabriella things she never knew. "Braxton and your father were very close at one time, almost inseparable. One day they just fell out about something and nobody knew what it was about and they never spoke to each other again."

"I wonder why Braxton even decided to come." Clarissa said. "The way the old folks told the story, Braxton wanted to kill your father one time after they fell out, but your father would never see him again because he did not want to hurt Braxton. He really loved him...so I was told," Clarissa said.

"Why did you want to know who he was?" Clarissa asked Gabriella," It is over now. Your father is gone and you never have to see these people again. Besides, he never really did anything for you anyway and now he never will."

Before Gabriella could answer her mother's question, the kitchen door swung open full width and Braxton barreled in. He had a smooth swagger to his walk and his eyes were still fixed on Gabriella. As he came closer, Gabriella could see his magnificent blue eyes.

His skin was perfectly tanned in every way. She only dreamed of having such a tan but knew it would never happen. His shoulders were broad and he was a distinguished man with much confidence in his face. Before he could come face to face with Gabriella, she realized he was coming towards her and began to instinctively back away, as if to give him room to continue his stride uninterrupted. Her mother quickly blocked her daughter's path and intercepted Braxton.

She quickly stepped out in front of him like he was a moving vehicle and she wanted to commit suicide. Then she did something shocking, she grabbed him by the neck with both arms and was dangling from his body like a lifeless limb, all while giving him an unsolicited hug and kiss smack dab on the lips! It was the most brazen and bizarre move she had ever seen her mother make. They say that in a situation where people have lost a spouse, their sexual urges are heightened by the intimate loss. Maybe this is what it was about. Now even more so, Gabriella realized how she and her sisters had come about…her mother was very aggressive and didn't seem to give the man any time to approach her. She simply attacked him!

The strange part about this weird scene was, Braxton never hugged or kissed her mother back and never took his eyes off Gabriella who stood watching the silent movie like scene play out with her mother hanging from Braxton's neck like a rag doll. As Gabriella slowly backed away, Braxton lifted Clarissa from around his neck like a used bath towel. Even with the way she had attacked him, he spoke to her in a kind but firm voice.

"Hello Clarissa, it's good to see you too." Even his voice was powerful and commanding. But to Gabriella's mother, it sounded cold and unfeeling. Clarissa turned and looked at Gabriella and looked into Braxton's eyes, still fixed on Gabriella. After having plastered herself over this man, she now spoke to him and her daughter as if they both were her children. The old Mama was back and had snapped out of her sexual mode. She grabbed her daughter's arm and snatched her forward almost pushing her towards Braxton's arms and yelled, "Come over here and give your Uncle a big hug!"

She said the word "Uncle" so hard it echoed in the room and she probably was grinding her teeth when she said it. The old woman sitting in the corner of the kitchen at the table woke up and asked who was crying. Clarissa then thrust Gabriella into Braxton's arms, probably thinking he would stand there, like he had done with her and embarrass Gabriella the way she had been embarrassed by his rejection of her unsolicited affections.

To Clarissa and Gabriella's surprise, Braxton openly embraced Gabriella ever so gently. He briefly lifted her from the floor and held her with both arms and Gabriella could smell a faint aroma of his expensive cologne on his shirt. There was even a residual scent in his hair. The fine fragrance disarmed her and almost took her breath away. She had never been this close to a man before and certainly didn't understand all the feelings she was having in this strange moment. She could have melted in his arms as he enveloped her and could feel the fine facial hair on his face. The partial fade of a neatly trimmed beard was ever so smooth. The tenderness of his caress was almost sensual and she involuntarily closed her eyes for a moment, only to be snatched out of his arms again by her ever loving mother, yelling, *"THIS IS YOUR UNCLE!!!"*

Clarissa had to pry Braxton away from Gabriella because he wouldn't let go. Clarissa could not understand why Braxton had caressed her daughter so closely, knowing that they were related. Gabriella didn't understand why she had never felt this safe and warm before. She never had a father's hug or any man's hugs for that matter. It was as if he really cared about her and was glad to see her. Realizing she had never been with a man before or had one in her life. From that moment on, she would have something to remember in reference to how it felt to be wanted or loved.

CAMOUFLAGE

It was clear that Braxton was glad to see her. She wished for a moment that he was not related to her but realized that this was one of those feelings that could get a woman in a lot of trouble very quickly if they weren't careful, but careful was her middle name. Mama brushed it off as if it were just nothing. But knowing Mama, she'd be mad later that the attention was not on her. Gabriella was glad she had her own place. Braxton finally spoke again. He said that he wanted all of the family in the room because he wanted to make an announcement to immediate family only. He had to wait until everyone who was not family left in order to discuss this important matter that no one else could hear.

He spoke to Mama and asked her to identify only family members who would stay for this meeting and she felt honored and excited that he had asked for her assistance. She scurried around doing the chore that he had given her like it was a down payment on some future affection to come. Gabriella had heard that Braxton and his family were very wealthy at one time, but didn't know how true it was. She would soon find out the details of this family. She was curious about what he wanted to talk to the entire family about and a little nervous as well. By six o'clock, all of the distant family had to be ushered from the house in order for the private meeting and the reading of the Will to take place.

Author: Victoria E. Kain

When it was only immediate family left, all the women young and old alike were lined up giggling like Braxton was some king looking for his long lost Queen. Gabriella sank to the back of the circle once again as everyone gathered in the middle of the room and Braxton sat in the center of them all and began pulling papers from his brief case. There were two large men standing at the front and back door as if to guard it from anyone entering or eaves dropping. Braxton began speaking about Gabriella's father and himself and the business they had established some years ago that was very successful. He didn't appear to have ever had any quarrels with his deceased brother as her mother had indicated in the kitchen when she first spoke about him. He spoke endearingly about his brother as if he loved him very much and was deeply saddened that he was gone.

Braxton began telling the family what was in the Will left by his brother. He said the Will expressed a specific dollar amount of what was left totaling over 500 million dollars in assets from the business that the two of them owned with two other partners. When he said that, the room was now abuzz like an agitated beehive with hushed excitement. Everyone was comparing thoughts and thinking they were about to get a share of the loot and would go home rich.

One woman fainted, thinking that this was the case. They had to excuse her from the room, which disturbed her. Braxton quickly cleared the air about the money before anyone else fainted. The rest of the request from the Will was disclosed. It was very disturbing to hear what he told them next. He continued reading and stated that he now owned 51% of the business but 49% was owned by two ruthless silent business partners of his deceased brother. He further stated that in order for him to keep the 51 percent of this business he would have to buy out the other 49% lock, stock, and barrel and there was only one way he could officiate that.

The final stipulation was that his brother must have a "Male" heir or the 51% reverts to the business partners leaving Braxton and all of Carlo's children penniless. Having the male heir would give him the legal right to buy out the 49% and own all of the business. If there was no male heir, the business partners would then inherit it all. The problem was that it was known that Carlos only had daughters and no sons. Everyone's face was bewildered at this moment. They didn't see how they could get any of the millions that, to them was just sitting there for the taking. They all looked around the room and tried to figure out what Braxton was talking about regarding the "heir." Gabriella's ignorant sister Terra asked,

"What is an heir?" Braxton was too dignified to even answer her.

Someone whispered to her what it meant and she was silent for the remainder of the reading of the will.

CAMOUFLAGE

"How could we help with a male heir?" Gabriella thought. We are all related.

"For goodness sakes Braxton," her mother boldly said. "What are you talking about?" Terra, decided to speak again and blurted out, "So what do you want us to do? Tell, me and I will do it for one million dollars... you can keep the rest." Terra at least had a basic thought that there was something that needed to be done. She already had three kids by different fathers. She was on assistance from the state and had no job. Brenda was almost married and had scalded her last baby's daddy when he fired her from her job. He had been cheating on her with his ex-wife. She now had a domestic abuse charge on her record. Micah was completely out of the picture.

She wasn't sure what she wanted to do anymore after having her children. Braxton went on to explain the final part of the will. He once again got everyone's attention. The crowd was getting loud now, and some were trying to leave. When the noise quieted down, Braxton read the final part of the will and outlined the stipulation of the heir situation and everyone was in utter shock! The Will further stipulated that if Carlos (the deceased) did not already have a male heir, upon his demise, it now would have to be a family member willing to be artificially inseminated and carry the child to term as Carlos's only heir. It had to be a family member because anyone else would stand to become impregnated and then could decide to "Keep" the child and sue for any undisclosed amount.

It was considered that if a family member consented, they would stand to gain financially and would not want to keep the child because they would be doing this as a way to save the family fortune. Since Carlos was already deceased, how could an heir be produced? They all were thinking trying to figure it out. Braxton continued. "This would be done by artificial insemination," he stated. The older women of the family almost passed out. They were outraged and grumbled as they left out of the door.

"This is ridiculous! If a man wants a baby, why would he want to let someone else other than his wife carry the child?" All the old women stormed out.

Everyone understood that they made a good point, but realizing that in their day, artificial insemination was not heard of and they were infuriated and many left abruptly. No one objected to them leaving because there was nothing they could do anyway so their early departure was a plus. It only made it easier for Braxton to talk to the rest of the women that understood at least some of what he was saying.

Braxton went on to explain that the woman must meet certain requirements to carry this baby. She must be without other children and cannot have been married before. By having these ties, it was felt that it would jeopardize the money the individual would receive because spouses would be entitled to part of what the surrogate mother received and could put pressure on the pregnant mother. It could then be unhealthy for the baby as well.

This person could not be engaged to be married or in any contractual agreement with anyone to marry. Verbal or otherwise. By now, everyone in the room was bewildered, but they continued to listen even if though they knew they were disqualified because of one reason or another. Braxton then gave the final information on the process to complete the conditions of the will:

"After the person is inseminated, she would be checked after four weeks to validate a pregnancy. Then, if she is pregnant, she would go back the end of the first trimester to determine the sex of the baby and if it is a boy, she would receive an initial $200,000 dollars.

"Each month she successfully carried the baby to term, she would receive $100,000 per month. At the end of the 9 months and the child is born, the mother will receive one million dollars. It would be over two million dollars total with her lodging and medical. The child would then be legally adopted by Braxton and he would take over rearing the child as his son.

The company would then be turned over into Braxton's name giving him 100% control. The baby would become the legal heir at age 21 which would complete Carlos's estate and have complete control of all assets. Everyone sat quietly for a moment not knowing what to think. It was clear now on what was happening. Many wanted to leave but the men at the door prevented them from doing so until Braxton had finished reading the will.

There was one last part. He continued: "If the woman agreed to the terms and became pregnant and then was involved with another man, the contract would be null and void and the money received would be "returned." The woman would have already signed an agreement to give the baby up at birth and receive nothing further for herself, but the child would be adopted by a good family and taken care of very well. They would have a trust in their name that they would also receive upon reaching 21 years of age. Only "they" could claim these funds and if anything happened to that child that was considered suspicious, prior to or after reaching their majority, the money would go back to Carlos's Estate and the funds would go to a charity Carlos had designated.

Gabriella looked around the room at the young women looking down at their children almost angered that they were not in a position to carry out this request. Of all things to do for millions of dollars that women were doing for free and no one in the room except Gabriella would actually qualify…yet she was the one that would not even consider thinking about the offer. One person already pregnant offered to let them adopt the baby, which was going to be a boy. Braxton refused. The child had to be from Carlos's bloodline.

The family was in shock that this would be the only way to keep the family fortune, but they all whispered about who they thought could do this and some flat-out said it was ridiculous. The rain was pouring down outside and lightening came crashing over the house causing everyone to recognize that there were higher forces working outside than inside the room. Suddenly, the lights went out temporarily.

Everyone sat in the dark house sighing. It was almost a relief for most so that their sad faces could not be seen. They knew they would walk out today, still penniless when a candle was lit by Braxton as he held it up in the air and everyone could clearly see his shadow across the room as the whispers became a frenzy about who could produce a child to get this money. Gabriella sat quietly in the corner and didn't know what to think about this request at all.

"That much money could help so many people, 'Gabriella thought,' but, the only way to get it was to have a baby and not be married! It was out of the question for her. Even if it was an artificial insemination. Besides she did have a male friend from school she was sort of interested in, but they were not a couple. The room still was buzzing trying to figure out what family member could actually carry this child for the family.

All offers were declined by Braxton. He stated that Carlos had donated to a private reproduction bank in Switzerland years earlier in the event he did not have a son and if something were to happen to him. This would protect his fortune. That may have explained why so many women were at his services. Maybe Carlos was trying for a son and just couldn't make it happen. Many that day felt that it would be wrong for a family member to carry their father's offspring. Soon they realized that artificial insemination was a real and common procedure for reproduction or infertile couples. People were freezing sperm and eggs from men and women and using them later in life because they wanted to get their careers started and wanted the healthy eggs for later.

Also, surrogates were being used in many instances where mother's couldn't carry the baby for one reason or another but had the eggs. The person carrying the child would be artificially inseminated. There was never any physical contact with the father of the child in order to keep the marriage valid and removing infidelity. They just did not know who would qualify to do this. There was a lot at stake. Finally, Braxton dismissed the group and the large men at the door opened it and escorted everyone out as if they had been held against their will. Before Braxton left, he took Clarissa to the dining room and sat in the chairs along the wall with her. There was no one else in the room and everyone was leaving now since the rain had stopped and the reading of the Will was over.

Gabriella dared not go in where her mother and Braxton sat and interrupt whatever they were discussing. It appeared to be intense. Braxton had a very serious look on his face and now Gabriella was really curious about their conversation. She had never seen her mother look so confused. They talked for a long time and then when Gabriella saw Braxton give her mother an envelope, she watched her look into the envelope and began crying uncontrollably. It was then that Braxton embraced her and this time, he did not push her away. He hugged her close. She kissed him on the cheek this time and they both rose simultaneously from their seats. It was as if he told her something that had changed her life. He kissed her hand and she held his face and had the look of a mother's love instead of lust in her eyes.

He apparently told her things that he had told no one else. Gabriella figured her mother was happy with what she had received. "Maybe Carlos had finally left her something after all," Gabriella thought for a moment. "What if her mother was given enough money to help with her schooling?" She became excited at the thought that she might be able to go to school after all. Finally Braxton got up to leave. She finally saw her mother hug Braxton again and this time she wiped the tears from her eyes. They talked as they both got up and Clarissa had a bewildered look on her face and searched the partially empty room and locked eyes with Gabriella.

She stared for a long time and then looked away as if her child was someone she didn't know. Gabriella had no idea what the look was for as she watched Braxton get his jacket and his driver pulled the long black town car up to the front door. He brought an umbrella out for Braxton that looked like they were walking under a tent. Braxton got into the car and his driver closed his door. He then let the window down half way as the driver got in on the driver's side. Gabriella moved into the kitchen again and purposely stationed herself at the window. She wanted to get a final look at this new member of her family that she couldn't help feeling a bit strange about.

As she looked out the window through the rain drops that had begun falling lightly on the sidewalk, Braxton stared at Gabriella from the partially opened window of his vehicle as they slowly drove off. He nodded his head to say goodbye to Gabriella knowing she could see him too. The window slowly raised leaving only a reflection from the tinted glass that engulfed the vehicle. She watched until it was clearly out of sight. What a day...she thought. What a day this has been. She thought about all that had been said by Braxton. There was something she felt inside but didn't quite understand what it was. Everyone had been told not to divulge the information they heard to anyone or there could be trouble and none of them wanted trouble.

Who was this man that had walked into their lives and left a strange familiarity and strong attraction? A man who had rejected her mother in one moment but embraced her and made her cry in the next. These were the signs of a powerful man who could turn his emotions on and off and smoothly walk away leaving no trace of ever having been there except in the broken hearts of the people he had left behind who had been graced with his presence. He was also a man full of love and tender compassion. It would be the only vision Gabriella would have of what her own father would have been like if he had been in her life. To know the love of a father like that could have changed her life forever. But, she knew it was too late for that. It would be the one feeling she would take away from today's service and cherish it, along with the haunting memory of Braxton holding her for those few brief moments.

~ CHAPTER 4 ~

Eyes of the Beholder

Author: Victoria E. Kain

CAMOUFLAGE

THE EYES OF THE BEHOLDER

Weeks had gone by since the funeral and Gabriella found out that her mother apparently had received money from Braxton. She thought it probably was from Carlos' Will. Brenda, Terra and Micah bragged about how many new things they had received, and how much money their mother was throwing around. Funny thing though, Gabriella was never given one dime nor offered a cent of her new found fortune to help her with school. She was not even asked if she needed anything. After that hard blow, she felt angry and sad because she was being left out of whatever her mother had received.

Gabriella couldn't believe how she had been systematically lopped off as if she were a useless limb. She felt that she was being punished for moving out of the house and all she was trying to do was to better herself to help them.

She was hurt just thinking that her mother had forgotten about the fact that this man was supposed to be "her" father, and wasn't even the father of her other children, but they got to reap the benefits of his wealth. She finally reasoned that maybe he really wasn't her father after all and she was not deserving anything from him. In her quieting thoughts, she determined to let them have their spoils and would move on as she knew she had to when she moved out. Her rent was coming due soon and her tuition was to be paid the following week.

If these were not paid, she would not only be out a place to stay, but out of school as well. Though still determined to succeed, she was entertaining the thought of possibly moving from Chicago altogether. She didn't know where she would go and had no knowledge of any family to go to for help. Pride or whatever it was called had caused her to feel that she would not ask for anything else from her mother. She resolved from that point to make it on her own. She reasoned that if her mom gave her sisters gifts but not her, maybe that was the way it was supposed to be. Weeks later, everyone in the family was still buzzing about what they would do with the money Braxton had spoken about if they could produce the male heir needed to collect the funds.

Women in the family were still trying to plot lies about how they could fake an heir for the money. Gabriella went on about her business and racked her brain about how she could get back to school and make something of herself. Her friend Pallie was coming to hang out with her at her little apartment. She decided that even though she was in need, she didn't have to be alone as well. She didn't think that having a friend constituted anything out of the way for her and knew they cared about each other only as friends. Marriage had not come up yet for her because she wanted to be sure about who she would marry. For now, they were friends, with no benefits!

That evening, Pallie was to order pizza and they would do some studying on assignments from her last class. Pallie didn't know it would be her last class, because she wouldn't tell him, but she knew it was. She never wanted people to feel sorry for her either. She held her head high and pretended that everything was alright. Pallie came over right on time that day. He was a nice young man and very smart as well. He was majoring in engineering and did very well in it. He only had one year to go to finish his program and his parents were paying for his schooling.

"Hey Brella," he called her. "How's everything cracking over here on Brella Street?" he said, making a joke as always which usually was never funny but she always humored him by laughing anyway.

"Things are going well Pallie," she said in a cheerful voice. Knowing she had the weight of the world on her shoulders.

"How did you come out on the physics test you took?" she asked, making small talk. Lifting his collarless shirt and flipping it he added, "I aced it!" His matter-of-fact tone flaunted his success while searching her kitchen for something to snack on before the pizza arrived. He had already ordered it before he arrived, but was always hungry. Sometimes she thought he bought the pizzas for himself because he always ate the most of it and if there was anything left, he'd take it home with him.

They sat talking about classmates and professors and Pallie asked Gabriella about the funeral and how her mother was taking it. It was clear she didn't want to talk about it but said her mother was okay, but did not say anything about the reading of the Will or the heir thing. Pallie started making jokes about someone in town talking about the baby part. Gabriella pretended to know nothing but was shocked that someone was stupid enough to talk about it even after being warned that it was not safe to do so. Pallie made a joke again and said "Wow, you could have a baby and be a millionaire, too. Why don't you do it, Brella?" he asked, laughing at the same time.

Gabriella became infuriated and realized how immature Pallie was. That day, his name was permanently scratched off the husband list for her or anything else for that matter. Then there was a knock at the door and Pallie ran to open it knowing it was the delivery boy. He paid for the pizza and almost slammed the door in the boys' face. He hurried and sat down on the sofa and tore into the box, almost dropping the pizza slice on the floor. He was ridiculous when it came to food. Gabriella did not let his previous statement go un-addressed. It was no joking matter what he stated and Gabriella fired back at him while he was guzzling down the cheap pepperoni.

"You are so stupid, Pallie! I really don't know what you meant about this "having a baby talk" around town, she said. Gabriella actually had already had the fleeting thought and dismissed it.

Besides, she had not even been intimate with anyone, so what would she look like trying to have a baby before even being married or having relations with someone? She told Pallie he was crazy and that she wanted to save herself for someone special. He made another fatal joke and asked who that "special someone" could be. Gabriella really got mad at him this time and threw her slice of pizza at him and asked him to leave. She picked up some of the pieces off the floor and added those to his box, yelling at him.

"You are so pathetic!" He had tried to say he was sorry, but she still asked him to leave.

"Why don't you just take the pizza that you brought for yourself and eat it on your way back to the dorm? Better yet, eat it before you get to the first floor of this building!" she screamed as she ushered him to the door.

She was hurt and he finally left. She realized that Pallie was more of the scape goat for her frustrations. She slammed the door behind him and was haunted by the look of bewilderment on his face with cheese all over his hands. She was angry because he never took her seriously about how she felt about him. She had been referencing "him" when she said she wanted to keep herself for someone special and he didn't even get it. And now, he never would! Gabriella thought about the thoughtless statements he had made and she began to cry. It was as if no one thought about her or her goals. No one commended her for what she was trying to do.

No one ever helped her, not even her own mother. Brenda had tried but as soon as trouble came, she ditched helping her. She was mad at herself and reasoned that maybe that is what her sisters felt when they laid down with those sorry men who left them with all of their children as a consolation prize to marriage. She vowed still, that she would not let it happen to her. She laid across her bed still teary eyed with no one to talk to or comfort her, but she was used to that feeling and felt it would go on for the rest of her life.

About thirty minutes later, there was a knock at her door. Thinking it was Pallie coming back to apologize again, she was slightly happy knowing she really didn't want to kick him out like that, because she desperately wanted the company, but for some reason had become super incensed at him scoffing at the idea of what was presented to them by Braxton. She decided before she opened the door that she would accept his apology this time and save their friendship. She flung open the door in anticipation that it was Pallie and stepped back frozen in her tracks. She couldn't catch her breath for a moment, as she looked in shock to see Braxton standing at her door. She was too alarmed to even slam the door out of fear. She just stood there silent, looking up in his amazing face. He finally asked if he could come in. She hesitated and looked into his eyes and instinctively said "yes."

Now she could see that his eyes were cold blue and almost mesmerizing. She was ashamed of her little apartment and made silly excuses about why the place was a mess, even though it really wasn't. It was clean and very well kept. It was sparsely furnished, but it fit her just fine. She offered him a seat and he initially declined. She gave him a stern look, as if she thought he felt he was too good to take a seat in her modest apartment and he reconsidered and took a seat on the sofa anyway, in order not to offend her. He began recalling the details of the will to her once again and said that he knew she was the one, the moment he laid eyes on her at the funeral. Gabriella then snapped out of it and responded.

"No, you must be insane!"

"I don't want to have any children!" My sisters have too many and no husbands in sight and my mother has four of us and was jilted by all the father's to include the one we just buried and I am not going down that road!" she said, vehemently.

"Not even for money!"

Braxton looked perplexed and almost defeated, but continued to express his respect for her goals and decisions she was making for herself and her life. Gabriella saw that he showed a true interest in her and quickly squelched her previous thoughts of no one supporting her goals.

It was as if he had heard her thoughts and quickly soothed them, making her feel better about herself and now even wanting to trust him more. Although Braxton was clear about what he was asking of her, he did not let up on his proposal. Gabriella knew she had never been with anyone intimately, and felt this would be too much to fathom, even though intimacy was not involved in the procedure. It would require her to give up her body and this concerned her greatly. She wanted to finish school and get a good job and live her life the way she wanted to live it. She continued to rattle on about the goals she had of becoming a doctor someday. Somehow, sitting there talking to Braxton made those dreams seem possible. Braxton explained how important this was to him and Carlos and then he did something that Gabriella never expected. He took out his checkbook and began writing a check.

He once again appeared defeated in his relentless proposal and wrote a check out to Gabriella for 200k and handed it to her. She looked down at the check as if it were a snake and couldn't fathom that many zeroes on anything in her bank account. She knew her account initially only had enough money to buy food for the next week and she couldn't even pay her rent for the apartment she lives in. But with this much money, she could start her life over and move from Chicago, she even contemplated buying a house anywhere she wanted. With this much money, she could do almost anything she wanted to.

Now she could pay for her graduate degree, and complete the goal she started. She couldn't believe she was holding this much money in her hands when days earlier, she was preparing to move out of her apartment for lack of funds. As desperate as she was for money for school, not realizing what the money was for, she slowly handed Braxton the check back. Her life was flashing before her eyes and Braxton sensed her need and responded to her decision to give back the check.

"I know you are in school Gabriella and I know how important that is to you. Carlos wanted you to have this. I was to give it to you personally at the funeral services, but in light of the will being read and its contents, I thought it best if I gave it to you privately." Carlos instructed me to give this to you even if you did not choose to carry out his wishes. I was also to relinquish the 51% of his company to his partners and move on. Braxton then handed the check back to Gabriella and this time held her hand. Gabriella felt strange having this much money. In one second, her financial needs were being exceeded with the stroke of a rich man's pen and she didn't have to beg or do anything underhanded. The kicker was that the father she's never met had thought enough about her after all, to leave her something. If she took the money, how could she turn her back on his request and allow his entire fortune to be engulfed by his greedy business partner. This would be selfish on her part. She remembered how her mother had forgotten her as soon as she received money. Gabriella did not want to be that type of person.

"I don't know what to say, Braxton," she mumbled under her breath.

"I do want to finish school desperately, but I'm sorry I can't do this. I can't carry this child." I've never even been with a man, so how could I do this?"

Braxton was very calm, he made clear eye contact with Gabriella. When he handed her the check again, he seemed to linger holding her hand as if to keep contact with her as long as he could. There was something in his eyes this time that began to melt her spirit. Finally he spoke...

"I only have one other choice for this proposal and it is your sister Micah. She is unmarried, unattached and does not have a bad reputation, but I will have to monitor her closely if she accepts my proposal." At that point, Gabriella's antennas came up. She appeared a bit jealous of the fact that he would ask Micah to have this baby. Micah was very pretty and smart, but had simply gotten caught up in the syndrome of her mother and sisters dilemma. She remembered what it felt like to hold the check in her hand and knew what she would ultimately receive would be six times that amount. It could afford her enough to take care of her mother and her sisters as well. She knew that Micah would be radical about the money and was torn now, not knowing how to think about what she was considering. The option was there to take the money she had been given from her deceased father and walk away. But her heart told her that doing so would make her no better than the greedy people that wanted her father's money. How could she save his fortune and have a sense of being part of his life and possibly help her family?

Braxton could tell that Gabriella was in deep thought after he suggested asking her sister Micah to carry the baby. It was as if this was his trump card to get Gabriella to see the need that he had and he would stop at nothing to get that need fulfilled. He knew that it had to be a family member to keep a measure of loyalty to the project. However, if he could not find anyone suitable to save the remainder of Carlos's fortune, he would give up the shares to the partners and everything would be lost. She knew that Micah would say yes to this man for anything and still would breach the promise. She was not loyal to any man at this point in her life. Gabriella knew that Micah was attracted to Braxton and knowing he was not a relative of hers, she would be free to be with him if she pleased. There was a part of Gabriella that didn't want that to happen for some reason. Call it loyalty to family or something else. At this point, she didn't know what she was feeling. Finally Braxton spoke.

"Gabriella, I believe you could save Carlos's fortune by sacrificing nine months of school. You would be well cared for and you would never have to work another day in your life. Your family would be proud of you for doing this, and so would Carlos."

"No one would know about our agreement until it was over," he quietly stated. Gabriella had to think quickly. She realized that Pallie was still a boy and she had years left in school and could not continue working the way she had been and not making enough money to even pay her rent. She didn't want to be pregnant and end up like her sisters, but would this be different? She thought.

Braxton moved closer to her on the sofa and there was something strange that came over Gabriella. She felt that closeness she had felt at the repast when he hugged her. She kept reminding herself that this was her relative. How she wished he was not. He was a beautiful person from what she could see and what she felt about his sincerity and love for his brother was drawing her to him. Most family would have walked away, but he was not letting up. Braxton did not leave Gabriella that evening for a while. She asked him questions about her father. He was extremely evasive, but answered her questions. She felt that if he was brazen enough to approach her about carrying the child for the family's fortune, she should be able to get answers from him. There was a lot she was still confused about, but unlike others, he answered her questions.

"Braxton, you are aware that my mother thinks that your brother was my father, right?" Gabriella asked.

"Yes, I am aware." he replied bluntly, trying not to look at her when he gave his answers as if he were hiding something.

"Well, am I his daughter?" she asked nervously, hoping the answer was yes or no, but feeling confident that she was not going to get an answer at all.

"I believed what your mother stated was the truth as well, Gabriella," he said gently.

"Why does everyone lie so much to me?" Gabriella blurted out, showing a fiery spirit and a bit of immaturity.

"I like your spirit about wanting answers to unanswered questions," he said.

"I am the same way when I want answers or need to solve an issue, like the one I have ensuring that Carlos' wishes are carried out." Braxton looked away for a moment again, as if to remember his loss. Gabriella was not letting up. She fired another question telling what her mother had said about them falling out years ago.

"What was it you and my father fought about that caused you to want to kill him years ago?" Gabriella demanded. "Mama, told me about that fight you had with him."

"I want to be honest with you because this is important to me," he stated and began explaining as if he were on a witness stand and had been sworn in by a judge. "Carlos had thought that the partners he had were trying to kill him. We devised a scheme to make them think that we hated each other so I could leave the company and watch over him and the business and to keep them from harming him. We never were really angry with each other, but were so close that we would do anything for one another."

"I loved him very much, Gabriella, and I do believe his untimely demise was due to these partners greed." "I really need your help." He said with sincerity. Gabriella felt something very different now. The fact that he told her the truth about what happened meant a lot to her because she wanted to trust him. Her mother seemed to know him and this was a next step for her to take. She had more questions for him.

"I don't want to be pregnant, Braxton." Gabriella retorted. "My mother and sisters all have children, more than they can feed. I am in school and want to do better. By having this baby, it will change my life.

"The money is secondary for me, even though I do need it!" Gabriella was almost tearing up. She was torn between helping Braxton save the family's fortune and changing the dynamics of her own life forever. Even indirectly, this act would put her in a similar situation as her sisters. She would have a baby, give him up, have money, but not have had the father in the baby's life and still be a virgin in the biblical sense. How would she feel carrying this child even though she never knew her father who is now deceased?

People would view her just like her sisters and she didn't want that. She would have to view this in a special way. How would she do this thing? Braxton expressed his respect for her feelings and told Gabriella he would take her away from the Chicago and get another place for her to live.

He stated that he would be there to take care of her every need and would never leave her side. He also shared with her that he had not married for that very reason. He, too, wanted someone special, but also did not want Carlos to have died in vain for all his hard work. He reminded Gabriella that when the child was born, he would raise the child and whoever he married would have to accept the child as their own, indicating they both would be in a similar situation of sacrificing their lives.

She would not have to raise the baby, but would carry the memories of carrying and giving birth to him. It was important to be able to trust the person that he was with. Braxton took out his phone and sent a text message. About thirty minutes later there was a knock at the door and Gabriella became nervous as she rose from the sofa to get the door thinking it was Pallie. Braxton gently caught her by the arm and halted her approach before reaching the front door.

"Let me get that for you. I know who it is," he said calmly. Gabriella was surprised by his statement of knowing who was at her door but accepted his kind invitation to intercept the visitor. Braxton opened the door and the pizza guy handed him a hot pizza with beverages. He tipped the delivery boy and closed the door. Gabriella smiled, knowing she was still hungry from throwing the pizza at Pallie earlier that day.

"Are you hungry?" "You must be. I see pieces of pizza on the floor over there." They both laughed and opened the box. Gabriella smiled sheepishly remembering how the pizza got on the floor. She noticed that this pizza had Italian sausage, anchovies, mushrooms and all the good stuff Pallie couldn't afford. Pallie only ordered pepperoni on his pizzas or just cheese. Braxton got up and cleaned up the pizza off her floor. It was something about him taking off his jacket and neatly laying it across the chair at the table. When he rolled up his sleeve to clean the floor, it showed humility which she didn't expect from someone that was as wealthy as he was.

He then pulled two plates from the cabinet and put the box on the table, and they both sat and ate pizza and talked more about the proposal. By the time the conversation and the pizza ended, Gabriella was more comfortable with Braxton than she thought she ever would have been. Just as she was relaxing more, her phone rang and she glanced down at the screen, but didn't answer it. She realized it was Pallie and didn't want to talk to him again after having the wonderful conversation she just had with Braxton. He had said that he wanted to take care of her and promised to give her "everything" she needed. She would be protected by him, every minute of the day. This was something she had never heard from a man and it felt wonderful to have someone comfort her in this way.

Braxton expressed that he was part of her family and as such, this is what families do for one another. They stick together. Finally, it was getting late and they both were feeling full and mellow in their visit. Things seemed to be turning out well in their connection and Braxton made one final statement. "Gabriella, if you agree to do this for me, I won't let anyone near you until the baby is born. It will be me and you and I will protect you with my life," "I promise you!" he said, in a serious, but personal tone. Gabriella searched his eyes one last time and knew in her heart that she believed every word he had uttered to her. At this moment, there were no butterflies in her stomach and she felt confident that he would not let anything happen to her.

She knew she had one class left to finish the next week and then it would be summer break. Her tuition and next classes would start back in the fall. She considered the job she had which constituted her standing on her feet all day and night with no possibility of making more money to support herself. She knew she would not be able to afford the master's program if something did not change for her. This lifestyle was getting old, and she wanted to do something better with her life. 'Would this be the right thing to do?' She thought.

How could she be certain who the donor was for the fertilization process? She couldn't be certain. She would have to trust Braxton completely.

She had only known this man a few weeks and if what he said was not true and she agreed, her life could be ruined forever. The point that kept solidifying the proposal for her was that her mother actually knew who this man was, which validated him for her. It would have to be true, she thought if he proposed this plan to a room full of relatives. This was the thought process that was sealing the deal for Gabriella. She was also told she couldn't say anything to anyone and that he had taken care of her mother so she wouldn't have to worry about her wellbeing. This made Gabriella happy. Finally Gabriella finished deliberating and agreed to help Braxton keep his families fortune. She was mortified at the thought of carrying a baby.

Being a surrogate for someone was the furthest thing from her mind ever and she never thought she would say yes. But, this day she did. That very night in her tiny apartment, she agreed that she would pack a bag and be ready to leave the following morning with Braxton. He would pick her up at daybreak.

This would be a complete secret, espionage like tactics. No one could know where he was taking her and she had no idea where she would live. Her literal life was in this mans' hands. Not even her own mother knew she was going with him. It was very risky but she had given her word to be the surrogate! There was something special about this feeling she was now having for Braxton. She would go from not knowing a man at all to trusting him completely with her very life.

Her heart was racing as she gave him her word that she would carry it through. Once again, Braxton stood up and embraced her. She could feel his heart racing as she hugged him back feeling a strange connection that he apparently felt as well. This time, there was no one to pull them apart, but they slowly released each other after exchanging glances intensely one last time. Before she closed the door behind him, Braxton turned to Gabriella and stared deep into her eyes again and spoke one last time.

"You now belong to me Gabriella." He then walked away leaving her standing in the doorway with her heart pounding and her mind racing. "What is this I have done," she panted, now feeling he body shaking all over as she slowly closed and locked the door. "Who really is this man I have agreed to put my life in his hands and trust him? What is this I have done?

~ CHAPTER 5 ~

Race for Time

RACE FOR TIME

Gabriella didn't sleep at all that night. To her surprise, she cried some and even hyperventilated once when she became very afraid thinking about what she was about to do. Knowing she was still a virgin, she had no idea how this would affect her mind or her body. She knew the usual things about carrying a child, from watching her sisters go through morning sickness and everything else and hoped she didn't have to endure that. She was becoming a nervous wreck as she waited for Braxton to return the next morning. She thought about her mother and could see how she could have fallen in love with the man Carlos. If he was half as charming as Braxton, it would be difficult to keep from loving someone that was as kind as he was.

It would be humanly impossible to keep her personal feelings to herself, but she knew what she would have to do in this case. The fact that Gabriella's mother knew Carlos and Braxton was a main factor in her deciding to put her trust in him. This confidence in him had helped her make the decision she had made. This was the only thread of trust she had outside of what she was beginning to feel about the whole situation with her Uncle. Braxton picked Gabriella up early that morning before day break just as he said he would. It shocked Gabriella about the early departure, but she was ready to go when he arrived.

She put on a sweatshirt and jeans to travel black short leather boots for comfort because she didn't know where she was going. When she walked out of the apartment, she looked back one last time and then approached the limousine. It was the first time she would have been in one and she had mixed emotions about how she would feel. Strangely enough, as she sat on the soft leather, it was very comfortable and felt like she belonged there. The driver closed the door after Braxton entered the vehicle and he greeted Gabriella with a big smile which was heartwarming for her, seeing that this was only her third time seeing him. "Good morning," he said, and then immediately asking her if she wanted anything special for breakfast. Her first inclination was to say no, but then she realized she had only had pizza the night before and really was getting hungry.

Braxton gave her a menu for her to look at and she was amazed at the restaurants that were on the list. They were five star places that she would never have been able to afford to go to before today. Braxton then made a call to the restaurant she chose, and placed the order. While they waited for the driver to take them to pick up her much needed meal, the man sitting in the second seat who was on the phone when they entered the limousine introduced himself as Braxton's attorney. "Good morning Ms. McPherson, I am Seth Harrington, Mr. Chavarezs' attorney. It's a pleasure to meet you," he said, and immediately taking another call.

Gabriella shook his hand and greeted him politely. He had scores of papers for Gabriella to sign for the agreement to be made official. Braxton explained to her in detail what she was signing and why. He also was watching every move his lawyer made as well which is what kept Gabriella calm. It was as if he trusted no one. He was watching over her like a protector. The driver took off for the highway to pick up breakfast and they continued the paperwork. While signing the papers, Braxton noticed that Gabriella was trembling.

He gently took her hand and had her put the pen down for a moment and just held her hand until she stopped shaking.

"I will be with you through every step of the way, Gabriella," he said, "and will never let anything happen to you. I promise." She finally stopped trembling and relaxed. After all the papers were signed Braxton told Gabriella that there were other papers to sign later and that the attorney would meet them at the new condo on Lake Michigan later in the day to finish signing them.

"Lake Michigan," she thought. This was the place only the rich or famous people lived. She sat quietly with her heart pounding in her chest, wondering what the place would be like where she would live. Braxton felt that Gabriella had been exposed to enough for one morning. They drove for a short while and dropped off the attorney and picked up breakfast for Gabriella. She only ate a small amount, but afterwards felt better.

Braxton and Gabriella talked about a number of things to include what might be going through her head right at that moment. He seemed to sense that she still had reservations and tried to comfort her the best he could. Finally they had travelled about forty five minutes or so to a beautiful secluded estate off Lake Shore Drive. Braxton exited the car and opened the door for Gabriella. He walked with her up the winding walkway that led to two gigantic doors. The doorman, standing straight like a Castle guard, nodded and spoke to Braxton.

"Good morning, Sir," he said, with a stern professional stance. "Good morning, Winston." Braxton responded, very politically correct, without smiling as all. Gabriella did not speak, but nodded her greeting to the man.

"Is this where I will live?" Gabriella asked, looking up at the high cathedral ceilings.

"This is where "we" will live." he corrected.

"We?" she replied.

"Yes, we." "I have a suite on the floor below you and the first floor is for the security officers, business office and infirmary."

Gabriella was blown away by the beauty of the building and the grounds. There were lush gardens, waterfalls, Rolling Meadows in the back. From what she could see, the place was on many acres of land. This was the most beautiful place she had ever seen. It was nothing like the part of the city where she grew up on the West side of Chicago. She had no earthly idea that any place existed as beautiful as this.

She was then escorted to the third floor and upon approaching the door, was greeted by a maid who took her suitcase and jacket. Braxton introduced Gabriella to her new staff and she was now in shock.

"I have staff?" she stated, with a surprised look.

"Yes, and there are more of them to wait on you hand and foot. "If not, let me know and they will be discharged," he said.

Gabriella was speechless as the staff came in one by one and introduced themselves. Then Orlando, her head chef, asked what she would like for breakfast since it was still early, not knowing if she had eaten already or not. She looked at Braxton and he nudged her playfully.

"Go ahead and tell him whatever you want. Remember, I am taking care of you and anything you want you can have." "I really mean it, anything," he said, with an adoring smile. He seemed to like the idea of spoiling her already. There was something about the way he looked when he was telling her she could have anything she wanted. No one had ever said this to her before and really meant it.

"Okay," she said sheepishly, not believing it was all real. Braxton reminded her that she would be seeing the doctor later in the day to have some initial tests run.

The infirmary was also in the complex, which was convenient. She nodded in agreement, becoming more comfortable with him making each decision for her. The upstairs maid showed her the living quarters. She took her to the bedroom, bathroom, private gym, and patio with a private pool. Gabriella was in awe of her surroundings. Everything was over the top in beauty. Braxton excused himself to give her some time to adjust and take it all in. He went to take care of some family business, he said. This would become a daily ritual for him. Gabriella was tired having had little sleep the night before and laid down gently on the bed as if trying to ensure she didn't wrinkle the covers.

She had forgotten that this would be her place as she looked at her two tiny bags next to the huge closet doors. She decided to go ahead and hang up her few meager things in the closet and to her surprise, when she opened the double wide doors, the inside of the closet was larger than her old apartment. There were shelves and shelves of clothing. Sweaters of all kinds, hats, shoes, blouses, even underwear. Her mouth stayed open so long it began to get dry. She didn't know whether to laugh or pinch herself because of her new life. Even more amazing than seeing this beautiful closet full of clothes was that when she checked the sizes, they were just her size! She was reluctant to touch anything, thinking it may have been someone else's place and they were coming back any minute.

After coming from having really nothing at all, she had to get accustomed to the idea of having someone waiting on her and having everything she needed. She decided to listen to Braxton's directions and called the maid to confirm that these things in the closet were bought specifically for her. She still didn't want to take any chances. The maid smiled, and confirmed that Mr. Braxton, as they called him, had ordered them especially for her weeks earlier. Gabriella was stunned that he had already made these plans weeks earlier.

How did he know she would accept his proposal to help the family with her father's requests? There was something strange about this new piece of information she received. It would become clearer much later as time went on. For now, she would absorb her new lifestyle and continued examining the closet with great interest. Some of the clothes she saw were maternity items. There were at least a hundred pairs of shoe, summer dresses, winter dresses and coats, swimwear, scarfs, suits. The bathroom had special lotions, soaps and even shampoo and everything a woman could want.

All the toiletries here, she only dreamed of having them at her apartment, but could never afford them. For a man who claimed to never have seen her before, he sure knew a lot about her likes. For now, she would allow herself to be pampered. It was not often that this happened to many women. But, it would take a little time to get used to it.

After the tour and a real breakfast, she noted how much better the Chef's food tasted than that in the restaurant.

She later took a bath to prepare for her first appointment with the doctor for the lab work that was required. She selected an outfit that was perfect for her size five frame and felt like a princess in it. Her hair cascaded down her back and it had a healthy glow to it. It must have been the soft water that made it so silky and soft, or maybe the expensive shampoo and conditioner. She was only accustomed to hard water at her apartment. She smelled delicious from the bath soaps and lotions she had pampered herself with.

"So this is what it feels like to be rich," she whispered to herself, gazing in the wall length mirror that gave her every angle of her figure perfectly in her dressing room. She remembered only having a tiny floor mirror she used to prop up against the wall in her apartment. The day was beginning to become comfortable to her already. She knew she had a big order to fill with carrying a baby, and prayed it would work out. Braxton came up to get her on time and commented that she looked amazing. They didn't talk much before meeting the physician but went downstairs to the ground floor of the Condo and there was a full hospital annex there. Again, she was amazed at the fact that this place had everything, even a small clinic! How convenient! Everything seemed to be in order. Dr. Luke came into the room where she had been seated and introduced himself.

The formalities took only a moment and they were informed of what basic tests would be required. Several blood tests and a short physical examination of Gabriella was necessary. Braxton agreed but he requested an ear bud microphone so that he could be privy to the conversation the physician would have with Gabriella in his absence from the room. Once again, Braxton was not taking any chances and literally stood guard outside the door. Dr. Luke began the examination and realized that Gabriella was still a virgin. She was sure that Braxton heard that part about her being a virgin and felt a little strange knowing that he knew this personal information about her. She reasoned that it was no big deal, and thought he probably already knew if he knew the size of her clothes already before she accepted the contract.

She still felt goose bumps when the doctor expressed it. Although that was not part of the stipulation, it was a plus that she was still innocent. The doctor confirmed that she was indeed fertile and this process should go fairly quickly. After the examination, Gabriella dressed and they left the office that day. Everything had gone well with Dr. Luke on the first visit. Braxton had a strange look on his face when Gabriella came out of the doctor's office.

He seemed elated about the news that she was fertile and still a virgin. He didn't say anything about it, but was almost giddy for some reason which was a bit awkward. Braxton told Gabriella that he wanted to take her to a new bank in another city a short distance away and have her open an account there for her funds to be deposited.

He wanted to ensure that her money would be safe as well. They went to the new bank and deposited 200k into Gabriella's account. It was a surreal feeling after they left the bank. He handed her the deposit slip and she realized that she would never have to worry about money again. Strangely enough, only a week earlier she was concerned about not having enough money for her apartment or her schooling. Now she had enough to pay for everything. It's funny how life can just flip over for you in one minute flat.

Dr. Luke had stated that they would come back in the next few days and review the blood test results and then schedule the fertilization process. Gabriella explained to Braxton that she was scared about being pregnant. They talked as they rode back from the bank. She decided to stop Braxton's giddiness and break the ice about the news of her being a virgin.

"Braxton, as you now know, I have never been intimate with a man. I am a bit frightened about this whole process still," she said, firmly.

"I understand," he said, very confident, and never letting on that his giddiness had been exposed.

"I know this is a lot to take on Gabriella, but I meant every word I said to you. I need you to trust me and you will be just fine." On the sex part, you really haven't missed much out there. Many couples are just superficial when they have their first encounters in a relationship and all too often women become pregnant and the man moves on."

He spoke with a kind reassuring tone, like a father would talk to his innocent daughter. It felt good to have someone explain things to her without hiding and lying about it. She was glad she opened up to him. She didn't know quite how to take this statement about men moving on, but quickly remembered her sisters and how they had been treated by the men they chose. He saw her discomfort and replied. "But, the good thing is that you have "me" right here by your side. I will never leave you, he said again, looking intently at Gabriella. I need you to trust me, "he said a final time in a very serious tone. She wasn't completely comforted and felt better knowing he had confirmed again that he would be there with her. She knew she could never hear those words enough. She even asked if he was going to be in the room with her during the insemination.

Braxton looked shocked in a pleasant way. It was as if he didn't expect such mature questions to come from Gabriella, but welcomed her expressions. He immediately answered in the affirmative, that he would be there to hold her hand during the procedure and would do anything else she asked of him.
She now was beginning to feel more confident and a sense of control with each question being answered. She was beginning to feel closer to him and wanting to trust him. As Braxton looked out of the window for a moment, she glanced at the deposit slip from the bank. She looked closely at it and noticed that another name was on the account.

She had been given a card that she could use to withdraw the money anytime she wanted but her instincts told her not to ask any questions at this time about the money. He promised her that he would always do what was best for her so she remained silent about this. Her trust in him was growing with every moment they spent together. The day had gone by fast and it seemed that she had almost forgotten about her little apartment on the west side of Chicago. She also had not thought of her friend Pallie either. Was it this easy to forget people when you had lots of money? Perhaps that is why people stay rich, because they don't think of anyone but themselves.

Gabriella didn't want to be that type of rich person. She would fight not to be that way. She had been raised the hard way will little to nothing. Braxton took her to a little place he had picked out to get a bite for lunch when she stated she was hungry. It seemed that she was eating more for some strange reason and she wasn't even pregnant yet. After lunch they returned to the condo for the evening. He escorted her to the third floor and performed a security check of her place before leaving to go to his suite on the second floor. They said their goodbyes with another hug. This was beginning to be a ritual now. Gabriella had a lot of thinking to do and she would write in her new journal all of the day's events. She would carefully express how comfortable it made her feel when she was hugged by Braxton and how she was beginning to look for those moments but waited patiently for each opportunity.

She didn't want to appear desperate for affection from a man, but understood that she never had a father's love and could only imagine that this must have been how it would have felt to have had someone hold her and comfort her when she was afraid. She would never forget the scene her mother caused at the repast when she swung from Braxton's neck trying to get his attention. Gabriella never wanted to do that to him and always would be the one to let go first. She was settling in quickly at her new place and the first day was ending very nicely. The next few days would come very swiftly. Braxton and Gabriella returned to see Dr. Luke again for the results of the bloodwork. Everything came up excellent and they were given a green light to set a date for the insemination.

The next week between waiting for the insemination procedure was spent with Braxton getting to know him better as family. They talked a lot about everything and seemed to have much in common. Gabriella chalked this up to them being related, but realized that Braxton avoided speaking on certain family matters about his deceased brother Carlos. Once again, Gabriella chalked it up to him still mourning the loss and pried no further. She would wait for a better time to delve into that subject again. Finally the next week came and it was time for the insemination procedure. Braxton came for her that morning as usual and took her once again for her appointment. This time it would be for the procedure itself and he would take every precaution with her.

Gabriella was nervous and knew this procedure would change her life forever. Braxton took her by the hand as they walked into the infirmary and continued on into another large building outside of that complex where they lived.

It was strange the way this new building was detached from the actual infirmary. As they entered to door, the nurse greeted Gabriella and prepared her for the procedure. When everything was ready, Gabriella scanned the room and visually examined all the instruments in place. She was nervous and her heart beat was rapid. It could be seen by her elevated blood pressure that showed up on the monitor. The nurse tried to get her to relax, but finally Braxton walked into the room and took her hand again and she instantly calmed down and her blood pressure began to drop to something normal. Dr. Luke responded, "It looks like someone calmed you down," she said, smiling. "I have that effect on young women," Braxton said, winking at her.

The doctor prepped Gabriella and took a needlelike syringe and began the procedure. She numbed her a bit since she was a virgin and prepared the serum. In moments, there was pressure like Gabriella had never felt before. She squeezed Braxton's hand and he cupped his other hand over hers. As she was about to cry, he leaned over and looked into her eyes, gently speaking to her.

"Everything is going to be alright, I promise you."

"I will never leave you." He said, and then kissed her gently on the forehead.

Braxton seemed to have a mesmerizing effect on Gabriella. She calmed down and didn't feel anything else. She only heard his words echo in her ear as Dr. Luke stated,

"Well, it is done, young lady. You did well."

Braxton had made Gabriella forget her pain. He then stepped out of the office and the nurse helped her get dressed again.

Braxton soon returned to the examining room and the Doctor gave him and Gabriella special instructions they needed to follow. Dr. Luke also gave them both a stern warning. Gabriella was to take it easy for the next 48 hours or she could easily miscarry if she became pregnant. Before Gabriella could respond to the Doctors orders, Braxton turned and swept her up into his arms and carried her into the elevator.

"Well, you heard the doctor, I am just getting a head start by not letting you tire out walking to the car," he smiled a happy smile. Braxton seemed very elated about the procedure that had just taken place. It was as if it was done for him and not his brother. Gabriella decided not to think so much about things she didn't understand but was relieved to get off her feet. The whole thing felt right for some strange reason and besides, Braxton was always the perfect gentleman. Gabriella was tired now from all the events of the day and wanted to go to her condo and rest.

She now realized that the clock was ticking and the contract was in full force. She said she wouldn't think about anything anymore but she couldn't help it. "I can't believe I have done this," she pondered. "I actually could have a child beginning to form in my body!" The thought was almost overwhelming. They arrived back at the condo and Braxton opened the door for her and she walked into her home. She still could not believe the beautiful things that surrounded her. In a speechless state, all she could think was, "Wow, this is very beautiful!" To top it off, her maid walked in and asked,

"Would you like something to eat mistress?" Gabriella looked around to see who she was talking to and then Braxton spoke and responded, "She is talking to you," he smiled.

Gabriella responded sheepishly "Yes please." Like a child who was hungry but afraid to ask for anything specific for fear they would get nothing, so they just take whatever is brought to them. Braxton spoke again saying,

"Tell her what you would want Gabriella," he said."

"Anything?" Gabriella asked.

"Yes, anything," he responded.

"Yeah right....Okay," she said, as if she would test out his words to prove him wrong.

"I want lobster with drawn butter, fresh sweet peas with homemade yeast rolls, a green salad (romaine lettuce only) fresh tomatoes, carrots, cucumbers and croutons with Italian dressing and lemon chocolate cake for dessert."

The maid responded in an affirmative without batting an eye and promptly left the room.

"She's got to be joking, right?" Gabriella asked Braxton again.

"No, she lives here and is paid to take care of you and to deliver you whatever you want."

Totally not believing him, Gabriella blurted out, "Whose house is this?"

He quietly replied.

"Yours," and held up three keys and dropped them in her hands. He explained to Gabriella that she no longer lived in her apartment and that he had paid the rent out for the year and closed the lease. He also had moved her things from her apartment into a storage Pod in case there was something sentimental that she wanted to keep from them. Anything she didn't want would go to charity. The storage was downstairs in the basement and she had her own key to it. She had a bewildered looked on her face as she glanced at him and finally realizing that this was all real, she asked him if everything he was saying to her was "really" happening. He assured her it was.

"From now on, you will be pampered, nothing is out of your reach an longer," he said. Gabriella had to sit down because she was in shock, still tired, but actually wanted to lie down first for some strange reason.

In light of the days' events, she quickly recalled that she had just had the insemination procedure and was cautioned by the physician that she would notice a difference in how she might feel almost immediately.

Her energy level might be affected as well. This mental recall helped her understand why she might be fatigued. Even now, her young body was beginning to feel the effects of the child she hoped she was carrying. Braxton realized that the procedure had made her a little weak and gave her a few moments to rest before he took her on a short tour of the property. This time, they rode in the golf cart for the tour of the entire condo. He didn't want her to become exhausted. He showed her all of the rooms and floors and took her into the kitchen where her three Chefs and two housekeepers were. The kitchen was amazing with all the utensils hanging neatly over the oversized stove with three huge ovens. There were two refrigerators a large convection oven and another wall oven. The head Chef explained what his duties were and expressed that there was no microwave in this kitchen per Mr. Braxton due to wanting to serve only fresh foods prepared as naturally as possible. After being introduced to her kitchen staff, he gave her a copy of their work schedules and explained that she could look it up on her special iPad that she was given.

The staff appeared happy in their roles working for Braxton and seemed elated to make Gabriella's acquaintance. Braxton then expressed specific orders to them. "Gabriella is your new "Mistress" and anything she desires, please ensure that she receives it promptly. He continued. "Do not wake her to get her menu for breakfast, lunch or dinner, but be prepared when she dials in to create whatever she requests.

If it is not within your ability to produce what she requests, contact me and I will authorize anything further that is not on the premises." The staff members smiled and agreed. Braxton was very comfortable giving directives to the staff. He turned and spoke to Gabriella asking her if she wanted them to turn down her bed each night. He insisted that she get plenty of rest and would not keep her up late. She would have a certain timeline to rest and she agreed that his request was feasible.

The Maids were to turn down Gabriella's bed each night at the appointed time to ensure that she did not have to wrestle with the large bed covering on the oversized California King sized bed. She could change the time for the beds to be turned down if she choose, but Braxton gave the order for a timeline to ensure they were doing as they were told. There was enough room in her bed to accommodate several people. Braxton then took her to another room that had huge double doors. When he opened them, they walked up two steps and she gasped at the size of the room. There was a large bay window overlooking a lake behind a row of huge oak trees that she had not seen on her tour. The area rug on the middle of the floor had a beautiful design in the middle of it that appeared to have a Persian look to it. She couldn't halt the inclination to bend down and touch it.

Casually moving to the other side of the room, Gabriella caught sight of another bed which was larger than the one she slept in. Braxton explained that this was a guest bedroom. They went into the bath room which was almost as large as the bedroom and had two bidets. She was in disbelief of the contents of this room. Her desire was to call someone and tell them what she was witnessing, but she remembered that no one could know where she was. Braxton exhibited playful antics as they perused the rest of the complex. He seemed proud to parade her around to each area and give her full authority over everything she saw. Finally, Gabriella expressed to Braxton that she was getting exhausted from the tour and needed to lay down for a while.

Again, being the perfect gentleman, he immediately took her back to her condo and she laid on the bed and closed her eyes for a moment. The sheets felt like nothing that had ever touched her body. Braxton came over to her as if he were someone other than a family member and sat on the side of the bed, gently brushing her hair from her face. He then touched her cheek softly with the back of his hand and she noticed him staring at her again like he did at the repast. This time, it was more intense than before. It was not the look of an uncle and Gabriella became excitedly nervous and slowly moved away. Braxton patted her gently on the shoulder and got up from her bedside. He spoke in a low tone so as not to arouse her with any unnecessary noise. "I'll be going now, but will be check on you in the morning. "We will need to go over some other things that are very important."

"Take it easy and don't lift a thing! There are many people here to wait on you," he said. It was as if he hated to leave and Gabriella thanked him for his kindness and he closed the door and walked out. Gabriella was still nervous. She realized she couldn't turn back the time and the insemination had been done. There was no one else in this with her except Braxton now and she had to get to know him very well and very quickly. She accepted that he was family and that was all that was important to her right now while she was longing to see her mom and sisters and even their noisy kids. Gabriella had never felt so alone and afraid in her entire life. She wasn't sure of her feelings and wondered if she had done the right thing. She lay on the bed caressing her stomach, realizing that if everything went as planned, she could already be pregnant.

"Was this a dream or a nightmare?" she thought. A knock came on her bedroom door. "Come in." The Chef rolled in a large food cart like the ones you see in the fancy hotels, white linen napkins and all. The aroma was amazing. As he lifted the lids on the multitude of plates on the dining tray, it revealed, Maine Lobster with drawn butter, fresh yeast rolls, romaine salad with everything she asked for and Italian dressing. The last lid lifted exposed the hugest slice of lemon chocolate cake she'd ever seen! She was stunned that her order was exactly as she had requested. "Oh, my god, is this what my life will be like as a wealthy woman?"

"Can I handle this?" she pondered. She knew she could never eat all of the food that she had ordered and felt bad for requesting it realizing that someone somewhere in the world was going to bed hungry. She wondered how she would fare in this new environment. As she ate, she had forgotten about the procedure she had just had. With each morsel she quietly thought back to Braxton and how playful he had been with her during their tour of the condo. She accepted that he had strategically selected her to be in this process with him but still wondered why she had been selected. What was this whole scenario all about? Only time would tell her the complete story of the family's history.

~ CHAPTER 6 ~

Facing The Ultimate Fears

FACING THE ULTIMATE FEAR

Weeks had gone by since the insemination and Gabriella was acclimating to her new staff in her condo and all the authority she had in her new surroundings. She didn't have to lift a finger and did whatever she wanted to do. She could ask for anything and it would be brought to her. It was an insane way of life for a girl who had been dirt poor from birth. As time went on, some of the maid servants looked at her with subtle envy when they came in to clean her bedroom and other parts of the house. Gabriella was becoming accustomed to this and ignored it, which would later prove to be a wrong course of action.

The day finally came for her to take her first pregnancy test to determine if the insemination actually was effective. She was nervous hoping it was positive. She didn't want to have to repeat the process which she had agreed to for up to three attempts. As she was looking in the mirror outlining her stomach to indicate how round it would be shortly, she stared at herself. It was as if she did not recognize the person staring back at her. She looked different even in this short period of time. The thing she said she would never do and had vowed not to do, had been done. It was different than she would have expected it to be, but the fact was, if everything went as planned, she would be officially carrying a child as an unwed mother.

This thought saddened her heart. It made her think about her goals and how she felt about her sisters and her mother having children out of wedlock. She would be no better than them except that she would be wealthy from having a baby and not poor like they were. Even thought it was not under the normal circumstances, she knew she was in the same boat as they were from a moral standpoint.

If the test was positive, she would officially be pregnant. She couldn't wait to get this part over with. Dr. Luke was going to examine her this time as well. She had heard that many women go back numerous times, but usually there are medical complications with them in the first place if more attempts are needed. Gabriella was young, in good shape, healthy and a virgin. That was a great combination. She had felt as if something was going on inside her body, even this early, but since she had never had a baby or been intimate with anyone before, she knew that something was different and wanted to know as well. Braxton came to pick her up for the appointment on schedule. Gabriella wasn't ready yet and Braxton patiently sat and waited. He read a magazine that was laying on the table, but since it was a girlie magazine, he quickly discarded it, neatly placing it back on the table. It was a nice but unusual feeling to have him sitting there waiting for her as if he belonged in the Condo with her.

Since she was not permitted to talk to anyone, not even her own mother, he had to listen to any and everything she had to say. He didn't seem to mind much, either. Braxton had explained to Gabriella that as the process went forward there would be different things she would have to do to keep everything safe and confidential. Today, it would be necessary to pretend that they were a couple when they were out for this appointment.

For some reason she had to pretend to be his fiancé. He placed a humongous diamond ring on her finger. He even went through the antics of a man asking a woman to marry him. Getting down on one knee, he opened the ring box and Gabriella gasped! She then turned up her lips when he spoke the words, "Will you marry me?" Realizing that he was a family member and this was a contract, she took the mock proposal as a joke, laughing along with him as he slipped the ring on her finger and told her it was fake. He also quickly told her not to hock it. Gabriella was smart enough to know that the ring was real. She didn't understand why he would purchase a real one instead of a fake one. She had looked at enough of the real ones in the jewelry store windows and remembered seeing the ones that cost thousands. This one was more than those most expensive ones she had seen. Also, the dead giveaway that it was real was the statement for her not to hock it.

After the ring incident, Braxton was waiting patiently for her to finish getting dressed and finally she was. She thought they were going to see Dr. Luke again for the pregnancy test results but for unknown reasons, they went to another place for a doctor to examine her. She didn't ask why they came to this doctor but went with Braxton. She was beginning to trust him more and more. They arrived at the location and entered the clinic. This time there were other people in the waiting room. Many were pregnant already and one women asked her how far along she was. Like a child, Gabriella looked at Braxton as if her were her father, not knowing what to say and he responded appropriately.

"We are here to see how far along we are," he said, gently placing his arms around Gabriella and pulling her close to him. The woman swooned over his amorous gesture and involuntarily began babbling.

"That is sooo sweet of you to come with your wife. My boyfriend is a jerk and this is my first baby," the woman said.

"I know I have made the biggest mistake of my life, but I'm going to love this child so much I won't even remember the father!" All the while, she was rubbing her belly like it was an Aladdin's lamp and she had just made her wish. Before she could go any further in her declaration, the attendant called the woman's name and she got up to go in to see the doctor. She congratulated them again and Braxton rushed up to open the door for her as a final husbandly gesture.

"My, my, you are certainly a keeper," the woman whispered to Braxton, all the while looking back at Gabriella in envy and giving her a wink of approval as she waddled through the open door. Braxton returned to his seat and Gabriella didn't say much. She was anxiously anticipating what was about to happen. Finally they called her mock married name,

"Gabriella Shavarez?" the nurse called. Gabriella naturally did not respond. They used Braxton's last name with hers as if they were married and she didn't recognize the last name with hers, knowing they were not married.

Braxton hurried and gave attention to the nurse, waving to her and coaxing Gabriella, "That's us dear," he said. Gabriella, now mortified that she had missed her important cue. She tactfully played it off by pretending to be playful as they approached the small hallway leading to the patient examination rooms.

Braxton went in with Gabriella again, this time posing as her husband. Now she understood why he gave her the ring when she noticed every woman looking at Braxton and then looking down at Gabriella's finger. He was really good at this, she thought. They were officially a couple and she was okay with the thought once she remembered what she was supposed to do. The doctor finally walked in the room and Braxton immediately extended his hand to the doctor, and talked to him as if he had done this before.

"Dr. Elliott, is it?" Braxton asked the man in the white coat.

"Yes, and you must be Braxton Shavarez.

Author: Victoria E. Kain

"That's correct, and this is my wife Gabriella."

"How do you do," Gabriella said, with a coy smile, now, looking up at Braxton adoringly as the doting wife as she leaned into his arms." Braxton was right on point.

"Dr. Elliott, we think we are pregnant," he stated, now looking back at Gabriella, hoping this would convince the doctor into believing Gabriella was his wife. Gabriella realized why they went to another physician. Braxton did not want anyone to know that this pregnancy was not natural. Dr. Elliott would only run the pregnancy test and confirm if she was pregnant or not. It was a perfect plan to keep anyone from knowing the results of the artificial insemination that took place, in the event there were any leaks in the communication. The business partners of his deceased brother Carlos, were known to be ruthless and had many contacts. It was a perfect plan that Braxton had set up. Gabriella was beginning to see the plan come into full view.

"Well, let's make sure that she is," Dr. Elliott stated. I need to ask your wife a few questions since she will be the one I will be seeing each trimester," the doctor smiled a crooked smile, not realizing that she would not ever see him again.

"Have you had any morning sickness abdominal pain cramps or bleeding?" he asked.

"No to all of the questions, Dr. Elliott but have been tired and a tad bit nauseous before eating a meal," but it usually subsides when I eat," Gabriella told him.

"Well, sounds like that's a normal reaction, if it's not excessive," he said.

The doctor then asked Gabriella to take a urine test and she left the room temporarily and left the specimen in the lab window. He also wanted her to take a blood test to be positively sure. When she returned from the examining room waiting for the two test results, the doctor continued.

"Can you get undressed from the waist down and put on the gown in the area here for an examination? I will step out for a moment." She played the part perfectly, knowing they were not married but Braxton excused himself with the doctor as well. "I have a couple of questions for you Doc," he said, as a way to leave the room without raising suspicion.

Gabriella undressed and robed for the procedure and called them back in. She approached the table and Braxton helped her up. Braxton positioned himself with his back facing the doctor so as not to make Gabriella uncomfortable because this was not the normal setting for them to be in given the fact that they were not married and she only knew him as her Uncle. The doctor guided her feet in the stirrups and begins his examination. Braxton talked to her to ease her discomfort.

The doctor completes his examination and expressed that Gabriella looked fine and noticed nothing out of the ordinary with her. He further added that she appeared to be very small during his examination and gave Braxton a strange look. Not mentioning the fact that she may have appeared to be a virgin, but he did notice that she was very agitated with the examination.

He looked at Braxton very briefly and they both exchanged glares and the doctor turned abruptly, removing his gloves and tossing them in the garbage. It was as if it were some sort of male stare down. Braxton didn't give in on the stare, but stated to the doctor emphatically,

"My wife was a virgin when we recently married," he said.

"It was difficult just to try to consummate the marriage and we haven't been very active since because she is still very uncomfortable with being intimate." The doctor's face lit up after he spoke.

"Okay, that explains it!" he said. "There are a couple of things I can prescribe for the two of you that might help with the transition." Braxton spoke immediately, trying not to give the doctor any more communication on the subject. "That would be super!" Gabriella, leaned in on Braxton's chest and played the demure virgin wife and sealed the conversation. The doctor then stepped out of the office for about five minutes or so. During which time, Gabriella got dressed and came out and sat with Braxton while waiting for the doctor's prescription. She was surprised when he put his arms around her again and pulled her close to him. He put his mouth almost on her ear as if he were going to kiss her.

Gabriella was beginning to tense up a bit when he whispered to her, "There is something strange about this physician. Don't answer any questions he may ask you when he comes back in. Pretend you are feeling nauseous or that you are going to throw up. I will make excuses for us to leave once we get the results. They also may be listening in," he said, smiling at her as he held her face close to his. "Act, normal also." Gabriella's entire face was covered with Braxton embracing her. She didn't mind at all, but was a bit nervous about what he had just said. She remembered that these ruthless business partners of Carlos might have had them followed or the Doctor could be working for them. They could not take any chances. This was becoming more serious than she realized at first, but she played along. It was as serious as he had said it would be.

The Doctor returned to the room and sure enough, he began asking Gabriella more questions just as Braxton had suspected he would. "Mrs. Shavarez, when did you have your last menstrual cycle?" Gabriella quickly answered, "I have always had irregular menses so I keep a chart…um, gosh, and I didn't bring it with me. "Honey, could you go out to the car and get my bag in the glove compartment" I can give the doctor the exact date. I am feeling sort of nauseated right now." She began to fake a hurl and the doctor grabbed the garbage can.

Author: *Victoria E. Kain*

Braxton jumped in, "Doctor Elliott, I think I need to get her home, can we call back the date to your nurse, if that's alright?" he asked. I sure wouldn't want her hurling on your nice clean floors and she had a big breakfast."

The doctor didn't seem to want that either and he looked at his chart with the test results and said, "Well, that would be okay, I guess, but please call back this number." He handed Braxton a card. "Congratulations, you are going to be a mother," he said. Gabriella almost fainted for real and Braxton caught her as she leaned up against him. Braxton was smiling like he was truly the father with this news. He shook the Doctor's hand so hard Gabriella felt the vibration standing next to him. The first thing that came to Gabriella's mind to ask was, "is it a boy or girl?" she said, then feeling a bit stupid.

"Well, since this is your first baby, you wouldn't know that it is too early to tell what it is." The doctor said giving her an excuse for the ridiculous question. Braxton played it off and laughed with the doctor and acted like it was a joke. "She knows I want a girl." He said winking at her, knowing that they needed this baby to be a boy for the contract she was under. Gabriella played along. The doctor looked suspicious though. Braxton was looking a bit strange as if the doctor was concerned about the relationship and the fact that her hymen was still intact. This was not abnormal for a woman to be pregnant and not be completely penetrated. This is where the dilemma was for the doctor. He knew it could happen.

Now that Gabriella was positive that she was pregnant, she had many questions. Dr. Elliott gave Braxton a list of things for morning sickness and some prenatal vitamins. Gabriella realized that the pregnancy was very real. They finally left the doctor's office and Braxton seemed to be in a hurry. He took Gabriella home and did not spend any time with her after the doctor's visit, but said he would be back after he escorted her to the Condo. Gabriella came in and went straight to bed. She really was feeling nauseous after the examination and wondered if this sick feeling would go away soon.

She tried not to think about it and rested for about forty five minutes and soon heard the door open again… and it was Braxton. He walked into her room with two dozen of the most beautiful pink and white roses and a giant teddy bear.

"This is for you. Gabriella, I'm so proud of you for the courage you've shown to have this child for me," he said, and he kissed her on the cheek.

"You are making me one of the happiest men on the face of the earth." A tear had formed in his eye. This was the oddest moment for Gabriella seeing that this was not his baby, but quickly realizing that he was very close to Carlos and keeping his wishes seemed to make Braxton happy.

She thanked him for the flowers and was really getting sick now. He finally put her to bed and she skipped supper that evening. It had been a long and tiring day and she just wanted to sleep. She couldn't help mimicking the woman in the doctor's office. Now she was rubbing her still flat belly knowing there was someone's baby growing inside her. That was a scary but happy feeling.

After confirming that Gabriella was pregnant, several weeks went by, from Dr. Elliott's examination, now almost two months pregnant. Gabriella was growing a little but not much. Being that her body was acclimating to the change it was going through, her brain had to catch up with everything that was happening to her as well. She wanted to be alone most of the time when she felt sick and was getting more accustomed to being pregnant. She talked a lot to herself and practiced in front of the mirror what she would look like as the pregnancy progressed. She put pillows under her small shirts and dresses and made a mess in her closet only for the maid to come in and when she returned from sun bathing at the pool side, it was all neatly organized again. She still wasn't accustomed to having maid servants and couldn't fathom that she was actually pregnant. However, as she sat and day dreamed about her life before the pregnancy, realizing it was very real and potentially dangerous. She wasn't getting out much because she had mood swings at times and just wasn't feeling up to having company.

Braxton tried to please her in every way and took her many places. If it were some place she didn't want to go, she declined and stayed inside. They spent many evening at the pool or playing other games in the garden by the gazebo. The nights were wonderful with Braxton. He was always great company. Gabriella was beginning to miss her family terribly and naturally wanted them to be part of the pregnancy. She wanted them to see her in her new surroundings and help them see that as mother's, they deserved to be treated the way she was being treated, but she soon realized that this was not a real situation in the sense of her not being able to keep the baby in the end. Her thoughts were noble, but unrealistic. Her loneliness began to get to her and she wanted more and more to go home to her mother.

It was a normal feeling to have but she kept fighting the urge because of the contract she was under. One Saturday, while sitting in her den, her cell phone rang for the very first time. It had not rung since she had left her tiny apartment on the west side of Chicago. She looked at the screen and it was Pallie! Instinctively she wanted to answer the phone due to the excitement of his name popping up, but quickly deduced that although she longed to talk to him, she dismissed the thought and remembered he had angered her the last night she saw him.

She then remembered that she was now carrying a child! How could she talk to him when she was actually carrying the baby that he joked about her carrying for the money! She was angry that Pallie had been right. She had done this, but it was not for the money because Carlos had left her two hundred thousand dollars whether she did this or not. It was the perfect thing to do to soothe her conscience. She knew that she did it because of Carlos's unselfishness. She couldn't walk away from giving something back to him. Now, she was getting bored sitting at the condo day in and day out with no one to talk to until Braxton would come back from wherever he went during the day. He watched her so closely that she was beginning to feel imprisoned, but understood that it wasn't safe to wander around.

He always wanted to spend time with her but she would refuse, partly because she didn't want to get too close to him because of their attraction to each other and believing they would never be a real couple. There had been strange people sighted around the condo and Braxton was taking no chances now that Gabriella was carrying the baby. She decided to let the phone go to voice mail and listened to Pallie's message. Pallie was apologizing profusely for what happened months earlier and sounded very sad that she had just up and left the area without saying goodbye.

She felt so bad that she reasoned that she should call him... after all, what would it hurt just to talk to him? She was already pregnant, so what harm could come from this. Besides, there would be nothing else going on between them. They were just friends now. She felt it would be good for her condition to be able to be close to someone since she couldn't be close to Braxton the way she wished she could be. Now ignoring all of Braxton's warnings about outside contact, she called Pallie back and began talking to him.

The conversation went well but he kept asking a lot of questions. He wanted to see her but she was not sure about that. He even said that he loved her for the first time and was totally open. Gabriella was surprised that those words didn't carry the weight she thought they would and she remembered how she wanted him to say them to her before, but now, all she could think about was Braxton. She fought that feeling as well. Pallie said he realized that she cared about him and admitted that he was trying to play hard to get until he saw how upset she had become the last day he saw her.

The conversation went well. Gabriella enjoyed the simple straight talk and he told her he was so sorry for saying the things he did that hurt her. They made up over the phone and he asked her if she would come to see him if he was not permitted to come to her. At this point, Gabriella was torn in her feelings of wanting to see him and breaching her agreement with Braxton. Pallie tried to coerce her.

"Brella, he said, calling her by her nickname, "it floored me when I came by your apartment and found someone else living there. I didn't know what to think! I even went by your mother's house and no one could give me any information."

If you had told me you couldn't pay your rent, I would have paid it for you, you know I would have." Gabriella pretended not to know that the rent hadn't been paid, but she was shocked when Pallie stated that the landlord said that she was evicted for nonpayment. She couldn't tell Pallie about being pregnant or where she was. She was still surprised about the lie about her being evicted and she wanted to question Braxton about it but didn't want to get Pallie in trouble. She would have to conceal her emotions on both sides from Pallie and from Braxton. Pallie was now trying to be the friend that she had always wanted him to be but couldn't. "Why did he have to get straight with her now?" she thought. She finally realized that Pallie really cared for her and she really thought she wanted to be with him before her life had changed so drastically. Was it the baby she was carrying now? Or was it her loyalty to Braxton and Carlos?

She was truly torn, but what she really knew was that she did not love Pallie like that. Not enough to mess up her contract with Braxton. Now, he truly was a friend and she could clearly differentiate between the two feelings. Gabriella knew she had to figure out a way to see Pallie since she was his friend. She wanted to make it up to him because of the way she kicked him out of her apartment. She knew she was not in love with him and didn't think it would hurt the situation.

She ended the call agreeing to see him. Besides, he had begged her to call him back. Each day the urge to see him became stronger. She had daily conversations with him and it seemed that they were getting closer than she had ever been to him before. She only wished Pallie had been someone she really wanted in her life in a special way. The day finally came that she would see Pallie. She evaded Braxton's request to take her out for the day and feigned not feeling well and hated lying to him. She felt she had to tell him something to get to see her friend. She waited until Braxton was away and called Pallie. Getting dressed was a snap with all the things to choose from. She would be able to impress her friend with all that she had. Besides, she was wealthy, but no one could know it. She got dressed very casually but in a nice outfit. After the deception had been planted, she asked the maid to call for her driver.

"Your driver is downstairs Mistress," the maid stated.

"Thank you!" Gabriella responded. Now taking full advantage of the authority she now was clear that she had. Once she entered the town car, she asked the driver to take her to the mall. It almost felt juvenile, but that's where she wanted to go. She had missed doing simple things like that, even though she never had money to spend like she did now. She told Pallie to meet her in front of their favorite store. As they turned the corner to leave the complex, she noticed a strange car on the street in front of her condo. When they pulled out, the strange car pulled out behind them. She tried not to think about it but realized that she was still in a dangerous situation.

She reasoned that nothing had happened so far, and maybe nothing would happen. When she arrived at the mall, Pallie was wandering outside the store as planned. He totally ignored the black town car as it pulled up, not realizing it was Gabriella. She finally let the window down just a hair and he caught sight of her. "Gabriella, is that you?" Pallie asked, jumping into the car like a teenager who had just been let out by their parents for the first time. There were all kinds of snacks in the back with them and he was like a kid... still greedy.

"Man, what did you do, rob a bank?" He was being silly again but suddenly remembered Gabriella didn't like that kind of talk. He quickly recoiled and said, "I am sorry, I didn't mean it like that."

"No, no bank, I have missed you Pallie," she said.

"I missed you a lot Brella," Pallie said, reaching over to kiss her and trying to grope her at the same time. Instinctively, Gabriella slapped his hand and realized she was agitated with his reaction, not accepting that it was normal for immature young men. He knew this was not her thing and she knew she was pregnant and could not be intimate, but she didn't see that it would hurt to have him as a friend. She was beginning to get the hang of ordering people around with her new found power from being rich. She instructed her driver to take them to the park and he immediately asked "which one Ma'am?" The driver checked his rear mirror to see behind him and witnessed what was going on in the back seat and quickly adjusted it to preclude evading the privacy of his passengers and his boss. Gabriella and Pallie sat and talked for a while and began kissing each other. Pallie was not a good kisser, but Gabriella was not the best, seeing she had never kissed anyone before and had only been kissed on the cheek by Braxton, just pecked.

Even with that memory of a kiss on the cheek and her forehead, it seemed that if it could have been more intense, she would know the difference in the feeling. Caring about someone would have to make a difference in the kiss you received from them, she thought. But, for now, kisses she received from Braxton on the cheek seemed to be better than what Pallie was doing. The light kiss was not anything to write home about, even for an amateur.

Pallie was a typical college student and thought this was his opportunity to make his move on Gabriella in case she disappeared again. Suddenly, there was a hard repetitious knock heard on the dark tinted windows. It startled them both and the driver began to get out of the vehicle when a police cautioned him to stay inside.

Gabriella let the window down and a police officer was standing at the window. "Is this your vehicle Ma'am?" he asked.

"Yes, it is," she reluctantly responded. Strangely enough, the officer didn't question her answer.

"We are looking for a convict in this area, have you seen anyone pass by in the last few minutes?"

"No, we haven't," she said. Pallie was scared and let Gabriella do all the talking.

"We are going to have to ask you to leave the area."

"Not a problem, officer," she said. Gabriella asked the driver to take off. Before they could move, they heard gunshots. Pallie was really scared now and the police came back to the car demanding that the driver and the two of them get out of the car because they were cornering the convict in the park and did not want anyone to get shot.

"How will you get home?" Pallie asked Gabriella.

"We will take you home Ma'am," the police responded.

Gabriella is now shaking and Pallie was just as afraid and helped Gabriella out of her car and into the back of the squad car. Just when Gabriella was thinking they would put Pallie in the same car she was in, the policeman drives off and Pallie was put in a different car. She could see the police officers talking to him as they pulled off. The police officer drove Gabriella directly to her condo. She realized something was strange because she had not given the officer's her address but here she was right in front of the complex.

She did not know how they knew where she lived. Both officers looked at her with a cold stare as she slowly exited the squad car and ran into the building as they watched until she got safely inside. Afraid and furious that she was being followed, she went to the third floor to her condo and locked the door behind her once she got in. Gabriella was mad to the extent that she wanted to call everything off. She realized that what she had agreed to was real and there was no turning back. The only thing she could think to do was call Braxton and ask him to come up to talk with her now. An hour passes by and Braxton finally arrives. The maid lets him into the condo and Gabriella is in full tilt anger. Before he can sit down and inquire about her day, she lets into him with both barrels.

"How long have you been spying on me?" She yells at Braxton.

He quietly answers, "Since you became pregnant with the baby," he said calmly, looking her deep in her eyes.

It was difficult for her to look at him when he was this calm. She knew she was wrong but still didn't like the idea of being watched. There was something else in his face tonight. It was a look of disappointment.

"Why are you spying on me?" she demanded, again.

"Because this is the agreement we have and I must watch you closely for your safety," he said, clasping his hands together as he sat down in the oversized chair in front of hers. Gabriella didn't know what to say to him. It was all too easy to blast him like she did Pallie with the pizza in her old apartment, but there was something different that made her not want to do this to Braxton. Though angry, Gabriella was confused. Braxton showed her all of the surveillance cameras in the house. When she saw them, she was furious again to the point that she stormed out of the room.

She picked up her jacket on the way and walked out of the building heading down the dark street. No sooner than she arrived at the end of the walkway, she realized she was being followed. The local convenient area was in the landing with shops and restaurants. She turned and went into a store and pretended to be looking for something realizing she was still being watched. Finally Gabriella decided that what she was doing was too risky and she quickly walked out of the store and hurried back to the condo. She reentered her place and slowly walked back into the den where Braxton was still sitting in front of the fire place, now listening to music with his head in his hands.

Gabriella sat down next to him. This time she was more controlled and mature in her approach. She was no longer ranting and tells him quietly,

"I can't do this, I can't be made to feel like a guinea pig. I want out!"

Very calmly he says without even looking up." I will arrange for the abortion tomorrow."

"Abortion!!!" Gabriella repeats in a high tone, almost hyperventilating. "We never agreed on an abortion!!!" she stammered almost in tears."

"This is the only way to end this," he said.

"Or, you can decide to keep the baby and we can end the contract, but you would return all but 200,000 that you received from Carlos's estate." Braxton was quiet, only saying what was necessary.

Gabriella didn't know what to say. She was frightened and confused after having stated she wanted out, not realizing how this would affect her.

"In a few months, I am having a baby. I have never seen my father alive and have never been with a man and you say that tomorrow you will arrange for an abortion??? This is ridiculous!" She screamed. "Fine!!!" She begins sobbing.

"Fine!" Braxton stated angrily and got up and left the room. Gabriella went into her bedroom and continued crying. She looked at her cell phone as it was ringing and she looked at the caller ID and it was Pallie. She began to pick up the phone to answer it and stopped herself.

Realizing that she was not a child anymore was becoming crystal clear to her. She had not liked Pallie's childish ways once, but now, she was exhibiting the same behavior with Braxton. She took her phone to her bathroom and took off her boots and smashed the phone to pieces. She dismantled it completely and realized that she was now carrying a child and her actions were completely out of line today. She didn't know what else to do after that except take a hot bath and get in bed. She didn't know how she would apologize to Braxton, but knew that for some strange reason, she wanted to.

The next morning, Gabriella was really sick. It could have been because of all the excitement the previous day. She started to get nauseous and wanted to throw up but made it to the bathroom. She was afraid thinking she might lose the baby which meant the deal would be off and she would go back home or wherever. She further reasoned that she still would have the 200,000 and could finish school, but what kind of life would she live after that? She called her maid for some hot tea to settle her stomach and she brought her several cups with different types of teas. Gabriella realized that the treatment she was receiving was beyond anything she could have imagined would be happening to her right now.

"I am actually pregnant," she said. She knew she had to call Braxton sooner or later about the night before and decided to get it over with. She had her maid call him up and he came right away. Braxton came in and stood this time, like a visitor, not taking a seat.

"Are you ready to go for the abortion? I have made the arrangements for you and I can have your things sent back to your old apartment and reset it up if you'd like. I can have the driver take you there after it is over." He looked away. Gabriella was stunned that everything was happening so fast. She was nervous thinking it would be over and Braxton would force her to have the abortion. She never wanted to destroy any baby she would have. She had to speak quickly.

"Well, I was sick this morning and wasn't sure what was happening to me." She said.

"That is what happens when a woman is pregnant, Gabriella."

That was the first time he had referred her as a "woman." She seemed to feel different all of a sudden. He further stated to her in a calm voice. "I thought about the abortion which was very harsh, but if you choose not to have the baby, you may stay here until you feel better after the procedure and then you can leave and take whatever you want from the condo with you." "You will be free to go and I will trouble you no further," he stated. There was something not right about that statement. Gabriella wanted to hear something different from him. She didn't like feeling that Braxton would somehow be out of her life. She was confused but mustered up the courage to speak.

"Well, what if I say, I don't want to go now?" she quietly stated, searching his face hoping for a positive response from him to reassure her that he still cared about what she felt. He was the only man that had ever said that he wanted to do "everything" for her, and she was beginning to see how good that felt, coming from someone. At this point in her life, it was all the love she knew and realizing that it could all be gone in a flash, she prayed that his response was something that she could handle. He finally spoke to her. He looked up and took her hand and lovingly stated to Gabriella, "Then, if you really mean that you don't want to end the pregnancy, I would ask you to get dressed and we will take a drive to the beach today to give you and the baby some fresh air." How does that sound to you? He then moved closer to Gabriella and gave her a warm embrace. This time he gently rocked her for a moment and kissed the top of her head.

"I am glad you made this choice," he said to her.

Gabriella's heart was instantly relieved that Braxton had not made her beg. She realized the mess she could have made by making the wrong decision. Before she went in to change, she turned to Braxton and humbly asked, "Do you think I could get a new cell phone today?" "I don't want anyone to have the number but you and the servants in the house?"

"I am sure we can make that happen," he stated. "And, you can have it in any color you like," he added. Gabriella had the biggest smile on her face ever.

She was instantly feeling better about her situation. The night before was soon becoming a blur to Gabriella and Pallie was ancient history to her. It seemed that being pregnant was maturing her faster than she had ever imagined it would along with it changing her entire view on life, all the while it was transforming her body. She realized she didn't want to put herself, the baby or Braxton in jeopardy again and would do whatever was asked of her going forward.

Braxton had referred to her as a "woman," and she felt obligated to live up to this expectation. She was beginning to feel like a woman which meant, she had to think like one. Carrying this child would require making other changes in her life that she never would have expected, but she knew that she had signed a contract and had to live up to it. 'This is how adults respond to things,' she thought. Braxton called the driver and had him bring the car around. They would spend the entire day to themselves out on a private beach. It was the most beautiful day Gabriella had ever experienced. She knew that the closeness Braxton showed her was to help her and the baby adjust to this special situation of her carrying a child and never having been intimate with a man before. The only bad thing was that it was becoming difficult to keep her feelings separated from family and personal relationships.

CAMOUFLAGE

As they walked along the seashore that night and watched the waves come in and go out. They laughed and talked about all the funny things they had experienced thus far. They even referred back to when Gabriella's mother was swinging from Braxton's neck at the repast. They both looked at each other as couples played on the beach and dipped in the water to cool themselves from the days' heat. Off in a distance, ships could be seen that looked like toy boats as they were sailing slowing in the evening as the sun was setting. Some smaller boats were seen docking at a nearby harbor.

They talked about many things that night and the day ended beautifully. It felt special to both of them but it was evident that they both were having major issues keeping their thoughts from drifting to the apparent connection they were having subliminally. Gabriella realized that having the baby would be the least of her problems as time went on. Remembering that this was a family affair would soon prove to be a daunting task, but for now, she never wanted the day to end. She was happier than she ever thought she could be. Gabriella knew she had to find a way to cope with her feelings but she didn't care at the moment and would treasure the time she had to feel close to someone right now, even though she knew it was not to be permanent for her.

She knew that in the end she would have to give up everything she loved and walk away. But for now… she never wanted this night to end. She wanted it to last forever.

~ CHAPTER 7 ~

Forgotten Memories

Author: Victoria E. Kain

FORGOTTEN MEMORIES

The incident with Pallie was long gone, never to be repeated again. Gabriella was clear now about the importance of the agreement she had signed with Braxton and as time moved forward, she was beginning to feel very pregnant. She knew that the clock had seriously begun ticking for her as soon as she was artificially inseminated and with every passing day was keenly aware that she could not turn back time or lives could be lost.

To fall into the grove of the situation, she began trying on some of her many maternity outfits that Braxton had purchased for her. Still being rather small, but showing just a bit, she was now having a little difficulty getting into things she normally would wear. Everything was from Paris or Italy and very stylish. One thing was for sure, Braxton had great taste in women's clothing. It seemed that after the Pallie incident, Braxton made sure Gabriella was never lonely. They travelled to private beaches in the Bahamas, to Las Vegas, Napa Valley wine country, Costa Rica, the Virgin Islands and many other exotic places. He realized the fiasco with Pallie was a cry for companionship and remembered that Gabriella was a vibrant young woman who had not yet tasted life or travelled the world. For the most part, she had never really been kissed before by a man. He knew he had to protect her from those emotions and showered her with as much affection as he could legitimately.

With her special circumstance, he knew that it was up to him to make her feel as if he was devoted to her, that she had his undivided attention. He now paid even more attention to her and put more excitement into her life. She was treated like royalty everywhere they went and Braxton paraded her about as if she were a princess and his personal pride and joy. Beautiful women envied her and as any woman would, she enjoyed the feeling of knowing that Braxton never took his attention away from her. He knew he had to convince her that she was the only woman in his life, even under these circumstances that were very strained. Each day she looked forward to seeing him and knew that she had to keep in mind that Braxton was a family member and not the father of the child she was carrying.

She began to see that her reason for trying to see Pallie was only to focus her emotions elsewhere. Being as strained as the relationship was with her and Braxton, she knew she could not express what she was feeling towards him and had no legal right to show any amorous emotions at all in the situation. Sometimes, this thought saddened her and it was difficult to remember her place. Many times she wanted to spontaneously hug him or hold his hand, but couldn't. She could see the restraint Braxton had to exhibit as well. On many occasions, he wanted to take that one step closer to pulling her into his arms, but he too fought the urge and pulled himself back.

Gabriella's biggest fear was always that she would not stop his actions, which would make her just as guilty as Adam was in the Garden of Eden for not refusing to take part in his mate's wrong doing. They had many constraints on their relationship that made the union difficult, but necessary. Being pregnant made Gabriella feel lethargic and really sick and weak at her stomach at times. She wanted Braxton to hold her when she felt bad and console her when she was lonely for family. He held her sometimes until she fell asleep in his arms. When he would let her gently go and cover her up, she would slowly open her eyes watch him walk away from her wishing he was able to stay but only listened as the door quietly closed. If he only knew how many nights she feigned sleeplessness in order to lay in his arms without guilt, just a little longer. To smell his cologne and feel his strong arms around her shoulders as he cradled her. After all, he was all the family she had now. This is why it is so important for a woman to be with the father of her child when she is pregnant.

Every emotion Gabriella has is now tied to this man and she can't help but love him and the baby more and more each day. This night, she was not feeling well and with this being her first pregnancy, she was taking no chances at all. She decided to call for Braxton and have him send for the doctor to examine her, but even though she gave the maid the order she never informed her of Braxton's whereabouts.

Unexpectedly, a new doctor showed up to see Gabriella. She thought Braxton may have been left a message of her not feeling well and sent a doctor. She figured since it was the weekend, it may have been difficult to get her regular physician to come to the condo, but although these were second guesses, it was still odd that Braxton never showed which was not usual for him. Gabriella began to think that the maid may have called the doctor for her and was afraid to tell her, so Gabriella tried not to think anything of it, but probably should have.

Braxton told her to call him if ever anything was out of the norm, and this would have been the occasion, but Gabriella didn't. He had been so wonderful to her that she didn't want to trouble him with what she thought might be trivial. The doctor came right away and examined Gabriella and asked her a few disturbing questions of which she answered very guardedly. She realized that Braxton was not there to buffer for her so she was very careful and vague in her answers. She also made a mental note of what she was being asked by this new doctor. Although the questions would seem normal in a regular situation, Gabriella knew her situation was nothing close to being normal. The doctor assured her she was just fine and insisted that she stay off her feet for a few days. She further warned that these were the months that many women who are having their first baby may miscarry because of doing too much when the body is not yet accustomed to carrying a child.

She told Gabriella to stay in bed and rest. Just as the doctor was about to leave the room, Braxton rushed into the condo. Gabriella could hear him yelling at the Maid for letting the doctor in.

"Is everything okay with you and the baby, Gabriella?" he demanded, totally disregarding the doctor's presence.

"Yes, we are fine, honey, the doctor wants me to rest a little more, and that's all."

Braxton looked at the doctor in a very peculiar way and asked her some questions. He didn't seem very happy that she was there.

"Are you with the Freeman medical agency?" he asked.

"Uh, no, I am not. The service dispatched me when Dr. Mesaoh was not available to make the call. They said it was a high risk pregnancy and he won't be back until Monday, so they asked me to come," she said nervously.

"My wife and I appreciate you coming over," he said to her and began to escort her out.

"Not at all," The doctor responded, hurrying to get her bag.

"Your wife will be just fine. Keep her off her feet for a couple of days and watch her diet and no rigorous sexual activity for a few days as well." She said, looking at Braxton with a side grin waiting for a response.

"Well, I will definitely curtail my desires for my wife for a few days doctor. Thank you for coming!"

The doctor was escorted out and Braxton got on the phone and questioned security profusely. There was something apparently wrong with the doctor being at the condo. She could hear him yelling from the other room.

"I need you to check out the physician that was just here to see my wife!!!" he said, to his head of security. Strangely, the maid was standing in the doorway and looked mortified when he responded that I was his "wife." The main, immediately left the room as if she was on fire. It was clear there was something strange going on.

"Call me back immediately, when you get the information on her." Braxton demanded. Gabriella was much calmer now that Braxton was there. She relaxed in her oversized recliner with all the plush accommodations. She waited for Braxton to come back into her room after he made his phone call. She was learning very quickly that he was all about the business at hand, which was her and the baby and would not let anything happen to her. She now trusted him enough to do anything he asked her to do for their safety. While she waited for him to come in to see her before she retired for the evening she wondered if he'd be in a better mood than he was when he first arrived. She didn't want him upset with her for not calling him as he had instructed her to do and she desperately did not want to disappoint him again. She was very concerned about his feelings now. Braxton left the den and came into the room where Gabriella was.

He told her he was going to have to leave for a short while and take care of some business, but would stop back in to see her when he returned. Walking towards the door, he did what all husbands would do with their pregnant wives…

"Can I get you anything while I am out?" he asked, hoping she would give him a request.

She accommodated, "Yes, could you bring back some sweet pickles please?" she said, smiling a sheepish smile. He winked and responded affirmatively and told not to go to sleep before he returned and not to let "anyone" in and he gave the same instructions to the upstairs maids. Gabriella was becoming accustomed to him leaving for short stints of time. She knew she was protected and was beginning to realize that what he did was for her safety.

She began wondering about the maid and why she did not contact Braxton for the doctor when she knew those were the instructions for them. Especially if it would be someone different. Gabriella had also noticed how the maid had looked at Braxton when he came in to see her each evening and when they came in from being out all day together. She always made it a point to come into Gabriella's sitting room when Braxton was with her. She pretended to see if they needed anything and would make herself visible as if to be seen by Braxton. He would simply send her away and tell her that we would call for her if we needed anything and not to disturb us further.

She thought back to the day his brother was buried and remembered what he said about the ruthless business partners and the fact that they did not want his brother, Carlos, to have an heir. She realized that these ruthless men could have been the ones in the park that day with her and Pallie. It could have been really dangerous for her and the baby. Gabriella was becoming more aware of her dire situation with the child she was carrying. The fact that she was now in her third month of pregnancy and visibly showing, it became very clear to her that it was important to adhere to Braxton's directives from this point on for her safety. For the last few months, they had been doing a lot of travelling.

He had taken her to all sorts of wonderful places. The last place they went before she was becoming more uncomfortable was the Swiss Alps. Although she didn't ski, she was there and enjoyed the lodge. He said he wanted the baby to remember having been there before he was born and wanted to have the special memories with Gabriella. She didn't know how to feel about this. Besides, it wasn't a bad thing to feel love for a kind and generous person, regardless of who they were to you. She also reasoned that what she was doing was not wrong. She was carrying a child for someone who was no longer able to have the child the traditional way.

People in the 21st century had been using the insemination procedure for some time now. There was nothing wrong with supporting couples or others who have special situations where they cannot carry a child and use a surrogate. There is no physical contact, therefore there was nothing improper with carrying this child. A further thought crossed Gabriella's mind as she rationalized her situation. The money would could come in handy to help her mother and sisters by purchasing a large farm house for them to raise their children. They so desperately needed more room, even though they didn't clean the small house they had, only God knows what will happen with more room to clutter and destroy. But, at least they would have the space to be safe and run free. Lord knows those bad kids needed to be in the woods somewhere so they can tear it up limb by limb. Gabriella was content with that thought as she read one of her magazines. She decided to take a hot bath before going to bed that night and called her maid to draw her bath water for her. After a short while, Gabriella soaked in the oversized bathtub. She glanced around the luxurious room and it was almost frightening to begin feeling comfortable in her new surroundings. At times, she'd forget and would become fearful of losing all the wealth she had acquired. It was not that she wanted to be filthy rich, but she didn't want to go back to the West side of Chicago either. It just wasn't a life she wanted to live. Very quickly she would remember that she was wealthy now and never had to go back to her old life under any circumstances.

It wasn't the worst place in the world, but it also wasn't the best either. Either way, she certainly did not want to live there for the rest of her life. She could easily get used to living like a queen in this wonderful place and thought how grand it would be to have a man like Braxton to love and care for her permanently. It was too bad he was her father's brother. Why should some other woman get the opportunity to have this wonderful man as her husband," she thought. She quickly dismissed the thought pattern to keep herself out of trouble. Thinking more about the matter, she massaged her stomach through the pretty bubbles in the tub and thought about Braxton holding her hand during the insemination process. Remembering how it felt just thinking he was the father made her giddy. For a fleeting moment, Gabriella felt that Braxton was closer to the child than he let on to be.

There was just something odd about how he had picked her out of all those women that were there at the services that day to carry this baby. She wondered for a moment about the surveillance and thought that maybe he had already checked her out and knew that she was trying to do better for herself than most of the young women in that area. As she slowly got out of the tub still vaguely pondering her initial thoughts, she dried off, while selecting the sweetest smelling oils and rubbed it onto her body and tummy area, trying to ensure that she didn't have stretch marks after she had the baby.

She knew she wanted to wear a bikini again and remembered how it felt when she sported the one Braxton bought her at a little boutique when they travelled to the Bahamas. Gabriella brushed her teeth and prepared herself for bed. As she walked out of the bathroom she caught sight of her image in the full length mirror. She could see a little roundness to her small stomach. She smiled, feeling wonderful. No one else could see that she was pregnant just from looking at her, but she could. She finally selected a pair of silk pajamas ensuring they were a little big so she would be especially comfortable. She didn't want her little one experiencing any discomfort as well. There was no better feeling than silk against her skin. She had never thought she would be able to have such nice things as what she was now exposed to.

She was beginning to feel proud that she was having this baby. Even though she was sad that she would not be able to keep it. In the back of her mind, she knew she was doing a good thing. It was the first time ever that she could clearly understand what her Mama and sisters must have gone through when they knew they were carrying a child. Once she knew the baby was inside her, she began to love the child regardless of who, what or where, the father was. In Gabriella's case, the father was already gone. Now her main concern was two-fold. Will the child be a healthy boy and who will tell the child who his mother is when it's time? This would be a difficult undertaking regardless of who told the child.

She knew this baby had to be a boy or the contract she signed would be null and void. If it is not a male, Gabriella knew that the next day would be the determining factor as to whether she would move forward with her contract. She was nervous about this part because, like Cinderella, at midnight her life would turn back the way it was before she started this journey. In her case she would go back to school and try to start her life over again. It would be a mess either way and she didn't know what to do. All she wanted right now was sleep. She got into bed and listened to the jazz that Braxton had left on the bedside table. She prayed that the next day would be the day that a baby boy would be announced to her and Braxton. Unlike before, she now desperately wanted to please him.

~ CHAPTER 8 ~

Playing For Keeps

PLAYING FOR KEEPS

The following day came ever too quickly for Gabriella. She was up at the crack of dawn preparing to see the doctor for the ultrasound to find out the gender of the baby. Oddly enough, she felt absolutely perfect. No sickness, not tiredness or anything. There was a glow about her today for some reason. She knew she was about twelve or thirteen weeks or so and although she felt just fine, she was still a little tired because she didn't sleep well thinking about the gender of the baby. Everything now hinged on that one factor. Other than those thoughts, Gabriella was in top shape. She had her maid prepare her clothing and she dressed slowly, trying not to hyperventilate before leaving. Once dressed, Gabriella waited for Braxton to call. A short time passed and she was getting nervous that the call hadn't come in yet from Braxton. She remembered the statement he made the night before about the doctor being there at her home when she wasn't feeling well. She had time to think back to that night and remembered briefly that she began feeling ill right after the maid had brought her something to eat. With the day's events, she had also forgotten to tell Braxton her thoughts on the matter as well. Gabriella didn't want to think that the maid had anything to do with her needing to call a doctor that evening, but was becoming more concerned.

Her thoughts were becoming clearer and she realized that Braxton also never came back that night as he normally would to ensure that she was already in bed before he turned in for the night. There was something strange about these turn of events that were out of the norm. Finally her train of thought was broken by the sound of the door bell ringing. The maid quietly announced that Braxton had arrived. Braxton came into Gabriella's room very chipper!

"Good morning, Princess." Braxton said cheerfully.

"Good morning, my Prince," Gabriella replied, curtsying with dramatic flair. She was in good spirits this morning and wanted everything to go well.

"Are you ready to go?" he asked.

"I am," she responded.

"Well, let's get this show on the road, as they say."

They turned to walk out of the door and Gabriella instinctively looked back. She thought about her earlier feelings about the maid's possible involvement in her becoming ill that night. Oddly enough, when she looked back, the maid was glaring at the two of them in a strange way. The look on her face was a look of envy and hate that she had never noticed before. Now, she realized that it was very possible that the maid had something to do with her feeling sick that night and having to call a doctor. Things were becoming clearer in her mind now.

Could the maid have had something to do with the way she felt that evening? Did she know that the regular doctor was not available or was she simply trying to get Braxton's attention? As they left the building, scores of thoughts passed Gabriella's mind. She began to wonder if she had not paid enough attention to the maids and servants assuming they were okay because they were selectively hired. From now on she would closely watch everything they did. Marcia always seemed to have a subtle negative attitude when Braxton was around her. Being the upstairs maid, she was the first one that found out that Gabriella was pregnant and she was always there when Braxton would come and sit with Gabriella or take her out. Once she found that Gabriella was pregnant, she acted differently towards her. It could have been that she thought that the baby belonged to Braxton and was jealous.

Either way, Gabriella and Braxton walked out of the door and took the elevator down to the first floor. The driver had the car pulled around. As they drove, they talked candidly about the feelings of Gabriella being pregnant.

"I want you to know that, whatever this baby is, it will be as beautiful as its mother. "Braxton said to her, trying to make her feel good about a possibly bad situation. They both knew that this child had to be a boy or the family fortune would be lost. "Well, I'd like to be able to say that the baby will be like his father except, I didn't know him," she said.

"However, I thank you for the compliment anyway and I hope it's a boy for the sake of your family," Gabriella replied, looking out of the tinted windows. She didn't know what to think and had wondered if she had done the right thing by doing this at all. 'Was it just about the money?' She thought. Or, was there something about the man who had asked her personally to do this thing? Either way, a baby would be born and would need to be loved by someone, even if it were not his birth mother. She reasoned that if it were a girl, she would keep her and tell her the truth when she grew up.

She remembered that Braxton had not asked her to have this baby in front of everyone at the repast, but waited and came to her privately. She always liked that aspect of why he decided to do it that way. He may not have wanted any distraction from others and wanted this to be confidential. Either way, they would soon know what sex the baby was and move on with the pregnancy or if it was a girl, move on with the rest of her life.

"Well, here we are," Braxton announced taking a deep breath.

"Wow, this is a switch from where we have been before," Gabriella stated as she got out of the car. They walked into the medical facility and no one was in the lobby. They were led down a long hallway and came to another office. Once there, they entered and saw a nurse come in from the back. She ushered them into yet another room that was set up for the examination. Gabriella and Braxton sat on the hard chairs in the small waiting room.

He held her hand and rubbed it continuously. He put his arms around her and held her. She was trembling a bit. Finally, the doctor walked in.

"Hello, I am Dr. Zorsinke."

"Nice to meet you." we are Mr. and Mrs. Shavarez," Braxton said. "You came highly recommended to us and we are here for the ultrasound."

"Well, let's get started," Dr. Zorsinke stated.

They had Gabriella lay on the table for the examination and as soon as they set the warm gel on her abdomen, they could hear the baby's heart beating louder than normal. They looked at each other, smiling, and still hoping it was what they wanted.

Dr. Zorsinke began the examination and looked at the monitor. They all could hear the baby's heart beat loud and clear. They looked at each other and finally, there he was. A tiny image and they could clearly see his face. Finally, the doctor continued to examine the ultrasound and determined the sex of the baby. "Well, it looks like everything is in order here. You have a healthy little boy on the way. Congratulations!" he said with a slight smile. He tried to get one more look at the ultrasound of the baby, but for some reason, the image disappeared. The doctor thought nothing of it, because he had done this so often, and many times the picture might disappear.

His statement about the baby's sex was mundane. It seemed to be nothing to him. Probably because of saying that same phrase to thousands of women over the course of his career. But for Braxton, he almost hit the ceiling. He grabbed Gabriella and kissed her for the first time on the lips before he realized it. It was a spontaneous move and he couldn't take it back with onlookers about. It shocked Gabriella, but she too was careful about her reactions towards affection from Braxton in public because they had to pretend to be a couple for the sake of the contract and the baby. Gabriella immediately recoiled her actions.

"Now, now, honey," she said, totally playing the role of his wife.

"We have to wait until your son is born before we can try for a little girl," she said. Embracing his hand squeezing it gently. The doctor cleared her to get dressed and prescribed plenty of rest but no other restrictions were given. The two of them left the office that day and were on their way back to the condo travelling by way of cloud nine. Inside the car, they laughed and talked as they rode down the highway like teenage kids.

"So, mommy, how does it feel to have a healthy baby boy on the way?" "You did it! You did it!" Braxton exclaimed with the biggest smile ever on any man's face. You would have thought this was his baby by the reaction he gave. This reaction would be puzzling to Gabriella for a time. But finally her thoughts conceded. She understood how this might make him feel because it could have been a little girl which was not what they needed to satisfy the contract of the Will.

Gabriella felt very elated about Braxton's reaction to the child she was carrying. She had hoped that if she married some day and had children of her own, the father of her child would be as happy as Braxton was today. This reaction would be the one she would set the standards by for having another baby for anyone in the future. She was growing closer and closer to Braxton and the baby in a disturbing way. Going into her next phase of pregnancy would bring more challenges to face but she knew she could handle it now with him by her side.

"I feel very proud to be able to do this for your family Braxton." Gabriella said, trying to keep her mind focused on the fact that this was a business proposition and not personal. She really was feeling good about being in a position to positively affect her father's fortune. She was becoming less concerned with what people thought about her or the decision she had made and felt that this was the right thing to do.

"I am proud as well." Braxton said.

"You mean more to me with each day you carry this child to term, Gabriella. You have no idea what this means to me," he said. "I understand how this might feel or look to some people, but you and I know the truth and know that it is the right thing to do." Gabriella listened quietly, absorbing every word of sincerity.

"I appreciate all of what you are doing for me as well."

He had that same look in his eye that he did when she first met him. It was the same look he had when he came to her apartment and asked her to carry the child for the sake of his deceased brother. Gabriella was feeling something strange but wonderful with these internal thoughts she was having. It was leaving a void in the pit of her stomach. It was difficult enough to think of Braxton as her Uncle while she was carrying a baby that would make them all related. She was clear that it was not incestuous because of the artificial insemination. What she was doing was for the sake of creating and preserving a bloodline heir for her deceased father who was wealthy and did not have any male children to satisfy the stipulation on his business partnership agreement. Without this Heir, all of his fortune would be lost to these greedy men who would stop at nothing to get rid of them all.

Braxton was willing to put his life on the line to do this for Carlos. Gabriella couldn't help but wonder why the fortune could not go to one of his daughters, but after further pondering, she decided not to rack her brain with the mundane thoughts anymore. She would enjoy the rest of the day with Braxton, knowing that she was carrying a baby boy and this seemed to make him extremely happy. For a moment, she forgot about the contract she had signed. Getting the extra attention because of the good news about the baby was their reason to celebrate. But they could not share the news with anyone but each other. For a moment, it felt like it was their baby and Gabriella tried not to hold onto that thought.

She was still nervous about the partners her father was said to have had who would not want this baby to survive. She prayed that it would be alright and felt safe with Braxton nearby knowing he would give his life to protect them. She knew she had months before she would deliver the baby and was anxious to have it over with knowing she could move on with her life. "Maybe I'll have a family of my own someday," she thought. She could tell that Braxton wanted to tell someone about the baby, but knew he couldn't. Gabriella felt that he was more in tune to the baby than he should have been, since he was only the uncle to this child. She still felt something strange and realized the baby was moving inside her.

"Hey, want to feel something neat?" Gabriella asked Braxton, smiling, trying to break the seriousness of their conversation.

"Yes, what is it," Braxton responded promptly, wanting to cater to her every wish today.

Gabriella took Braxton's hand and placed it on top of her stomach. They both looked at each other intensely for a few moments and finally it happened. A hard kick from the baby caused the outward movement to her abdomen and Braxton could feel the baby kicking.

"Whoosh, what was that?" He asked, smiling very adoringly as if he was going to faint. "That felt like a line-backer kicking in there! It didn't hurt you did it?" he asked.

"No, silly." Gabriella responded, like she was a pro. "That was your baby." Sheer embarrassment struck her and she immediately corrected her statement.

"I mean "the" baby," she repeated, looking down at her stomach and shrugging her small shoulders. "That just slipped out," she whispered.

"Well, in a sense, it is ours," Braxton said to Gabriella. It was as if he wanted to reassure her that what she was doing was special and what she had just said was not all untrue. Braxton's feelings was the same as her and he wanted them both to be given the credit for making this situation possible.

"We are entrusted to care for this child like a father and a mother would," he said to Gabriella.

"This is exactly what we are doing. Even though he is not here yet, we have to show him the same love now, as he will receive once he arrives." That made sense to Gabriella and Braxton confirmed that it was okay to say that the baby belonged to them. She just had to be convincing to others. It was equally as important that she practice believing that the baby was theirs.

They both knew that what they were doing was part of the contract and ultimately Braxton would end up rearing the child alone if not with a nanny. Gabriella wondered for a brief moment if it might be possible for her to be in the baby's life after he was born. She would even consent to being his Nanny, but quickly dismissed the thought realizing this would breach everything in the contract and not be practical because she knew in her heart she would want the baby to know that she was his mother.

It would be too much to bear looking into his beautiful little face every day and holding him and never being able to tell him how much she loved him as his mother. She was beginning to feel awkward knowing she would not be able to watch him grow up. She wasn't sure how this was going to affect her having children in the future, knowing that one of them was missing. How would she feel having other children and never being able to see the first one that she gave birth to grow up? This was beginning to plague her a bit. She wouldn't let on to Braxton about how she really felt, but just at that moment, the baby kicked again and Gabriella smiled to herself. This time she didn't say anything to Braxton. She just savored the moments of feeling the child growing inside her and treasured the time she had left with her baby alone. Today was the most beautiful day ever. Braxton was looking out of the window, in deep thought.

He let the driver know to take the next turn to the Fresh market and gave him a list of things to get for the Picnic he was taking Gabriella and the baby on. The driver was very swift in purchasing the items Braxton asked for. Soon, they would be at the forest preserve picnic area in record time. It was a beautiful sunny day as they found a cool shady spot with a huge old oak tree with limbs that seemed to shade most of the park. They laid down a large plush blanket on the grass and soon after, Gabriella laid in Braxton's arms, feeling comforted and protected. He cradled her like she was an infant.

When she wanted to sit up, he laid his head on her lap, using it as a pillow. It was a perfect day for a picnic and this was everything Gabriella could have asked for being pregnant for the first time. She had a strong, handsome man by her side going through the pregnancy with her. If for no other reason than experiencing the utmost love and care during her pregnancy, she couldn't ask for any better memories as a woman expecting her first child. It was a shame she had to give everything up in the end. This still was proving to be a challenge she didn't know if she could face when the time came. There was nothing she could not have that money could buy. Women would kill to be in her shoes, but this is not how Gabriella wanted to bring her first child into the world. Braxton seemed to adore her and loved the unborn baby as if it were his own. Gabriella thought that he would be a wonderful father someday for some fortunate woman. It saddened her to think it could never be her.

He treated Gabriella like the royalty he knew she was. He would deny her nothing she wanted. She was like a princess to him and she had strong feelings for him in her heart, but knew he could never belong to her. In this instance, this was a family affair. Never knowing a father's love, this was the best opportunity to experience love in a most complete way. What she would take from this ordeal would be the love that was being shown to her from someone who knew her father intimately. It was the closest thing to having one.

This whole life change was amazing. To have only known someone for such a short time and to feel this way about them was almost unreal. She tried to attach these feelings to her deceased father that she had never known. She was beginning to feel a special kind of love for Carlos, even in his absence. Gabriella couldn't help lamenting that it was a shame to be related to Braxton. "Why couldn't it be that he was the father of this baby and we were really a couple, madly in love?" She thought many things that day as they walked down through the meadows and played games with each other like any expecting couple would. The wild flowers that grew in the fields smelled very pretty. He picked a handful of them and presented them to her along with a small bouquet for the baby.

Playfully, he laid them on her tummy as the sun beamed down on her beautiful face casting a glow to Gabriella's skin. Every so often, he would see the flowers rise and fall on her tummy indicating that the baby was moving around. He seemed like a man in love, if there was ever a scene to convey it. "You are a beautiful woman Gabriella," he said. No smile this time, but a serious, deep sigh followed his glance. This kind of look in any other setting would be accompanied by a kiss, but these circumstances only merited a "thank you," and a glance in return. Gabriella wondered why the serious look on his face fell each time he looked at her. She wondered what tomorrow would bring.

This day had been very special for both of them. It seemed that the pregnancy was coming along just fine. Gabriella had begun to show visibly but didn't know how that would make her feel. Not being able to wear any of her regular clothing was a ne feeling for her. She had heard her sisters talk about how their baby's fathers talked about them when they started gaining weight from the pregnancy and how bad it made them feel. She wondered if this would happen to her, deciding that she would be brave and ask Braxton a typical question a woman asks the father of her child during their first pregnancy.

"What are you going to think of me when my stomach is really fat and I can't wear a bikini anymore?" she asked, pressing her shirt tight to her tummy.

Braxton knew what to say to any woman in that condition.

"I am going to think that you are beautiful anyway and only look at you from your neck up." He laughed and she playfully punched him in the stomach. She noticed that she didn't fly off the handle with Braxton as she did with Pallie in her old apartment. She could see that they had a lot in common and Braxton knew how to make her laugh. Maturity was taking hold of her and she was maturing into a woman. Braxton then grabbed both of her hands and kissed them. "I truly love the fact that you are doing this for me, Gabriella," he said.

"This is no light task that you have undertaken. This is major," now looking longingly at her. He seemed to want to kiss her at that moment, but restrained himself under the circumstances. Gabriella felt him pulling back, and so did she.

They both had to continually fight the attraction they knew they had for one another. It was evident, but they knew they could not do anything about it. By the time they reached the town car from their short walk, Braxton's phone rang. It was a call from his security officers.

"Yes." he asked, beaconing for Gabriella to quickly head towards the car. Something was going on. Gabriella began to pick up the blankets and Jesse, the driver, stopped her and took them from her opening the car door for her to get in. He then picked up all of the food stuff and tossed it all in the garbage. It was a waste to throw away good food like that, but being rich was taking a lot of getting used to when you came from nothing and knew that people are hungry somewhere else in the world. Once the ground was cleared of the picnic items, Gabriella waited for Braxton.

She was peeking through the tinted windows, trying to read Braxton's expressions and his lips to see what was going on. It looked as if he was very upset. He could be very stern sometimes with the people that worked for him. After going on for a while on the phone, Braxton finally emerged from the roadside where he had walked away from ear shot of Gabriella and the driver. "Is everything okay?" Gabriella asked him, almost taking on the position of a wife.

"We have some concerns, but I don't want you worrying your pretty little head about anything other than delivering a healthy baby boy in a few months, you hear!" he stated, tapping her lightly on the nose with his finger and sealing it with a wink.

"Ok, that's fair enough." Gabriella responded.

Braxton then spoke to the driver and asked him to drop Gabriella off at the condo because he had somewhere else to go for a short while. Gabriella wanted to ask him where he had to go, but knew that this was not the right time or thing to do. Her job was to carry the baby and she was becoming very good at doing this.

They arrived back at the condo to drop Gabriella off and Braxton did his usual routine and checked the place out down stairs. He took Gabriella upstairs to the third floor and a surprising thing happened when he opened the door. A different maid greeted them.

"Who are you?" Gabriella asked, now exercising her full authority for her new home. She was shocked knowing that her other maid Marcia, was not to be off today.

"Where is Marcia?" she asked the woman, looking at Braxton for the answer. She had become accustomed to Marcia and was now becoming very concerned. Braxton immediately dismissed the new maid Kaitlin and took Gabriella into the sitting room to explain the change of events in her servants. Once in the room, he asked Kaitlin to bring Gabriella a cup of hot tea.

"Yes, sir," the maid responded swiftly as she left the room to carry out his wishes. Braxton began to explain some of the changes he needed to make. "We had to relieve your entire staff, but you have a new staff now."

"Why?" Gabriella asked.

"Because of a security breaches," he responded.

"What kind of breach?"

"Well, nothing for you to be worried about. But remember I said there would be many changes during this process and we cannot become too relaxed with the information about the baby possibly being leaking out. We have several months before the baby is born and must be extremely cautious." In light of the days' events with the announcement of the baby and the beautiful day in the park. Braxton was taking every precaution. He knew these business partners of Carlos's were close on their trail and he wanted nothing to happen to Gabriella and the baby.

"Do you still trust me?" he asked Gabriella, looking directly at her with a seriousness in his eye. She didn't hesitate to answer with conviction.

"I do, Braxton," Gabriella responded.

"Then I want you to relax, change, and get ready for dinner tonight because I have a surprise for you. A smile immediately erupted across Gabriella's face. All her fears disappeared when she heard Braxton's final words. She was beginning to enjoy his authoritative way of taking charge of things in her life. Kaitlin, the new maid was summoned back in with Gabriella's tea.

She was then given a proper introduction by Braxton and dismissed once again. After a further brief conversation and finishing her tea, Braxton left her condo and made sure Gabriella was secure. She did notice when he left out of the door this time, there was a security officer outside. It actually made her feel more secure, but a bit nervous. Braxton prepared to leave Gabriella to get dressed for the evening. She was becoming accustomed to having maid servants and immediately requested Kaitlin to run her bath while she went into her walk-in closet to select something to wear for the evening. Having no idea where they were going, she wanted to be practical in her selection of clothing and wanted to be comfortable as well.

The further along in the pregnancy she became, she noticed that she didn't want anything too tight around her tiny waist, even though she was not showing that much. It appeared that there were hundreds of outfits in this walk-in closet and she could not begin to imagine what to choose. Everything fit her perfectly which made it more difficult to select. She had no idea where he would be taking her and she didn't care, as long as she was there with him. In these few months, Gabriella's life had taken a full ninety degree turn. Everything in it seemed to be going well and she was only months away from delivering a baby that she would never see grow up. For her, this dream be ending soon turning into a nightmare for her and it would all be over.

There was a small measure of fear that accompanied the thoughts she was having. Not knowing when something would change for the worse was ever present with her. But, for now, she was elated and trusted Braxton to take care for her and the baby. Tonight would be special as she looked forward to whatever had been planned for them. It was funny how things happen when you are wealthy. You don't seem to worry as much on a daily basis. You just know that whatever comes up you can take care of it. What a night and day difference from her previous life. Even though the whole fiasco was going to take a massive hold on her, she didn't feel bad at all knowing she would never have to work again in life.

While Gabriella was pampering herself getting dressed, the baby kicked constantly. Motherhood was taking a hold on her and she was beginning to treasure the moments. She wondered if the baby was kicking because of her excitement about the evening or if it was from nervousness about the "what if's" about what Braxton had said about these murderous men that might come after them. Tonight, it didn't really matter to her. With her heart now beating with love for the two new people in her life, she accepted that they were the only family she had in the whole world. That was alright with her...

~ CHAPTER 9 ~

True Love Is Forever

TRUE LOVE IS FOREVER

Time soared the next few weeks and they only had minor incidents during that time which created no major issues for Gabriella and Braxton. For a month, they had noticed that they were being followed by someone suspicious. Braxton's security was very well trained and assured him that no one or nothing could get close to Gabriella. It was as if Braxton were the President of the United States and Gabriella was the first lady.

It was fast approaching the time for the arrival of Gabriella's baby. These months had caused the two of them to become inseparable because of the need for close scrutiny on their safety. Being together most of the time caused them to become more attached to one another as they should have been under the current conditions. It was difficult for them to maintain their relationship as family in the public eye, when they had to pretend to be a loving couple expecting their first child.

Even in the public eye, they held to their standards and crossed no moral lines as per their agreement. At times, when there was trouble, Braxton slept in the spare room in Gabriella's condo to be closer to her for protection. He took no chances and knew that she needed to feel safe and loved if she was to deliver a healthy baby. The baby boy was growing perfectly and kicking constantly which let them know that he was ready to come home.

Gabriella still wasn't showing as many women would be in their final trimester. Given that this was her first baby, it was common not to show as much for some women and Gabriella happened to be one of them. She looked radiant as any woman would in her final months of pregnancy and would go back for a final checkup for herself and the baby soon. With only a short time left before the delivery, they agreed that Gabriella would pick out the child's first years' clothing. Braxton knew that she was becoming attached and gave her any concession she wanted to make her feel comfortable. They both decided that she would pick out a name for the baby with Braxton as well. They agreed on the name "Jonathan" which was said to be the name of Braxton's grandfather and it was his middle name as well. They would also give the child the middle name of "Carlos," which was his late brother's name and donor. This made Gabriella happy to know that she could have this special part in naming the child she would not be able to keep.

Gabriella then busied herself with picking out everything baby Jonathan would wear from the bed he would sleep in to the shoes he would wear on his feet during summer and winter. There were rows and rows of tiny booties for him and he would want for nothing. It was sad to think that she would not know Johnathan as a mother should.

Everything was going as planned with the pregnancy and fulfillment of the contract. In the process, Gabriella had become a very wealthy young women in these past months. With each month she carried the baby to term, she received $200k which was deposited into her account. She was already a millionaire and had not thought about it. It was strange how only months earlier, she had stressed about how she would pay her meager rent and get money for books for school. Now, when she returned to her life, she would be able to pay upfront for anything she wanted with no issues. It's amazing how money can change someone's life overnight. Oddly enough, the money had become secondary to her current feelings. Regardless of how it was changing her feeling, with each passing day, she wanted the baby more and more for herself. She was fast becoming numb to the financial gain of the whole situation realizing that her life had completely changed over these months of being pregnant and living the life of luxury with Braxton.

Now she had many concerns about the staff in her condo. There always was someone being let go for various reasons. She was scheduled to go for her check-up with the doctor since she would be delivering by caesarian. They did not want to take any chances with her ability to deliver the child successfully. In a month, it would all be over. She slowly began getting dressed for her appointment and rested in between. Her thoughts were, if she moved slower, it would prolong her ability to keep the baby with her longer. She felt silly, but kept the thought anyway.

The new maid Kaitlin came to her while she was still resting and gave her a suspicious request.

"Ma'am, Mr. Braxton called and stated that he wanted you to meet him downstairs at the car." Gabriella didn't think anything of this statement because she had learned to trust Braxton. He was often detained for business reasons so she wanted to do exactly as he instructed. She had disappointed him once and never wanted to do it again. Being tired due to the pregnancy, she dismissed the thought that she couldn't completely trust the servants. Now the situation was becoming dangerous.

She adhered to the request given to her by the Maid and got dressed and walked out of the front door as requested thinking that these orders were from Braxton. As she rounded the hallway and walked to her private elevator, two very strange men approached her. She didn't recognize them and was guarded in her reactions but when they called her by name, it gave her a slight measure of comfort.

"Ms. Gabriella, Mr. Braxton has asked us to escort you downstairs to the limousine," they announced. These men were not familiar to Gabriella and they didn't look professional. There had been so many changes in staff that she couldn't keep up with the new faces and didn't want to appear too suspicious but wanted to question them anyway.

"What are your names please? Are you new here?" she asked, cautiously. "I don't think I have seen you here before." She wanted to see if they would tell her that they were new and that Braxton could be called to verify their identity, but that didn't happen. The second man appeared nervous and kept quiet after Gabriella spoke, but the first man responded. "We are not new Ma'am, we are the ones that watch you wherever you go. We are paid to stay out of sight," he said, chuckling.

"Well, why can I see you clearly now?" She stated, smiling a half smile, making a quasi-joke but not really feeling like conversing with the two goons. They didn't seem to fit the description of any of the other security officers Braxton had working for him. She still did not completely trust these unfamiliar men.

Just before the elevator came to the third floor, she instinctively looked back at the front door to her condo and the new maid Kaitlin was seen peeking out of the door. It was apparent that she knew the men at the elevator. When she saw that Gabriella had spotted her, she quickly closed the door. It was odd for her to be in the doorway at all. Now, Gabriella was really frightened. Her heart was pounding and a strange feeling came over her. Instinct told her that this might be part of Carlos's business partners scheme to harm the baby. She immediately tried to divert the men in order to get back into her Condo.

"Uh," I need to get my vitamins, guys," she said nervously. "This will only take a minute."

CAMOUFLAGE

The men picked up on Gabriella's nervous tone and quickly replied. "No, that will not be necessary Miss, I will bring them to you."

"No, I need to get them, I have different ones," she stated, as she tried to bolt to the front door of her condo. The large man realizing that she was on to them, placed a large gun barrel to her side. Now Gabriella was clearly aware that these men had not been sent by Braxton. She became weak in the knees and nauseated as they roughly pushed her into the elevator holding her up to ensure she didn't fall.

"Who are you and where are you taking me?" she demanded boldly. "We all are going for a little ride, lady," the man said. She noted their change in tone. "I have an appointment today and they will be expecting me," she said, nervously, trying to think fast. "If I am not there, they will surely let Braxton know." She then demanded they let her go again.

"Little lady, you are going to your appointment today, but it's the one "we" set for you. Gabriella was in full fear now. She knew that her worst nightmare had begun. The thing she had feared most was now upon her.

She had once doubted that there was any danger at all for them, but now knew that everything Braxton had told her the previous months was true. These men had watched and waited until they could be sure that Gabriella was pregnant to attack her.

They worked for the men suspected of killing Carlos for his fortune and now they were there to kill her and the baby. These men were the same ones that did not want the baby to live because they wanted to take over the company that was now worth millions. Gabriella was visibly shaking and almost hyperventilating. She realized that soon her life and the baby's life could be over. They reached the first floor of her complex and walked out of the building unstopped. The security guard paid no attention to them at all as if he worked for the two men with the gun to her side. They left the building and got into a black limousine and took off. Gabriella tried to look around for Braxton or someone she recognized and this day, there was no one around she recognized. Finally the man with the gun spoke again.

"Don't worry, little lady, we are not going to hurt you, yet. We have to be there for the examination to see if your baby is a boy, that's all... "If it's a girl, you go free, if not, well, let's say, that will present another problem." "You just might need an emergency delivery."
Gabriella's heart rate was still racing. Quickly thinking that if she diverted their attention again, she might be able to get away somehow. Realizing she had worn her pink shirt which represents being pregnant with a girl, she threw out a vague distraction pretending she was not afraid, but still was shivering in her boots.

"As you can see, do I really look pregnant?" she asked them, patting her stomach hoping the baby didn't respond. Knowing well that she was very pregnant, but to most people she only looked a little pudgy. Everyone always had to ask if she was pregnant or not. The doctor had said that her size was great because he didn't want her gaining much weight and the baby would be just fine.

She continued to try to fool the two men who had abducted her.

"So, you say you are taking me to my appointment?" she asked.

"Well, we are taking you to get an ultrasound," the man answered, smugly. "We need to verify that you are actually pregnant and if so, if it is a boy."

"Why is that important to you," Gabriella asked, hoping to get some answers herself and trying to stall to find a way to get away from them. She only knew what was told to her by Braxton. "Well," the man stated, pausing for a moment and then speaking…"just say that there is a bonus in it for us."

Gabriella was afraid now. She knew that as soon as they did the ultrasound they would know that she was pregnant and was having a boy. The sky was beginning to get very cloudy outside. The forecast had predicted a thunderstorm for the area later that day but it was beginning to get dark already. They finally reached an old abandoned building. She wondered why they didn't blindfold her, but knew in her heart that they wouldn't need to after they verified that the baby was a boy because they could kill her anyway.

She wanted to cry at the thought, thinking her life and her baby's life would be over just like that. What a horrible decision she had made, she thought. She felt the baby kick and this time she wanted him to be still. She couldn't even enjoy knowing she was carrying a beautiful life inside her as she had months earlier. As close as the men sat to her, she hoped they did not feel the baby kicking and confirm that she was pregnant. She put her arms to her side to shield the baby's kick.

"Where are you Braxton?" Gabriella whispered under her breath. "Please find us... Please!" She didn't know what to think. She prayed that they would survive this, but knew the chance was slim. They had taken her purse and keys from her on the elevator and she couldn't call anyone. She wouldn't even be able to give the money to her mother because no one knew where she or the money was. This was horrible! The sky was black now and the wind had picked up as they got out of the limo and walked into an old abandoned building. They walked into a corridor with concrete floors and walls. Broken glass from two windows was on the floor and it crunched under their feet as they scurried along. The two men held her tightly, almost dragging her to a small room...they walked into a back room and entered another door. This room was more sterile than the first one they had entered but still did not meet any sterile requirements for a hospital setting. Gabriella was praying very hard now. She was angry with herself and thought about the wonderful times she had enjoyed with Braxton.

She knew that she loved him and realized that she didn't know how she could feel this way because he was said to be her uncle. He had been more than an uncle to her. He was kind, sweet and even loveable. She felt that she could express her feelings now, even in her heart because she would never have thought these things out loud before. Believing she would never see him again she asked God for forgiveness for what she had felt in her heart about him. Now was as good a time as any to pray, one last time. Gabriella sighed a deep sigh and bowed her head:

"Lord, I know I haven't been living long, and I didn't get to know you well, but I heard my mother pray when our lights were cut off and they soon came back on. When my sister was sick and my mother had no money to take her to the doctor, a neighbor came and took her and paid for her shots. I haven't done much in my life but I'm sorry I left home. I wanted to get my mother and sisters out of their situation with all the kids they were having. I was a good girl and have never been in trouble or with a man, but I am pregnant, trying to help a father I never knew. Please forgive me for this. I didn't know what else to do. I needed so much...or I thought I did. Forgive me for not being satisfied with what I had. I am sorry for thinking the way I did about Braxton. I know he's my uncle, but I love him and I don't know how to feel about that. I guess it is best that this didn't go any further. I am sorry for any wrong doing so please if you can read my heart please answer my prayer now...Amen."

Gabriella had tears in her eyes and had gained the courage to face whatever was to come next. When they finally opened another door, Gabriella's eyes were still filled with tears, when suddenly Braxton and two other men barreled through the door…One was in a white physicians coat. Gabriella's eyes lit up like a winter fire pit.

"Braxton!!!" "You are here! "What is going on?" Gabriella yelled, relieved to see him, but quickly realized his hands were cuffed behind his back.

"Don't be afraid Gabriella, these are the men I told you about. They want to verify that you are pregnant and to see if you are carrying a male child," he said, in a solemn voice. "I am sorry this had to happen to you."

"What do you mean?" Gabriella asked, crying again.

The men lifted Gabriella up onto the table for the doctor to examine her.

She began resisting them, kicking and screaming. She realized it wasn't good for the baby, but wanted to go out fighting these men any way she could. Braxton began to try to break free because the men were standing watching the doctor prepare to examine her. He was becoming almost violent and Gabriella had never seen him like this before. Finally realizing he couldn't break free, he yelled at the men at the top of his voice. "DO NOT EXAMINE HER WITH THESE MEN PRESENT AND LOOKING ON!!!! I SWEAR IF YOU DO, I WILL KILL YOU ALL, I PROMISE YOU!"

Braxton's eyes were crimson from intense straining and yelling at the top of his voice. There was a vein on his temple that mysteriously appeared and looked as if it were ready to burst any minute if the men had stayed to watch the examination. It was immediately apparent that his statement was not overlooked and the doctor appeared to be afraid with Braxton in the room and demanded that they all step outside in the hallway while he conducted the examination. Though frightened, Gabriella felt a sense of comfort knowing that Braxton was there with her even though it looked bleak. She was still afraid and very silent now. She pleaded with the doctor to allow Braxton to stay in the room with her, but the men refused the request and they all left the room still trying to contain an out of control man. Gabriella had never seen Braxton this way before and realized it may be her last time seeing him at all.

You could see fear in their eyes as well. The doctor then had Gabriella lift up her blouse and began his examination. The weather outside had gone from bad to worse and the storm was in full throttle. It was horrible now with the thundering and lightening. The doctor had the ultrasound set up and began his examination.

"I need you to relax Ms. "he said.

"I can't relax knowing you want to kill me!" She screamed.

The dimly lit room was beginning to get darker with the rain pouring down. Thunder and lightning was all around them. Finally the lights went out momentarily and everything stopped working.

Then there was yelling and bumping in the hallway. Gabriella prayed the equipment didn't work. It sounded like someone was falling, but there was no way to really tell what was happening with the condition of the storm outside. The doctor was getting nervous and Gabriella was trying to see if there was any way to escape from the little room. She realized there was no way out. The only window had bars on it and it was not a full window. The lights soon came back on and the doctor appeared relieved and continued the procedure. As he examined her, he had a puzzled look on his face. Gabriella had calmed down thinking her life would be over soon.

"I don't see anything." The doctor said, confused, realizing that he should have been able to see the baby. He called the men in from outside that had brought Gabriella in and had them look at the monitor to prove to them what he did not see. The men, still scared from Braxton's threat, covered their eyes as they walked in the room remembering what Braxton had told them as if they really believed Braxton would kill him.

"This woman is not pregnant. The doctor stated. "There is no baby in there!!!"
Gabriella prayed the baby didn't kick at that moment.

"What do you mean, no baby!!!!?" the man stating, raising his voice at the doctor as if he were a mere clerk.

"See for yourself!"

"Look at the monitor, look at it!" he shouted at the top of his lungs," Clearly angry about the culmination of events.

"Nothing is in there! She's just fat!" the doctor stated.

"That can't be." The man said. "Kaitlin, the maid for this woman stated that a doctor had come to the house to examine her and said she was pregnant!!!" The doctor looked him in the eye and responded.

"THEN SHE LIED TO YOU!!!" "Where is my money for this circus act I just performed?" the doctor demanded, turning red in the face and reaching in his pocket for something.

"Was any money promised to the maid for this bogus information?" The man with the gun scratched his head in disbelief. "How could she be this stupid?" He then called the other man to bring Braxton back in the room.

Gabriella was worried that she had miscarried. "Where is my baby?" she asked herself in her heart. She felt as if she would burst with the pain of thinking she had miscarried after coming along this far.

"How could he have just disappeared?' she thought. Finally, Braxton was back in the examining room with her. He looked on the monitor and was in shock along with the others in there, but didn't let it show, knowing that she was actually pregnant. Right before Gabriella was about to become hysterical, her mind raced back to the many stories her mother had told her about what happened when she was born. She remembered the newspaper clippings her mother kept about the 'phenomenon" that happened at the hospital.

The doctors could not see Gabriella as an embryo in her mother's womb on the monitor but they could hear her heart beat the same as they could hear her baby Jonathan's. She further remembered that they had called her mother crazy and fat as well stating that she wasn't pregnant. But she knew she was. Life came back into Gabriella's eyes as she realized that she must have had the same phenomenon her mother had when she carried her. She was elated and her eyes lit up like a flood light. She had to act quickly before Braxton said or did something wrong to spook the men about the situation. She put the worse scowl on her face and yelled at Braxton causing him to become disturbed.

"Braxton, did you tell these men I was pregnant!!!" I hope you didn't because you swore that if I gained weight you wouldn't lie about me being pregnant because you were ashamed of me. "DID YOU SAY THAT ABOUT ME? She yelled...Gabriella began to cry and Braxton didn't know what to think but had to play along until he could figure out what she was doing. He knew the statement from Gabriella was strange along with her actions, but he had no idea what was happening. She continued the act, trying to convince the men who were frustrated about not getting the news they sought.

"I hate you Braxton!!!

"If I get out of here I never want to see you again!"

"You and your stupid family can go straight to hell!" She threw her shoe at him deliberately missing him and told them to let her out of there. The men were dumbfounded and told Braxton that they would see him in court to sign over the company to the partners since there was no heir to take over Carlos's shares of the company per the agreement and partnership. Braxton sighed and held his head down in sadness and agreed to meet them to sign over the company and they let both of them walk out of the building unharmed. The man handed Gabriella her cell phone back along with her keys and purse. When they were out of the door, Braxton took Gabriella's cell phone and called his driver. Braxton grabbed Gabriella and hugged her and he kissed her. "Oh, my God, I thought they had killed you," she said.

"No, the maid Kaitlin worked for one of Carlos's partners. They faked everything to get her employed at the condo. I am not taking you back to the same location, it's too risky"

"We have to leave right now," Braxton said.

"I am not taking any more chances with you and the baby, especially now that they are watching us this closely." Gabriella was feeling a bit of relief as soon as Braxton's driver arrived and they left the horrible location.

They sped away and Braxton kissed Gabriella again and this time it was on the lips. It was not the kind of kiss from a relative and while Gabriella wanted to reciprocate she remembered the prayer she had prayed for forgiveness of any impure thoughts and pulled back, reminding him of their relationship.

Braxton apologized sheepishly and said that it was just that he was so afraid that she and the baby had been killed that he was over joyed that they were safe. Braxton had the driver take them directly to the airport where they boarded a private jet. They flew for several hours to an island he owned in the Bahama's. They had visited there months earlier, but this was a totally different place. He felt it was the best place to stay for the next few weeks until the baby was born. There, he could control who came in and went off the island and it would be secure. The flight was comfortable, but they both were exhausted from the earlier event.

Braxton couldn't help but keep watching Gabriella, even when she wasn't looking. They refrained from any physical closeness but Braxton held her hand very tight and kissed it often. It was as if he was remembering when he thought he had lost her and this seemed to trouble him deeply. Gabriella was tired from the day's ordeal and the baby was now moving about for several reason. She was glad he had been quiet through the whole ordeal which actually saved them from being exposed.

It was as if the baby knew something was happening and he simply slept through it all. Gabriella closed her eyes for a while and as she dozed in and out of a shallow sleep, she could hear Braxton whispering under his breath when he thought she was fast asleep, "I don't know what I would have done if anything had happened to you and the baby." She never let on that she heard those beautiful words from the man she was not permitted to love.

She was just thankful that they had made it out alive and wanted this to be over soon. They both felt better knowing they were far away from the men that were trying to kill them. Knowing they were still watching them, Braxton felt fairly safe that the men believed there was no baby so they would not be looking for them right at that moment. He still took no chances. Once they landed safely, upon arriving at the Villa they checked into their private suite on the top floor of the building. On this floor, there was no way for anyone to come in or out except by way of doors that were heavily guarded by trained service men. There was a helipad on the roof in the event it was necessary to move Gabriella and the baby and Braxton was also a pilot as well. If something were to happen and his personal pilot was not there, everything was in place. They were greeted by the servants who took care of all of their needs. Gabriella once again was treated like royalty but this time the people that worked for Braxton seemed more genuine in their loyalty to him. It would be a few days before Gabriella completely relaxed but finally she was coming down off the fear from the kidnapping. The days that followed before the birth of baby Jonathan were wonderful. The island was beautiful and Braxton took Gabriella around and showed her all the special places he remembered visiting as a kid with his parents.

It was odd that when Gabriella asked him about his own father, he refused to talk about him. She didn't pry, but found it strange that he politely skirted any information about him. They spent nights walking on the beach watching the sun set. They took night swims in the warm waters of hidden springs that only Braxton knew about. Braxton never left Gabriella's side. He finally discussed the delivery of the baby with Gabriella and stated that he had a local midwife there with them who was actually a licensed physician that would deliver the baby when it was time. He knew he could trust her because she had attended Carlos while he was ill and loyally stayed with him. He was not taking any chances on anything else going wrong and vowed to give his life if necessary to protect her and the baby.

He did not leave Gabriella's side until the day she was to deliver. This time, they shared the same room and he would not let anyone or anything come near her. When the maid brought food in, he would even sample the food first before she would eat to make sure no one had tried to poison her. He gave her special instructions that if he should die first, she was to flee with the baby if something should happen to him. She was to take the money she had from the account and go far away with Jonathan. She would then be contacted by someone that he had sworn to secrecy that would bring her an envelope with further directions to be taken care of for life.

That was a lot to digest for Gabriella and she tried not to think about it being so close to delivering the baby. Since they could not leave the island, Braxton found things for them to do. They played games on the beach at night with their trusted security officers who were like family and hey had cook outs and their own Luau. Gabriella felt that these would be their last days together as a family and they were all too short lived. She was sad knowing it would all be over soon. She enjoyed the festive nights and the beautiful sunny days and would remember them always.

Finally, the day was upon them. They were walking on the beach, looking at the beautiful waves in the ocean, when Gabriella felt a sharp pain she didn't recognize. She knew it was time! Gabriella was in full bloom ready to give birth to the baby. Nervous, Braxton was right by her side with each contraction and calmly took her to the hospital and called the Midwife. They were instructed to meet in the special delivery room that had everything in place. They gave the number of the delivery room but went to another to thwart any possible issues of the information being leaked. This room was sterile and secured with two sets of guards at the door and at every entrance to the building. Even on the roof. Braxton had his helicopter pilot ready just in case anything came up and Gabriella had to be taken to a larger hospital. They would be at the big island within minutes.

Security had been instructed to fire upon anyone coming into the complex that had not been cleared by Braxton himself. He was now standing beside Gabriella as she was told that they would soon put her to sleep. Gabriella looked up at Braxton and firmly stated "No!" "I want to deliver the baby naturally," she said, looking weak from the contractions she was now having very close together. The doctor looked at Braxton for his permission and he looked at Gabriella and saw a woman about to give birth to her first child. Even after all this time, he still could not deny her request for anything she wanted. He knew at that moment that he was in love with her.

He nodded, yes to the doctor. It was clear to everyone in the room that they were in love with each other, but no one knew their true relationship. The process had begun as they checked the ultrasound monitor again to see the position of the baby. The doctor was concerned that she still could not see the baby and was nervous about the delivery. She felt that this was not going to work having a natural childbirth when she could not see the baby's position and recommended again, a cesarean delivery. She needed to be able to see the baby. Finally Gabriella told her, the baby would be fine. She had another hard contraction and they prepped her for the delivery. Braxton was standing at her side as she began delivering the baby. The doctor was very nervous, but with her examination, she could feel the position of the child, and with Gabriella's first push she could now see the baby's head crowning.

"It's almost here," the doctor said," "I will need to make an incision for the episiotomy and then I will need one more push for the baby to come out!" "Are you with me Gabriella???" the doctor stated. Gabriella was getting tired and was now panting and screaming between each breath she took and was beginning to have trouble breathing normally. "Try to breathe in and out calmly Gabriella, you must try or this baby could be in trouble!" The doctor was emphatic. Braxton had become too nervous and was almost in a panic when the doctor asked her to relax again and take short breaths. She knew if she couldn't get Gabriella to cooperate it could be disastrous since the baby's head had crowned. Gabriella couldn't do it. The fact that this was her first child and she had never been intimate prior to the insemination, her body was rejecting the ordeal and shutting down completely. This was a bad idea and Braxton was in full fear at this moment. Gabriella's felt as if her body were on fire. She was not receiving enough oxygen. The doctor was very concerned because Gabriella was a virgin and her body was not responding. The baby was almost there and could be injured or die if she did not push "NOW!" "Try one more push, Gabriella," she demanded in a stern voice knowing the baby's life and hers was at stake. Braxton was horrified. He began to perspire and was about to leave the room not wanting to witness losing either one of them when the doctor told Braxton to take Gabriella's hand.

"Take her hand!!!" she yelled at him. "Tell her you love her." She yelled again. "We've got to calm her" NOW" or you may lose them both!" Everyone in the room was on pins and needles. The nurses that assisted were frantic and tried to coach Gabriella as well. Finally Braxton, looked down at Gabriella's face in full panic…tears were now in his eyes and he grimaced and shook his head as he grabbed Gabriella's hand….

"I love you Gabriella, I've always loved you!" He said, over and over again. He kept talking without being prompted. "I loved you from the first day I saw you. I knew you were the one."

"PUSH ONE MORE TIME!!! Gabriella," the doctor demanded, "One more time!" she yelled, manipulating her anatomy to ensure the baby would not get lodged in the canal and be strangled on the umbilical cord.

"You were always the one for me, Braxton continued his plea. "I want to hold you when the sun comes up in the morning and when the moon shines at night. I want to love you with all my heart and never let you or the baby go." "You have my heart Gabriella… don't' leave me now or I will surely die. Gabriella was in extreme pain and exhausted, but those last beautiful words caused her tiny frame to give all it had. For that moment, these words were what she had wanted to hear from the time she became pregnant. Now, these words would save her life and her baby's life. Braxton leaned in to her and kissed her again and told her one last time.

"I will love you for the rest of my natural life and will make this right for you, I promise." Gabriella looked at Braxton with tears in her eyes and the doctor yelled to her, "PUSH ONE MORE TIME GABRIELLA!!!" NOW! Gabriella let out a death growl and screamed as she pushed one last time, "Aaaaaaaaaaaaaaaaaah!!!!"

The doctor grasped the baby and pulled him forward and cradled him in her hands safely. Everyone in the room applauded and baby Johnathan began to cry immediately!

"Good girl," the doctor said. "Good girl. "Congratulations, you have a healthy baby boy!" Braxton grabbed Gabriella again and kissed her. This time, he didn't care whether it was right or wrong, he did not pull back and neither did she.

In the heat of the moment, it was the natural thing to do. Gabriella was crying and laughing all at the same time which indicated she might be going into shock. The natural birth had been too strenuous for her, but she did it! The doctor placed Johnathan on her chest and she held the baby close to her. She kissed him and knew it would be the last time she would see him. This pained her more than the delivery itself. The baby was in perfect health according to the doctor's examination. In a weakened state, Gabriella thanked the Doctor for her assistance before she left the three of them alone in the room for a brief moment. Braxton couldn't take his eyes off the baby or Gabriella.

He was in a full stream of tears as he looked at the woman who had given him the most precious thing in the world. Marveling at the fact that she came through as she did, he desperately wanted to say something more to her but couldn't. She had created a miracle that day in the midst of chaos. The ordeal was proving to be too much for the natural delivery and she became extremely exhausted. She was happy that the baby was healthy but sad that she had to let him go. They let her hold him for a few more minutes and then the nurse came in and took Jonathan away from her. They would not permit her to feed the baby at all because they knew she had to be medicated. Gabriella's first instinct was to hold the baby and not let go. Her thoughts were becoming diabolical.

She was trying to see how she could escape with the baby and hide out on the island so that she could keep her precious little boy. Now, through her tears, her eyes searched Braxton's, hoping he would understand what she was about to say. She began begging and pleaded with him to keep the baby. Her tears were becoming too much for him because he hated to say no to her. It appeared she was going into hysterics and Braxton quietly pressed the button to call for the doctor. He knew she would need something to sedate her, and fast.

Gabriella was now in full tilt when the nurse came in and administered a sedative to her. She initially tried to refuse, but Braxton assured her it was for the best. She had learned to trust him over the months she had been with him and like a little child, she conceded and permitted them to inject her with the needle. Before it would take full effect, she poured out her heart to him one last time. With labored breathing, she whispered out a mother's plea for her child.

"Braxton, I can't do this! I thought I could, but I can't give my baby up! I don't know what I would do if I have to go home without him."

"Please, let me keep him. I will give you all the money back and would pay you back for everything you have done for me."

"On my life, I promise you!" she desperately pleaded, but would not stop begging to keep her child.

"Once you get your company and the money, give him back to me…give me your word, please!" She begged, because I know you won't break it. Knowing that if Braxton told her he would concede to do so, he was a man of his word. Braxton was in tears now as he looked at the woman he had fallen in love with. His eyes showed that he wanted to say something more but couldn't say a thing to console her.

They shed tears together as he demanded that the nurse assist Gabriella to calm her down. It broke his heart to see her in the state she was in knowing she had done it all for him. He knew that as long as Gabriella could remember that the baby was in the same place where she was, she would not rest as any mother wouldn't have. Rest was what she needed. Gabriella soon was in full distress as she lay on the bed. This was her first baby and she was truly distraught thinking she would never see her him again. The doctor then came at Braxton's request and gave her another drug for her pain and exhaustion and something to make her sleep. Her ordeal was over and it had taken its toll on her.

As she became groggy, she remembered vaguely the agreement she signed and chuckled to herself under the effects of the drug she had received. She recalled in her mind that she had agreed that after the baby was born she would give it up and go away for a while and then return to her pervious life. Even though she reminded herself of this promise she had made, as any loving mother would do, she still fought for her child and continued to plead with Braxton until the drug would take full effect on her and she would remember nothing.

"Braxton, what am I going to do?" she asked, holding onto him now. No longer caring how it looked or felt. The drug was in full affect and she was now talking in and out of her head.

The doctor checked her one last time to ensure that she was not going into shock before she left the room again. Braxton had not left her side that night. She expressed her feelings to him completely.

"I want you to know that my life is a mess now." Gabriella was now slurring her speech trying to tell the man she knew she was in love with goodbye, not knowing how to do it.

"I know I am not supposed to feel what I feel for you, but I can't hide these feelings I have any longer."

"No matter where I go, and I plan to go far away from here because if I don't, I know I will be in trouble and I don't ever want to feel this way again about anyone,"

"Why did I have to be related to you?" she asked, still going in and out of consciousness fighting the effects of the drug. Not wanting him to leave her sight. It was evident the drug was taking affect because all of her inhibitions were gone. She said everything she couldn't say before. Braxton had poured his heart out to her before she delivered the baby and now he listened through quiet tears and took everything in that Gabriella confessed to him.

He wanted to ensure that he stayed with her until she was asleep so that she would always remember that he kept his work and never left her side. Gabriella was quiet now and accepted that life as she had come to know it was over. She would fade into darkness and could no longer form the words to express the love she had for the man that stood before her.

Before she closed her eyes, there was a long intense gaze from her. She wanted him to see her strong and trying to defy the effects of what she knew was inevitable. The drug that was rendering her helpless now was in control. Finally, she gave up and let the quiet sleep take over, as she lay one final time in his arms. Braxton kissed her again and left her room. She had faded to black and would not awaken until the next day...

"Gabriella, Gabriella," the voice kept saying.

"Can you hear me?" The night had ebbed away and the next day had entered quietly. It was already evening as Gabriella was awakened from what appeared to be a nightmare. The doctors had monitored her closely throughout the night because of the trauma she had experienced. By the time she was cognizant, the day was almost gone. She had slept for many hours after delivering the baby. When she had fully awakened, she was still tired and in much pain from the ordeal of the natural delivery. The episiotomy was affecting her as well and she had a very bad headache. Soon the doctor came in to examine her before she would let her get up from her bed. Everything checked out for her except the cramping she felt, which was normal. She finally remembered the events from the previous day and sheepishly asked the doctor if she could see her baby. Deliberately denying what she remembered about the contract she had signed with Braxton. She hoped it was all a dream and her baby was in the nursery like all the other babies were waiting for their mothers.

The doctor looked at Gabriella for a moment and then looked away with sadness in her face. She knew the pain Gabriella must have been experiencing knowing she would never see her baby again. The doctor then reached in her coat pocket and handed Gabriella an envelope and walked out of the room. Gabriella felt like a criminal being given privacy to read her mail. As she slowly looked at the hand writing on the letter…she put the envelope to her chest before she opened it. She realized it was from Braxton. Slowly she opened the letter and read it in an undertone.

To Gabriella

"My dearest Love, I know that by now you are fully awake and realize that Jonathan and I are gone. This is a very complicated situation we are in and I can't give you all the details in this letter. I promise to do so in person. The things you said to me last evening after giving birth to this beautiful baby touched my heart. I could not speak because of being filled with pain from the ordeal you had endured. As I look at his beautiful face, my heart skips a beat. He is the most precious thing I have ever had the privilege of holding, except for you. My love, know that it was necessary to take the baby in order to create court records showing his birth on short notice. This was to finalize the contract and complete the requirements stipulated in Carlos's Last Will and Testament.

It will revert all legal papers to turn the company back over into my name and Jonathan's name. To keep Jonathan and you safe, I had to take him to a private place while all of the paperwork was being completed. The men that kidnapped you had found out we were on the island but were too late. I had the hospital change your records to show that you had delivered a child but that it did not survive and the record stated for them that is was a "girl." While you slept, my security watched over your room because we knew they'd be looking for the baby. I immediately took Jonathan from the hospital. Once I met with the attorney's and Carlos's business partners, they thought they were there to receive the full ownership of the business. When the attorney told them that "Carlos" had an heir, a son, they were outraged and demanded a DNA test. We immediately presented the papers with the DNA test results from the documents that had already been put in place. The test showed him as 99.9% the rightful heir the partners were outraged. They still believed it was a hoax. My attorney asked them what else they would accept other than the legal proof from the DNA testing proving that Carlos had an heir. They boldly stated that they needed to see the child and if they could see the baby, they would accept the terms. They didn't believe Jonathan existed. The attorney was clever and had a quick statement drawn up to this affect. They signed the statement, saying that if we could produce the child, they would give up the company, but if not, they would take possession immediately.

They gave us 24 hours to produce the child. Once they signed the document, the attorney beckoned for the security to let the nurse into his chambers. She brought Jonathan in and when the partners saw him, they were incensed! They accused the attorney of fraud and bribery. But they had signed the paperwork and were escorted out by security. They left the office ranting and raving about suing the company. Fortunately, the company is back in our family's hands thanks to you. Dr. Falcon states that you will be going home from the hospital tomorrow. I will need to see you one last time to finalize our portion of the contract. Your final payout for one million dollars has been transferred to your account. Once you sign off on the contract as having fulfilled it, everything will be concluded. There is more, but I must go now. I will have my driver pick you up and bring you to me as your benefactor one final time. Thank you for everything you have given me that I didn't have. I await the opportunity to see you again tomorrow before Jonathan and I prepare to leave the country. I do have one question to ask you when I see you again. I hope that you will choose to see me when I return.

Braxton

Gabriella dropped the letter on the white sheets of her hospital bed. There was deep sadness in her heart. Tears welled up in her eyes as she quickly wiped them away when a nurse came in and asked if she felt up to taking a walk down the hallway for exercise. Gabriella was feeling used after reading the letter from Braxton, but tucked it under her pillow and accepted assistance from the nurse to leave her bed. As they walked down the hall, they passed the nursery. She could see all the new fathers with their babies. Some with their faces pressed to the glass windows. Some tapping on it, trying to get their baby's attention as if they could identify their parents. Some were holding their wives as they both looked on in joy at their new arrival. Gabriella told the nurse that she felt sick and wanted to go back to her room. She really wasn't sick, but couldn't take watching the other families have the opportunity to love their children when she had no one to love or to love her.

The only thing she had to remember about her child was the pain of giving birth to him and the wonderful pregnancy she had with Braxton by her side. The natural deliver, which almost took her life was what she wanted in order to feel what it felt like to give life. She had decided to never have children again and wanted to relish in this thought. Once she was back in her room, she cried herself to sleep that night knowing that the next day would be equally as difficult for her to contend with.

The night was long, tiresome and sporadically painful. The morning would come much too soon and would not relieve any of the pain she previously felt. She arose and slowly busied herself with gathering the few things she had left. It reminded her of what she felt when she had first embarked upon the agreement to carry the baby. She tried not to let anyone see her internal pain, and finally the hour had come for her to be discharged. They wheeled her down to the front of the clinic the same as all the other mothers, but she appeared to have lost her child since all the other mothers had their babies with them. They gave her the sad look and held their babies tight, feeling sorry for Gabriella.

The island had become home to her for this short period of time and was abuzz with tourist and residents busying themselves on the street with their wares that were all for sale. "I guess everything is for sale," Gabriella thought. She sat in the lobby and watched mothers being greeted by their husbands with smiling faces. Scores of bouquets of flowers were being given out... even candy to some. Others brought other children to see the new addition to their family. Gabriella lovingly watched them exchange kisses and hugs. There was smiling, chanting and puckering for the first kisses on their grandchildren's tiny faces. Gabriella sat quietly waiting for Braxton's driver to show up for her, remembering that he once was her driver, but no more.

She waited for 15 minutes which turned into 30 and finally determined that no one was coming for her. Her heart became even heavier at that moment feeling as if she was nothing more than a surrogate. She had no right to feel good about what she did or to even give herself permission to take credit for anything. She was beginning to accept that another woman would raise the child she gave birth to along with loving the man who had once cared and loved her. She couldn't believe that this was happening to her and looked for her phone to call the only friend she had, Pallie. Though she knew she didn't love him, right now she just needed someone to be there for her. She found the cell phone and began to dial the number and realized there was no sound.

The cell phone was dead and she couldn't make any calls. "What now," she thought, wanting to cry but realizing she was tired of crying. She decided to get a nurse or the people at the help station in the lobby to get her to a phone to call Pallie to meet her once she came back to the States. She couldn't bear the thought of being on the island and running into Braxton and Jonathan with another woman on his arm as his wife. Death would certainly engulf her. She knew her old friend Pallie would help her out even after all these months of no contact. Frustration was now taking over and panic was settling in along with postpartum.

She was thinking that Braxton had abandoned her when he had promised he wouldn't. Now breathing labored with frustration about what she had done with her life, realizing she had lost the two people she loved more than anything in the world. She knew she had to learn to cope.

"What am I going to do," she asked herself. "My God, what am I going to do?" She decided that she would not call Pallie, realizing that she now had the means to take care of herself. Just when she was beginning to get her mental bearings and leave the hospital on her own, she heard a voice from behind her call her name. The voice was familiar to her but she dared not be fooled again by anyone and refused to turn around, but the voice came closer.

"Gabriella, are you waiting for someone?" the voice asked. Without turning around in the direction of the man speaking, she responded. "Yes, I'm looking for a phone to call a taxi to get to the airport and leave this dreadful Island. I am going home today," she said, her heart now palpitating. The man continued to speak without revealing himself.

"Well, why would you want to go home when everything you want is right here on the island?" the man stated, now standing right behind Gabriella's wheelchair. Finally, she could no longer play the cat and mouse game. She knew the voice, but hesitated to turn around, believing that this would be the last time she would see Braxton's face.

The thought of that feeling left her unsure as to whether she wanted to turn around at all. She now believed she would have to watch him walk away from her forever this time. Secretly, she wished he hadn't come back at all. Her heart would no longer permit her to wonder and she determined to turn to say goodbye forever to the man she believed she could not have as her own. Closing her eyes one last time and asking God to forgive her for what she believed was a misplaced love for a man she had no right to love. She turned her wheelchair around to face him one last time. Braxton was standing over her like a giant, with a dozen red roses that he placed in her arms. Her eyes searched his face for answers to his actions as he kneeled down in front of her chair. People were now watching this wonderful man lowering himself to her. He put the lock on the wheels, so that nothing could interrupt what he was about to say. Gabriella began to speak to him directly. "Thank you very much for the flowers, Mr. Shavarez," she stated subtly, trying not to make eye contact.

Now stuttering, she continued to speak, trying to be strong. "If you will give me the papers to sign, I will sign them and let you be on your way. I know you now have a son to care for." Gabriella's voice was breaking horribly, but she did not waiver in her message to him. She felt sick and light headed saying the things she felt she needed to say to close this chapter of her life once and for all. In these months, she had become a woman and a mother and it was as if she was burying someone that was alive in her heart.

The words Braxton would speak would further confuse her, but she listened, hanging on his every word.

"Don't you mean 'we' have a son to care for?" Braxton asked.

Gabriella was getting frustrated and physically hot, hearing these words knowing how hard it was to give her child up. She could take no more of the mystery of this entire scenario.

"Stop it!!!" she yelled in a hushed voice so as not to bring undue attention to their conversation and destroy the beauty of other families uniting with their new babies.

"I can't take any more of this, Braxton! Just stop it!!! You know we can't have anything with each other. My father was your BROTHER! What kind of relationship would that be?" she asked, knowing the answer.

Braxton stopped for a moment: Her heart would skip a beat with his next words.

"What if I told you I am not your uncle?" He quietly asked, never taking his eyes off her. Gabriella thought she would faint, but spoke anyway...

"Then, I would be happy to hear that, but, you said that the donor for the artificial insemination was Carlos, who was supposed to be my father which means the baby is not ours!!! How could you ever fix that Braxton?" She asked, still searching for something concreate to hold on to.

"What if I told you, the fertilization was not by the man you were "told" was your father?"

Gabriella was becoming frightened now thinking that the baby she had given birth to was by some other man that she had no clue about at all. This was becoming morbidly disturbing to her. Fear and anxiety was mounting in her heart. She couldn't take any more suspense and made one final plea to Braxton.

"Braxton, I am weak right now and cannot take much more stress than I have already endured. Please, tell me all of the truth… now, or let me sign the papers and walk away from me forever. I must know what I have done to myself and this child, and I will beg God to forgive my error so that I may go away from you both forever. I must know, now," Gabriella quietly pleaded with him. Braxton unlocked the wheels on her chair and swiftly moved Gabriella towards an empty room as the doorman scrambled to unlock the room for him. He realized her delicate condition and knew that he had to tell her all of the truth…and it must be told to her now or he would lose her forever.

He sat down on the sofa nearest the door. Gabriella's chair was placed next to the window. He began to speak… "Gabriella, there were many things I could not tell you in the beginning. I had to wait until the baby was born before I could divulge the rest of the information to you. You see…the man we buried in your home town months ago was "my father," not yours. My stepmother and father had a very difficult marriage.

They lived separately. Father lived in one city and my stepmother and her two other sons lived in another city. My stepmother hated me because my father had been in love with my mother before she died and he favored me as his only son. She tried to trick father into adopting her sons but when he refused, she was angered and vowed to destroy me and my father.

"My father was a very wealthy man, but when he found out he was ill, he had a Will prepared. The original Will stated that all of his possessions were to be left to me... his only natural son. Because he and my step mother had a pre-nuptial agreement, she would receive nothing after his death. "At first, my stepmother never knew about that stipulation that I would receive everything when my father died, but when she did find out about it, she sought out an attorney to try to overturn the will, but couldn't. The attorney's told her that she could add an addendum to the will adding special stipulations about my father's only heir, which was me. My Stepmother then had the addendum state that the only way I could inherit "all" of my father's fortune was if I had someone to succeed me to carry on my fathers and grandfather's name. My fathers will and the addendum was then officially in place but needed his signature to hold up in court. My father was aging and his ill health was catching up with him. His eye sight was failing him and my step mother tricked him into signing the addendum and it was then that it became official. "When father found out what my Stepmother had done, he was furious and put another plan in place.

He knew that my stepmother would stop at nothing to get rid of me so that her sons could inherit my father's fortune, leaving me penniless. She would be one of the wealthiest women in the world. Before that time, father met your mother Clarissa, during one of his business trips to Chicago. After getting to know her, he found out she had broken up with a man that she was with but he, too was married and had worked for the same company with her. My father fell in love with your mother, but knew that my stepmother would never have given him a divorce.

"When the relationship continued, father was very happy with your mother and one day she told him she was pregnant with you. She really believed he was the father and he believed it too. I was 18 years old when my father told me about your mother being pregnant with you. He told me I would have a sibling but he did not know if your mother would have a boy or girl. He also told me I couldn't tell anyone about the pregnancy. I loved my father very much Gabriella and would do anything he asked, so I said nothing. Father had two business partners that also were relatives of my Stepmother. They were greedy and wanted father's fortune as well and they were instrumental in helping my stepmother scheme to get his money. Your mother never knew that I was Carlos's son. We devised a plan to create a fake argument and fight which made it appear to everyone that I hated him and I never wanted to see him gain.

Everyone bought it and my father then sent me away so that I would be safe. Father sent your mother money each month through me to care for her during her pregnancy with you and asked me to keep an eye on you all until you were born. I did as he asked. I never saw my stepmother again. After you were born, we found out you were a girl. He then had the attending physician do a DNA test which confirmed that he was "NOT" your father. So we are not related."

"I remember being in the hospital that day when they gave me the news from the DNA test for my father. I cried that day and the nurses were coming to me consoling me thinking I had lost a child. I felt the hurt for my father knowing that you were not his child and how much it would hurt him knowing you were not his and Clarissa had been unfaithful to him. Someone from the hospital leaked the information to my Stepmother and she threatened to have you and your mother killed. Your mother did not know why father never saw her again. I knew that father wanted you to be his child because he loved your mother very much. He knew they would have a difficult time even if he had married her, but he would have lost all of his fortune in the divorce.

"I felt compelled to keep watching you grow up from afar. You had become the only family I had. I knew you were a good person Gabriella, and when you entered college, I knew I was becoming attached to you. I wanted to know you better as a person but didn't know how to introduce myself, knowing that your mother knew me as Carlos's younger brother, but I could not divulge who I was since father was still alive. It would be too risky for him.

The last thing my father said to me after finding that you were not his biological child, was, that if anything happened to him, I was to give you $200k dollars and to help your mother financially. He felt she deserved it. She had given him love when he had no one else and had asked for nothing in return. She deserved a better life. I think that is what made me begin to want to know you better. Your mother had captured my father's heart and I knew you would be the same kind of person. Gabriella was stunned with the revealing of this information, but the pieces were finally coming together. Braxton continued…

"Father knew my Step mother was cruel and told me to be careful and never trust her. He said that I should preserve my lineage and sent me to a physician in a reproduction fertility bank in Italy where they collected samples from me and my father. This was in the event that father or I died. He had others who would carry out his wishes even after he was gone.

"What I read in the Will at his repast, to everyone was partly true. His business partners did want his fortune and we felt they had something to do with his demise. Before I saw father take his last breath, he told me to act swiftly. He knew that my stepmother would not stop until she had moved me out of the picture completely any way she could so he had arranged for his services to be in your home town where your mother was. He knew I would naturally have to come there knowing my Stepmother would not attend.

"He also knew your mother was a good, honest woman and he would have given up everything to be with her if you had been his child. My Stepmother believed that my father was in love with your mother and was afraid that you were his child and that's when she threatened to kill you. We later suspected that she had my father poisoned. After he died, I did as my father instructed me to do. Having the services in your home town allowed me to be officially introduced to you and it not seem strange. That was the day your mother placed you in my arms and I never wanted to let go." "We embellished the truth and made the request of the surrogate from the man you thought was your father. I knew that if I could convince you to be the surrogate you would be mine forever." When you finally agreed to the contract, I had to act fast because my Stepmother knew I did not have any children of my own and to have a male was a fifty fifty chance of happening since I did not have any suitors at the time."

"The day you said yes, to the contract, I fell in love with you then. It was very difficult not being able to tell you that I was the father of our child, but I knew I would never let you go." Braxton paused from expressing the whole ordeal to Gabriella. She sat silenced in the small room in full shock, trying to digest what she had just heard. Now knowing that she had given birth to Braxton's son. This was a massive undertaking and relief to her. It was as if something had stopped her heart from beating and now it could beat again. "So you really are the father of my baby?" she asked, searching his face waiting for the final answer.

"Yes, I am the father of our baby Jonathan. I wanted you to have no doubt so I brought the DNA paternity test with the results. Dr. Falcon did the swab on you as well. Here are the results. I want you to know all of the truth from here on out. I know Jonathan is ours.

"When you delivered the baby, I had to take Jonathan the next day to the attorney's office when they were reading father's will to the family. I walked in and my Stepmother and stepbrothers were there. The attorney began reading the will stipulating that if I did not have a male heir, my family's fortune would go to my Stepmother and her sons.

However, when they came to the part about the male child, he added that I had presented him with Jonathan's birth certificate. My stepmother fainted and her sons called me a liar. My stepmother revived herself and agreed that I was lying that the paper was a forgery. She did the same as the greedy business partners had done that I wrote you about."

"I then called the nanny in with Jonathan and presented our son and the DNA results. The attorney immediately entered the information into his records and stated: 'It is further deemed that Braxton Shavarez is the sole heir of Carlos Shavarez's estate and inherits his entire fortune. He leaves nothing further for distribution to his wife and stepsons." My stepmother fainted again and her sons walked out of the attorney's office and left their mother on the floor. They called her stupid and said they knew her plan would not work. I know this was a lot of information to digest, but it is all over now, Gabriella.

"Braxton, what are you saying?"

"Gabriella, there was no other way to do what I did. It had to be done this way. I had to have an heir in order to keep my father's fortune and let his name live on. I fell madly in love with you in the process," he exclaimed.

Braxton understood that Gabriella had heard a lot and he restated the basic facts for her to digest. "The man we buried was my father, not yours." He told Gabriella.

"The insemination was from me and not my father. So the baby is ours, yours and mine." He paused for a moment to collect his thoughts and feelings and continued filling her in for all the gaps of information Gabriella had not been denied during the entire ordeal. I now own the penthouses, the condo's, the servants, the drivers and everything is mine and will be ours... if you will marry me." Taking her hand, again, he asked her the same question, but this time with more sincerity.

"Will you marry me, Gabriella?" Gabriella looked out of the window in amazement almost ignoring his proposal and captured the view of the nanny standing, holding Jonathan and gently rocking him. Gabriella was again feeling weak. The nurse was beaconed to bring their son inside to them. The nurse entered the room and Gabriella tried to rise from the chair to reach for her baby and opened the blanket. Jonathan looked like a little prince. He had eyes like Braxton and was simply beautiful. She kissed him and hugged him and looked up at Braxton. Now, everything was becoming real to her.

"He has your eyes." She quietly said, through tears of joy.

"He will have your spirit, Gabriella." Again, Braxton pleaded with the woman he loved... "Will you marry me?" He asked a third time.

Finally Gabriella came to her senses after trying to digest all of what had happened in her life. Now realizing that Braxton was not her uncle and Jonathan was truly "their" son. Smiling, she answered him... "Yes, yes, I will marry you." she stated, reaching for him.

CAMOUFLAGE

"I love you so much, Braxton," Gabriella said, as she kissed him for the first time without feeling any guilt. The heavy weight had been lifted from her heart. No longer did she have to think that she was doing something wrong for all the right reasons. They left the room and came back in the hospital annex. The people in the lobby smiled when they saw that Gabriella now had her baby like all the other mothers. Braxton took his new son and fiancé back to their home on the island. The house was abuzz with the servants preparing everything for the wedding festivities that Braxton had arranged that evening. Braxton could not wait any longer to make Gabriella his wife. They knew it was sudden, but they didn't want to wait a minute more to be able to openly express their love for one another. It had been far too long that they had hidden their true feelings from each another for the sake of protecting their baby.

It was clear that the sacrifices they made were done so unselfishly because of the love they had for one another. Trusting the word of her mother, Gabriella had trusted a man she had never met before. She had humbly submitted herself to this man's request and allowed herself to be artificially inseminated not knowing who's child she was carrying. She had no idea she was destined to be this mans' wife. But now, she understood why he was so attentive to her needs. Braxton had already fallen madly in love with Gabriella when he first saw her. He knew that she was the right one for him from the beginning. That evening, they would have a small private wedding.

FYCORE PUBLISHING   www.fycore.com   305

Braxton had Gabriella's mother and sisters, along with all of her nieces and nephews, flown to the island to witness this beautiful occasion. He wanted them to meet their new cousin, Jonathan. Clarissa approached Gabriella before the wedding and was amazed at how she had grown since she last saw her.

"You have become a beautiful young woman Gabriella," her mother said sheepishly. She was amazed at what her daughter had accomplished in such a short time. It was a reminder that the man that she once loved was now very much alive and part of her life by way of his son and her daughter. This made her happy. "I knew you would always be the one to do something very special that would affect all of our lives in a positive way. I am proud of you and happy for you, Gabriella." she kissed her daughter and hugged her.

"Mama, I didn't do anything except fall in love with someone. I finally understood what you and my sisters must have gone through having the children you had. Even though their fathers were not in their children's lives."

"It almost killed me to think that I had to give Jonathan up and never see him again." Gabriella was tearing up now and her mother lovingly halted her tears. "Now, now, you're going to smear your makeup before the ceremony. We'll have plenty of time to talk about everything later. I promise you."

"Mama, I know what it's like to love someone and want them to love you back," Gabriella said. "Well, I loved Braxton's father very much and now, I will have a chance to have a part of him in my life through Braxton as my son-in-law. At the repast when Braxton and I talked, he told me that Carlos was his father. That is also why I didn't pay for your college from the money I received. I didn't forget you, but Braxton promised me you would be taken care of and so you shall be.

"You took a chance Gabriella, and now, it has paid off. I didn't take the chance when I had it and I knew Carlos loved me, but I made a mistake because I was afraid to trust him, fearing he would walk out on me like the rest of them did. I guess I didn't know how to trust. He would have given everything up for me, but I blew my chance for happiness, but you didn't. Now, I want you to be happy."

"I love him so much, Mama," Gabriella said, holding her mother's hands. "I know…and I am sorry for not telling you all of what I knew. I am really sorry for that, I truly am," Clarissa said, wiping a tear from her eyes now. It was a happy but emotional moment for them both. They realized that they would always be taken care of now and Clarissa would never have to work again. Finally it was time for the ceremony to begin. It would be elegant and quiet. Braxton did not want Gabriella on her feet more than a fleeting moment.

She needed her rest and he would ensure that anything she wanted would be given to her from now on. Everyone was in place for the ceremony. There were many people from all over that were family and friends of Braxton's. It was clear that he knew many prominent people. He had known all along that he would marry Gabriella and had planned the entire event. The music began and everyone was seated. They had the traditional walk down the aisle on a white carpet in their hotel that Braxton owned in the Bahamas. He even invited Pallie to the wedding. Gabriella was happy that Braxton invited her best friend Pallie to walk her down the aisle. Pallie was proud to do so as he took his position in the ceremony. "I figured since you were not going to be my wife, I would do the honors and walk you down the aisle as your best friend." Pallie said, kissing her hand and receiving a furred brow from Braxton at the other end of the altar where he awaited his bride-to-be.

Braxton wanted all the people in Gabriella's life that were important to her to share in this moment. She heard later that Braxton paid the rest of Pallie's tuition anonymously. He had a kind heart that way. The ceremony was underway and they walked down to meet the minister at the altar. The vows taken were sincere and heartfelt...they were pronounced husband and wife. They tenderly kissed each other knowing they would never have to hide their love from each other again. As they walked down the aisle and back to the reception area, all their guest witnessed them hugging each other all the way.

The Nanny followed close behind with their son Jonathan so he could see his parents and every few minutes his mother turned to look at the child she thought she'd never see again. They would share everything together as a family going forward and never leave each other's side.

"I love you Mrs. Shavarez" Braxton whispered to his new bride.

"I love you more," Gabriella said to her husband, hugging him tenderly. Her petite hands trembled as she touched his face validating that he was real to her now. The night was aglow with the wonderful festivities and the love they both shared for each other. The nuptials were elegant. The food and dancing warmed the hearts of all their guests and everyone there could see the immense love Braxton and Gabriella had for one another.

Gabriella held Jonathan close to her chest. She never wanted him to leave her side ever again, but her husband insisted on one dance for the evening. Their wedding day was the best day of their lives. It would be a happy ending to a troubled beginning. The entire night was beautiful…they would recline that evening as man and wife. In light of her delivery ordeal, they would lay close together that night, talking quietly about the rest of their life into the wee hours of the morning. The nanny slept in the room with baby Jonathan to give his parents time alone. The next day, Braxton arranged for the three of them to travel to their new home in Hawaii. Gabriella said her goodbyes to her sisters, Brenda, Terra, and Micah. She hugged Pallie, and her mother. They all wished them well. As they got into the car heading to the airport, Clarissa kissed her Grandson Jonathan and told Gabriella something special.

"Don't forget to write and send me lots of pictures of him."

"I will Mama. I will." she said, smiling like she had never smiled before.

"Mama, I want you to know that I always loved you and appreciated all that you did for me. I couldn't have asked for a better parent than you. You were always my inspiration." Clarissa now began to cry and hugged her daughter one last time. Braxton had to break up the conversation because it was time to depart.

"Mom, Gabriella, you both will be seeing each other soon, I promise." he said to both of them, unclasping their hands, as if to pry them apart.

"Goodbye, mama, I love you," Gabriella said. They put the luggage in the trunk and the doors were closed by the driver. Gabriella could see the looks in her family's eyes as they slowly pulled away. It was a look of sadness but happiness and good wishes on top of a bit of envy, in a good way. As they left their hotel, Gabriella took one last look around and realized this was all hers now. She had forgotten all about the account she had with over a million dollars in it. Funny how life can change and shadow what is important to us. The money was always secondary for her. What she had gained was more valuable than anything else in the world. The driver took off and quickly entered the expressway and soon they were at the airport. Braxton held Gabriella's hand and kissed her all the way there.

He simply could not keep his hands or lips off her. They arrived at the airport which was not far from the hotel. Gabriella assumed they were boarding a commercial flight this time, but the driver took them to a special hanger where they would depart. She was patient as she exited the town car to a private entrance to the runway.

As she looked up, there was a massive private jetliner. Gabriella looked at Braxton.

"You didn't?" she asked, looking up at the Jet with the name "Camouflage" boldly painted on the side in bright letters.

"I did do that," he happily responded. "This is the first present of many you will receive from me, my lovely wife," he said, giving her the keys to the air craft. Her mother had told Braxton why she had named her Gabriella after the doctors confirmed the phenomenon they called "Camouflage" effect.

The other sisters did not have this experience with their children. It could only be passed on to a female child that was born camouflaged. They immediately boarded their private jet and Gabriella was introduced to her pilot. "Mrs. Shavarez, I am Captain Benjamin. It's a pleasure to make your acquaintance. "We will be taking off shortly and the weather looks exceptional in Hawaii today Ma'am. You can expect a smooth flight."

"Thank you Capt. Benjamin." Gabriella stated. She was stunned. Within moments, they were seated. There was a special seat in the middle for Jonathan that held him perfectly secured between his parents. There was a private sleeping area where Gabriella could rest if she needed to. A full bathroom and kitchen with a chef. They also had the nanny come along and she sat in another cabin behind them to keep an eye on Jonathan.

They finally begin their taxi down the runway. Gabriella looked around the cabin and secured her baby in his seat one last time as he lay sleeping. Just knowing that she had her first night and now the first day with her new husband, overwhelmed her with happiness. She felt satisfied knowing she had the best of everything...sheer elegance. She looked at her precious baby again and covered him with a light blanket. Special ear buds had been designed for him and she placed them in his tiny ears to keep him from experiencing the change in the cabin pressure during take-off. His father had had thought of everything and would stop at nothing to protect him. Like a loving father and husband, Braxton checked Jonathan's seat belts along with Gabriella's. Once secured, he took his wife's hand and kissed it.

"I love you, Gabriella. You and Jonathan. I will love you both, always."

Gabriella leaned into his chest and he kissed her again and they relaxed as the jet engines revved up to begin to taxi down the runway. The jet turned facing the sun as they slowly moved forward. They paused for a moment, getting their clearances from the air traffic controllers. Soon, the jet began moving faster and faster and finally it swiftly lifted off the ground. You could feel the weightlessness of the plane. Gabriella looked longingly at the ground as it became smaller and smaller until she could no longer identify anything on it.

Her heart was racing as if she would lose her breath at any moment from the sheer beauty of the sight of the billowing clouds that surrounded them. She had a flashback of memory looking over the year's events that had led up to this one euphoric moment. It was like something out of a story book. She had never dreamed in a million years this would be happening to her and wondered if it all was a real. Finally, it was clear that it wasn't a dream and she could accept the reality of it all with her new husband and baby. She would later pen the words of her life in a book to tell her children of how she and their father fell in love. She would tell them about how their grandfather Carlos had put them together years earlier before she was even born. With each altitude change, her fears and sad memories were completely erased from her thoughts until they all had dissipated in the jet stream they left behind.

She was no longer afraid of anything. The roar of the engines were quieted by the accomplished pilot and Gabriella reclined and took a deep breath. The doctors later determined that the phenomenon of "Camouflage" effect would never happen again. Gabriella could look forward to a normal pregnancy with the other three children they would soon have. Gabriella had finally accomplished her original quest to break the cycle of unwed mothers in her family. She knew that she would have a long and happy life with her new husband Braxton. She would put away forever, the heartache and pain of her past, only remembering that seeing is not always believing except through the eyes of fear.

~ THE END ~

Author: Victoria E. Kain

I'LL BE RIEF ™